Family
Found

Letitia Mason

Shellness Publications

Copyright © 2023 Letitia Mason

Shellness Publications, London

ISBN: 978-1-9168800-0-9
Printed by Kindle Direct Publishing

ACKNOWLEDGMENTS

Thank you to my husband, Howard Mason, for his support and my local writing group, Aspiring Writers. Thanks also to sons Alex and Jon, and friends Ruth Sander, Shirley Powell, and Anna Murphy. You have all given me encouragement at difficult times.

CONTENTS

Nyadena's journey to Juba

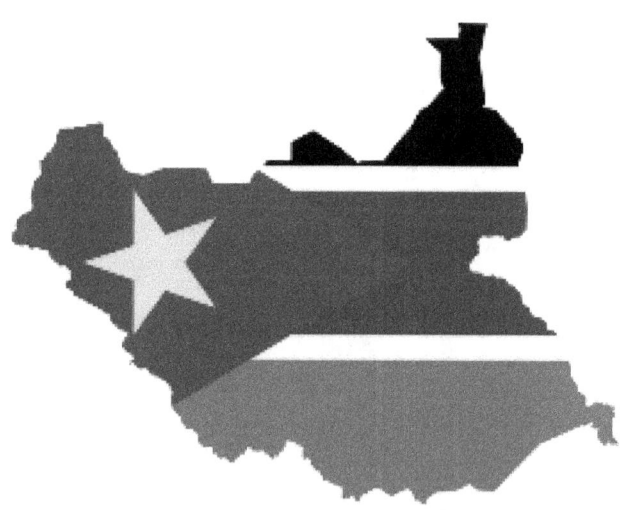

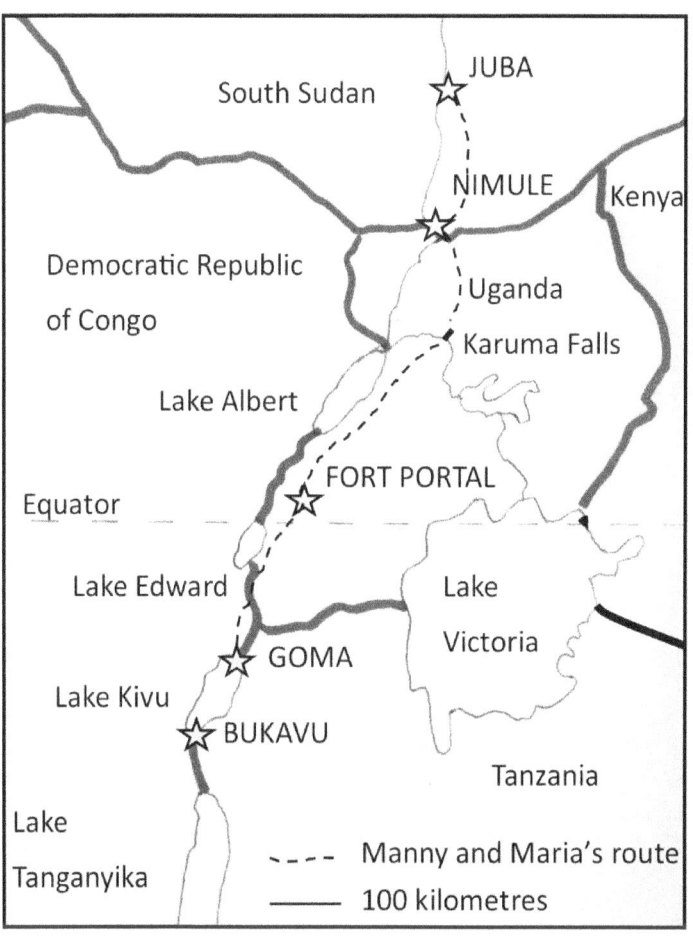

Manny and Maria's journey to Goma

JUBA
South Sudan

NIMULE
Kenya

Democratic Republic
of Congo

Uganda
Karuma Falls

Lake Albert

FORT PORTAL

Equator

Lake Edward
Lake
Victoria

GOMA

Lake Kivu

BUKAVU

Tanzania

Lake
Tanganyika

- - - - Manny and Maria's route
——— 100 kilometres

Maria's family

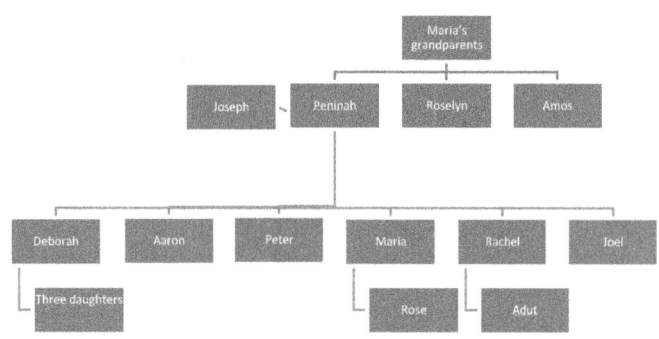

Manny's family

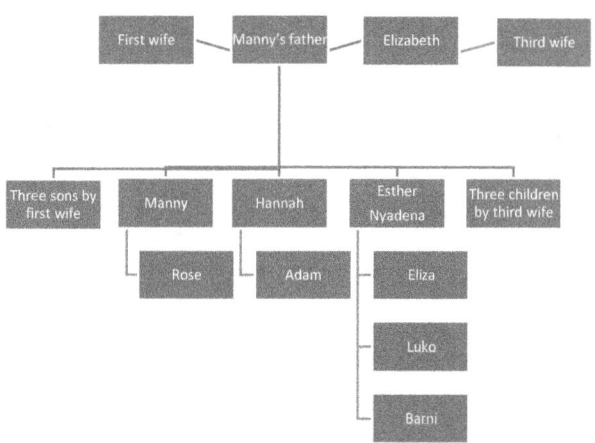

1 KING TAHARQO

The air on the London streets is spiced with sleet, and the pavements are slushy and dark. I am glad to be back in the city where I lived and worked for many years but yesterday when I left my home in Juba, temperatures in South Sudan were in the high thirties, the tarmac melting on the runway. The political temperature is similarly hot and stormy. I miss the heat of my own country, but I welcome the peace and safety of London.

'You want me to show you the way to the British Museum, Maria?' The colleague I am staying with asks me.

'No, I'll be fine, thank you, Paul.'

'Have a good day. Supper at seven tonight.' He has been so kind, letting me stay at his place rather than a hotel.

The pavements are wet with that damp oily smell typical of English cities. There are no leaves on the trees, and the branches drip steadily. I went out this morning and found a thick coat in a charity shop, and a pair of knitted gloves. The coat is bright red, the colour of the berries on the bushes around Paul's block of flats. I have my cotton scarf tied in a turban, African style, and a pair of shiny black court shoes that I bought years ago and took to Juba with me when Manny, who is also South Sudanese, and I returned there to be near our families. Despite the weather there is plenty of traffic and the spray from vehicle tyres has blotched my shoes with mud. I had forgotten how British weather penetrates to the bones. I shall be glad to go inside, to meet with Jane, my boss, but also my friend. I am looking forward to hearing the news of Avon View House, the hostel for trafficked young people in Bristol, where I used to work. Life in Juba is very different. I am happy to be near my family but for Manny it has not been so easy. He is in touch with his father, but there is no trace of his mother or sisters and he is convinced they died in the conflict with the Sudan government in the when he was a child.

People are standing on the stone steps at the entrance to the museum, holding cups of coffee steaming in the chill air. There are colourful banners hanging from the front of the building. A man leans against one of the pillars at the top of the stone steps, raincoat flapping open as he eats a sandwich in one hand and scans his phone, held in the other. I wonder if he will notice the blob of mayonnaise on his tie.

I pass through the double doorway into the stone entrance hall. I am taller than most British women, but I seem to shrink in size. This building is massive. The hall is gloomy, the roof so high the ceiling is lost amid the shadows of the pillars. I narrowly avoid bumping into a plastic box, full of crumpled notes, with the Museum's appeal for cash signposted above it. These stone columns are disorientating. Jane said to meet at the cafe in the atrium and I wander around wondering where to go. There are stairs on either side, one with a label saying Africa, but Jane said to stay on this level, so I keep straight ahead. The stone pillars open into a vast, sparkling cave. Above me triangles of glass stretch away from me in all directions, each one a different shape, so that the roof seems to curl around the central stone column. I stand, overwhelmed. I sense the spirit of the British people strongly here. There is pride, ambition, confidence, but also a questing spirit, a longing for other nations. What strange people, so restrained and reserved compared to African peoples, so unaware of the spirits of their own nation and those they conquered, yet they build these towering homes for them.

A movement attracts my attention and there is Jane, waving on the far side of the cavernous space. Our eyes lock and we move towards each other across the vast and embrace.

'Maria, you look wonderful, what a beautiful coat.'

'Jane! It's so cold! I went shopping this morning. The coat is warm, but itchy.' She laughs.

'It looks like pure wool. How was your flight, and your family?

'It was fine. And Manny and Rose are coping without me!'

'She will be bossing him! It goes with being a two-year-old.' Jane laughs.

'Yes, she has a strong spirit. Is Carlye okay?' I ask after her daughter.

'Winding her father and stepbrother round her little finger. Look, sit here by my bag and I'll get us some lunch. Is a salad okay, or would you like a sandwich?'

'A cheese sandwich, please. It's hard to get cheese in Juba. -and a cup of tea, thank you.' She goes to a serving hatch and joins a long queue. She is thinner than when I last saw her, and there is a touch of grey in her dark curls. Her face looks pale and tired, her leather messenger bag, her constant companion, bulges with papers. She is one of those who works harder than her spirit can bear.

I gaze around at this extraordinary place. In front of me a cylindrical stone column has book shops and gifts shops at the base. The windows are tall, with elongated pillars at either side of the glass, decorated with gold. I can see families mounting the stairs inside. To my left there is a stone wall and a doorway through which people amble, guide maps in hand. To my right the serving hatch is busy and the smell of coffee drifts across, together with something older, mustier, difficult to identify. On the next table an elderly couple are consulting a map, and an earnest young woman is typing into a laptop. Other tables have families seated with their lunch boxes, munching steadily to fortify themselves for the afternoon's activities.

'Here we are.' says Jane. 'Has Paul been looking after you?' Paul manages the London work of the Olaudah Trust, the charity for whom we both work, consulting with the National Referral Service for victims of trafficking.

'Yes, of course. He's very kind.'

'How's Manny? Is work going well?' My husband was nicknamed 'Manny' when he went to the USA as a youth but he was baptised

'Emmanuel'.

'Tense.' I reply. 'The Unity government is not fully in place, even though the peace was signed over eighteen months ago. There is no minister for Manny's department and the funds are held by the President's aides. There are many things he cannot get on with, while the money is used for guns.

'I have read the reports on the corruption and gun running.' she responds.

Manny is in the government ministry responsible for the many lost children in South Sudan, working to reunite them with their parents or find them a home. My country was at war with the Khartoum government for three generations and there are many families who have lost their relatives, and children who are separated from their parents. My purpose in coming to London is to share my own story of being forced into labour and brought to the UK.

'It is very sad,' I agree with Jane, 'but we do our best to make things better.'

'How is the hair dressing salon?' Jane asks.

'Doing well. Ladies come with their husbands to Juba, and they like to have their hair done. And you, Jane, what about you?'

'Busy. We have a new grant for the work at Avon View House and are at full capacity. I will email you the latest numbers. We have a new cook, but we need to recruit more part-time counsellors.'

'We used to cover that work ourselves.' My role at Avon View House was to manage the running of the household but I spent many hours with troubled people, helping them make sense of what had happened to them.

'Yes, but we need a more professional approach.'

Jane replies. 'We have had younger people recently, who need more support than our usual programmes can give.'

'And Rory and the family?' I ask. Jane married late and has a teenage stepson and a young daughter.

'It's an adjustment,' she admits 'after so many years of being single. There's so much to plan just to come away for a couple of days.'

'It will be okay, Jane. Small children take time, I spend most of the day watching Rose, and teenagers can be exhausting too.'

'Just being married can be challenging!' She comments. 'Do you find that?'

'I'm happy that we are together after so many years but Manny is frustrated at work. He can be irritable.'

'With you?'

'No, with how different things would be if he were still working in the USA. He had a big office in Baltimore and a justice system designed to protect family life. There's no court for gender or child justice in South Sudan.'

'Do he ever think about leaving Juba and returning to Baltimore.'

'We discuss giving up but then something changes, and we have hope again. There are many reports of corruption, and people suffer, but we hope now that there is peace things will improve.

'I'm sorry, Maria, I know it's tough.'

'We came back to South Sudan because Manny wanted to trace his family, but we've tried the Red Cross and other agencies and there is no evidence of them. He believes his father is right that they died. He seems to have given up but I am urging him to keep looking. We know his womenfolk made it to Uganda after the conflict in Bor. There is no trace of them in the camps in northern Uganda but they might have moved on from there.

'Oh, how painful not to know.' Jane responds, touching my hand with hers. Jane has worked in Juba and knows that many families in South Sudan have been torn apart by the conflict.

'At least I feel I am doing something useful.' I add. 'The Trust helped me find my mother and my sisters and now I help other families.'

'We must hope that something will turn up to for Manny's family.' says Jane and adds. 'Would you like more tea or a dessert?'

'No thank you,' I reply, 'I've eaten enough.'

'Let's get going. I want to show you one of the collections here.' Jane sets off across the shiny floor, her rubber soled boots make a dull thud, but my shoes have hard heels that clatter. I try to look dignified but in truth the scale and grandeur of the museum makes me feel like a small child. We pass through a vast door and cross several rooms of statues that are more than life size.

'These are statues of the kings of Egypt.' says Jane. 'We go through here to get to the Sudan Gallery.' The statues have stern faces and tall crowns. Their chins are elongated, or perhaps it is a kind of beard. The stone is carved to show the folds of their garments. They sit still and silent on stone thrones, but their spirits are strong and present. I sense their strength and power. Jane leads me up a massive flight of stairs and into a smaller room filled with glass cases where pots and ornaments are displayed.

'This is the Sudan and South Sudan gallery.' she says.

In the centre of the room, in its own glass case, is a black marble statue with the head of a man and the body of a lion. The face is strong with high cheeks, wide nostrils, and deep furrows from the nose to the corners of the mouth. There is a spirit of great power in this figure that shines from the stone as if it were alive. The eyes are blank but seem to stare into the distance. Two cobra heads, their hoods deployed, ready to strike, adorn the front of the crown. In my land Dinka chieftains are crowned in a lion skin cape, and a snake is a symbol of power and black magic. This man inhabits the strength of a lion and is crowned with power.

'Who is he?' I ask.

'King Taharqo.' Jane reads.

'He is a man from the south.' I observe. 'See, he has the face of a Dinka or a Nuer.'

'He was king of all Egypt.' Jane points to a map. 'Look! Egyptian rule stretched from the Mediterranean to the fourth cataract north of Khartoum.' I feel confused. This man of South Sudan was a big chief, who ruled in the north. My grandfather and father fought against the rulers of the north. Why is she showing me this king with his powerful magic? The room seems warm, and I feel dizzy. Did this man, whose features remind me of Manny, rule in Khartoum?

'What is it, Maria?' Jane asks.

'That king! He is a deserter! He went to the north. He sided with the enemies. Why do you show me these things?'

14

'No, no, Maria. It is thousands of years ago. He ruled soon after the pharaohs in the Egyptian Gallery.'

'The pharaohs in the Bible?'

'Yes, I suppose so. I'd never thought of it like that. I'm sorry. I didn't mean to upset you.'

'Was Taharqo a pharaoh?'

'Yes, but hundreds of years later than the pharaohs in the Bible, when the empire covered the whole of Egypt and Sudan, about six hundred years BC. I puzzle over what she is saying. I make that two thousand six hundred years ago. There would have been many kings and chiefs since then. I try to work out how many ancestors would have lived and died in that time, but it is too many.

'Why is the statue here?' I ask.

'I'm not sure. One of the notes said it was excavated in the 1930's, it would have been brought here for research.'

'But how can they study without the stories of the people?'

'I don't know. Archaeologists are interested in the Egyptian pharaohs, and I suppose it was seen as part of that historical period.' Jane stares down at her old messenger bag. She has looped the leather strap tightly round her wrist, the other hand twists the opening flap.

'I'm sorry, Jane, you wanted to show me, and I have spoiled it.'

'It's me who should be sorry. You are right. These things are not understood well in our culture. Nations are asking for their items to be returned.'

'It's good that it's been kept safe here during South Sudan's war, but one day, when there is a place for it, the king should go back to his country.'

'Yes, that would be the right thing.' Jane sighs

heavily. 'I've always loved this museum. My grandfather brought me here as a child to see the precious things from different nations. It was part of what inspired me to work for the Olaudah Trust. But you're right these items do not belong here.'

'That's okay, Jane. One day there will be a South Sudan Museum. We will tell our story with dance and drumming, which is how we pass on our history. We will tell the stories of our chiefs and how we fought for freedom.' Jane has released the strap of her bag. Our eyes meet.

'Shall we find a meal somewhere?' she suggests. We pass through the forest of colonnades to emerge into the fading light. The man eating his sandwiches has gone. The streets glisten with rain, reflecting the lights of the bars opposite.

We step off the slippery pavement and cross the busy road. Car wheels churn in pools of mud, pushing water up onto the pavement. The cold and damp suck the energy out of my veins. We seat ourselves in the corner of the Museum Tavern and take off our wet coats. I stare through the frosted glass at the steps we have just come down. How strange that an ancient ruler of South Sudan has ended up in this palace of western culture. What would the man crowned with twin cobras have said to that? Aie Aie, this is a strange world.

The waitress takes our order. 'How's Rory' I ask. Jane met her husband when he moved to Bristol after his first wife died of cancer. He left his work as an international journalist. He is a

Kenyan whose father lives in Nairobi.

'He's getting new commissions for his writing and may have to travel to the Democratic Republic of Congo soon to report on the conflict in eastern Congo.'

'Perhaps he will not need his City Council job?'

'I hope he'll be able to be a freelance journalist again, that is what he'd like.'

The waitress brings a salad and a glass of coke for Jane and an omelette and tea for me. Things are comfortable between us now.

'How are you feeling about the conference tomorrow?' Jane asks. 'Do you know how to get to Old Street?'

'Yes, Paul has shown me. I spoke with the organiser today and they have my slides ready. Do we know how many are coming?'

'A hundred and fifty.' she replies.

'So many, even in this cold weather!'

Back here behind the screens, I cannot see the people filling the hall, but I can hear them. Metal chair legs scrape on the wooden floor. Paul is on the Welcome desk, asking people's names and handing out badges and programmes. There were sporadic bursts of chatter to begin with but now there is a steady hum of conversation. The hall must be full. The blond woman next to me smiles.

'Ready to go on, Maria? Just a couple more minutes.' I smile at her and nod but inside my stomach is churning. A demon has gripped me and is squeezing the breath out of me. I do not know if I will be able to speak. I say 'Good morning, I am Maria Kuol Deng from the Olaudah Trust...' to myself. What comes after that I cannot recall. I hope I will remember when my slides are in front of me. The blond woman nods in my direction, and I follow her onto the stage. Four others come behind us. They told me their names, but I am not used to English after four years in South Sudan and my ears did not catch them. I know the blond woman is Jenny, because it sounds like 'Janey,' which is Rory's name for Jane. I look out across hundreds of faces, some talking, others turned to the stage. Jenny indicates a seat and I sit down cautiously, making sure my long legs do not knock the table, which is covered with wires and microphones. The faces below are a blur. People at the front are sitting at round tables. Further back the seats are raked, like a theatre. I finally spot Jane on the third row and smile, but I cannot see if she smiles back, it is too far away, and the light is strange, slightly green, which makes most people look pale. It makes my skin appear even darker than it is.

Jenny stands and moves to the lectern. Her black skirt and patterned jumper seem to flicker. There is silence as everyone turns their faces towards her.

'Good morning. Welcome to our first London conference on child slavery and trafficking. We have called the event 'Out of Sight' because many children are lost through conflict, poverty, and exploitation.' A latecomer enters the hall, full of apologies. I see Paul put his finger to his lips and point towards Jenny.

'The purpose of our conference today is to hear stories of these children and to identify how we can work together as international charities to address this terrible trade. Our first speaker is Maria Kuol Deng, who is the South Sudan representative of the Olaudah Trust. She is going to tell us her own experience of being trafficked and about her work in Juba. Maria.' I feel my body move from the chair to the lectern, but I do not feel in control of myself. It is as if the spirit in Jenny is drawing me towards her, somehow triggering a polite burst of clapping as I move. She adjusts the height of the lectern, opens the laptop, clicks on the first slide, and resumes her seat.

I look out into the hall and find Jane, who nods in encouragement. I pray that the words I prepared so carefully will return to me. Someone at the audio-visual desk turns a knob and the hall lights dim, whilst the strip light on the lectern brightens. The gold tones of my skin reappear and the fabric of my green dress shimmers slightly as I grasp the sides of the lectern, draw a deep breath, and smile blindly at the listeners before me.

'Goood morning, ladies and gentlemen.' My vowels sound very African with that long oooo. Where has my English accent gone?

'My talk will have two parts. First, I will tell you how I came to London as a child. Then I will speak of my work for the Olaudah Trust.' The screen displays the Trust's logo, a vertical blue wavy line, with a circle each side of it. It expresses our aim of preventing child trafficking along the Nile, but it also looks like a child's face because every victim is an individual, torn from their family and their place.

'My family come from Torit, south of Juba. When I was a small child, my father was a teacher and kept cattle in the traditional way. I am a Christian, like many in South Sudan, my parents were taught by evangelists

19

from Uganda.

'The government in Khartoum is Muslim. They ordered that we in the south must learn Arabic, study the Koran, and obey Sharia law. My father and most of the men in my town went to fight for the Sudan People's Liberation Army. We fought against the Sudan Armed Forces, SAF, for the right to our own culture and beliefs. The Khartoum government forces bombed Torit. My family fled to the caves and then to my uncle's house at Nimule, on the border with Uganda. On the way there, Government soldiers captured me and forced me into a "relationship" with the colonel who sent me into slavery in Juba.' I hear a gasp and stop for a moment, but it is okay, they are just shocked by my story.

'I was sold to a family in Khartoum. They brought me to the UK to visit relatives and left me here when they returned. I escaped but was tricked into joining a drug running gang and sent to prison. Thanks to the help of a teacher and a pastor I was released and given counselling support. I worked at a hair dressing salon for many years where, by chance in 2014, I met Jane and joined the Olaudah Trust.' I pause for a moment and then start on the second part of my talk.

'The mission of the Olaudah Trust is to end slavery along the White Nile. We do this by looking after people who have been trafficked to the UK, and referred to us, at our main centre, Avon View House in Bristol. We have a beautiful Edwardian mansion, given to us by a wealthy Bristol family, and converted into offices and a hostel. We currently have five adults and five children staying. Here is Abulufa. He is seventeen years old. He landed on the Kent coast in September with a group of older men, when their inflatable washed ashore. He thinks he left South Sudan when he was thirteen. He has been in the hands of smuggling gangs since then and is severely malnourished. He has no memory of how the journey started, or maybe he is full of trauma and cannot tell us. At Avon View House we check his health. He will be given the food he needs to make him well, and counselling. He will be trained in a skill, horticulture, or carpentry or administration. Eventually, if the peace holds, he will return to South Sudan.' I notice that the people in the front row, the only ones visible to me, are looking intently at the photo of Abulufa.

'I live in Juba and my work is to support people who have been trafficked abroad and then returned to South Sudan. I help them trace their relatives and find work. I make sure they have the correct papers and help them adjust.

'Another part of my work is to consult with our partners in South Sudan to prevent children from being taken.' I watch the upturned faces at the tables. Some look sombre and concerned. Others shuffle their papers. I glance at my notes, take a deep breath, and continue:

'South Sudan became independent in 2011. Many people planned to build a better country, but the leaders have been unable to agree. Since 2013 there has been war between the forces supporting President Salva Kiir, and those supporting the Vice President, Riek Machar. Fierce fighting broke out in Juba in July 2016. Over one hundred people were killed, and many buildings and roads were destroyed. Families have been scattered and businesses damaged. Children have been captured and taken into the army. South Sudan has policies to protect children and families, under the peace agreement signed in August 2018 but until the new government is agreed, there are no ministers to implement these policies and no child justice system. Many charities help, but we must bring our efforts together to make sure no child is lost. Today we can share our experience in how to do this. Thank you for listening. Now there is time for questions.'

The rest of the day passes in a whirlwind of talks, workshops, rest breaks and a final panel. Jane and I answer questions and join discussions until at last the guests leave and we can speak freely.

'Well done, Maria, your talk went well.' says Jane.

'Yes, well done.' agrees Paul. 'Let's get you home for supper and a good night's sleep before you fly back.'

'I'll see you for the conference in Nairobi at the end of March.' adds Jane.

'Yes, see you soon. Bye, Jane.'

We were not to know that the world would change fundamentally before the end of March and that it would be two years before we would meet again.

2 PAGAK, SOUTH SUDAN

Grasses two metres high bend their tall stems over the Sobat River, as it flows north to join the White Nile. Raindrops beat the ground with venomous blows, sending up a spray of mud. Nyadena tightens her shawl around the child tied on her back and hurries home. The water sounds angry, each drop a cannon shot, punching holes in the roofs of the homes she passes. The thatch is worked in layers, trimmed into steps, and capped by small terracotta cones, but in a tropical storm no amount of skilled work prevents water accumulating. The straw flattens, rivulets form and drip on the floor.

The rains have come late to this north-eastern corner of South Sudan and torrential showers punctuate every afternoon. The river level is high, the soil waterlogged. Fine Nile silt dries in the heat of the morning sun. In the afternoon onslaught it becomes a gluey paste that sticks to the feet, making them heavy and clumsy.

Nyadena slams the corrugated iron door of the *tukul* shut, unties her shawl, and places the sleeping child on the double bed to the left of the doorway, tucking her shawl tightly round his small dark body. She bends down to scrape her bare feet with a stick, piling lumps of mud by the door to be dealt with later. Rope lines are strung from each corner of the hut and tied to the central wooden pole that holds the roof up. She reaches up to fold washing that has hung there since early morning. The extreme heat has dried the clothes, but they will become damp with the humidity of the afternoon, unless folded and put away in a box. She avoids from habit the onion strings, cooking implements, lantern, and towel, which hang from other sections of rope. She collects a knife and basket from the shelves on the back wall and sits on a plastic chair in the square of light from the single window to dice tomatoes and greens for supper. She hopes the school will keep her children indoors, it would be dangerous for them to walk home in bare feet, there might be sharp objects concealed in the mud. She would like to buy rubber boots for them, like the pastor's children, but their father is a soldier, based in the barracks in the town. His pay is erratic, they have nothing to spare, and no family to help them. She has lost touch with her family as a result of her husband's promotion to army chaplain and posting to this remote spot. She wishes she had made more effort to keep in touch, but it is too late now, she has not written or tried to phone in years.

'Mama, let us in!' She sighs and opens the door. A boy of eight comes tumbling through, followed by his older sister carrying a sodden piece of cardboard over her head.

'Stand still.' Nyadena yells as she struggles to get the door shut after them. 'Don't move till I've dried you.' She tackles the younger boy, Luko, first

24

stripping off his wet Superman T shirt and shorts and towelling his damp legs.

'Hold your foot up so I can check for cuts..... No, you're fine.' She lifts him onto the bed, gives him a stalk from the greens to chew. Eliza waits patiently, her hem dripping steadily on the earth floor, until it is her turn to take the towel and dry herself.

'Sit on the bed and wait for your cup of tea.' says their mother. 'Eliza, wake Barni and help him with his cup.' She takes the large thermos flask prepared earlier in the day and pours them each a mug of hot, sweet tea.

'Drink up and don't spill it while I find your dry clothes.' The rain pounds incessantly on the roof. She must tell their father that the thatch needs patching. She steps carefully round the greasy puddle forming in the middle of the earth floor. In the town centre it is worse, homes are flooded, and people are sleeping without a roof over their heads.

'Get dressed quickly but stay on the bed and don't go walking on the floor till it's dry. Mmm?'

'Yes, Mama.' She measures out a portion of millet flour and finds the small jar of oil. She cannot light the conical metal brazier filled with charcoal on which she cooks their meals until the rain stops. It is too dangerous to cook indoors. At least if the children see her getting supper ready, they stay calm, knowing they will eat eventually. Less determined mothers would be daunted by the challenges of Pagak in the wet season, but Nyadena has worked and stayed in many places, since she left her family, and this is where she has come to feel at home, surrounded by the warmth of friends and the beauty of the area.

'Dear Lord Jesus don't let him be posted

somewhere else.' she mutters under her breath. 'What would I do without my friends?'

The children sit quietly drinking their tea. She rests for a minute. The beauty of this swamp land in the dry season awes her, the hamerkop birds, the cranes, huge and brightly patterned butterflies, the tall grasses by the water courses, the croaking of frogs at night and the rapid growth of sorghum, squashes, and onions in the dark and fertile Nile silt. The local school is well run. It is half an hour's walk to the Ethiopian border where there is a good hospital in Gambella. Best of all there is a wonderfully supportive group of women, brought together by the local Mothers' Union leader. She worries about stories circulating in the barracks and shared by other wives. The platoon is to be posted to Juba. The men will be sharing accommodation, there will be no room for wives and children. She will be left here on her own. Reuben will not discuss these rumours, merely says:

'Wait for my posting. It will be fine. The commander is a good man.' Nyadena sighs, and glares as a scuffle breaks out on the bed.

'Sit still, or there will be no supper.' she warns them. 'Eliza, start a song. Luko and Barni, you clap.' Eliza sings sweetly but her voice is soon drowned by the energetic clapping of the boys who jostle and push against each other in their effort to be loudest.

'No wriggling, just your hands move.' warns their mother. She chops greens and tomatoes and mixes them to a paste. She cuts boiled fish skins left over from yesterday's meal into strips and lays them across the top of the paste. Her hands smell of fish and tomato juice; they are sticky with scales. She rinses them with water from the kettle and dries them on the towel she used for the children.

'Luko, see if the rain has stopped.' She tells her son. The eight-year-old scrambles off the iron bed and jerks the door open.

'It has.' he confirms.

'Open the door, and let's get this floor dried.' Water still drips through the thatch. A weak shaft of light falls through the open door and casts shadows across the uneven floor. The sun is dropping rapidly in the evening sky and will be gone in half an hour. Nyadena fills her brazier with charcoal.

'Eliza, bring that pan of millet, please.' Mother and daughter pick their way carefully over the raised threshold as a clamour breaks out behind them.

'Boys, keep clapping. I want to hear a good rhythm or no supper.'

The simple meal is soon cooked, and peace reins. The children play around the hut and Nyadena washes the pans and puts them away. She longs for family to support her. Most of the other women in this north-eastern corner of the country have mother's, aunts, cousins, but her mother and sister are in Congo, on the western border. She has not seen her father and brothers since they fled the massacre of her hometown, Bor, when she was a baby. Her father left them during the conflict, and she has no way of contacting him. At least Reuben is a good husband. He works hard, and rarely drinks.

The following Sunday Nyadena and her children sit under a large cassia tree, the meeting place for the village, watching the national flag being raised. It is an important occasion. The district commissioner and the bishop are here, as well as the commander of the regiment. Reuben has completed a weeklong training to be an army chaplain and will be awarded his certificate, along with forty men and women from the armed forces, the Ranger Service, the Police and Fire Services. He has never discussed his beliefs, his faith seems to be a label, but it has enabled him to get this additional role and Nyadena senses that his curiosity has been roused this week. The district commissioner will present the certificates and the bishop will lead a service of commitment for the chaplains. It is a solemn occasion, but the children are fidgeting and giggling with their friends.

'Eliza, Luko, Barni' Nyadena hisses. 'Sit still. You will shame your father.' They subside into furtive kicking of the wooden bench in front of them; she can see their attempts to be good will not last long.

'Look at the flag,' she tells them. 'Barni, what colours does it have?'

'Red!' yells Barni. It is his favourite colour. 'Shush.' Their mother puts her finger to her lips. 'Answer quietly.'

'Green and blue and black.' hisses Luko rapidly. 'And…?' Nyadena queries. 'White!' Luko adds. 'Lellow,' Barni finishes.

'You can tell us what the colours mean, can't you?' Luko shuffles his feet and withdraws his attention from a school friend he has spotted at the far end of the bench.

'Green is for the trees and grass of South Sudan,' he says, 'And black is for people.'

'Well done.' Nyadena commends him. 'Eliza, can you remember what the other colours stand for?

'Red for the fighting and white for peace.'

'You are right!' says her mother. 'And there is one more part of the flag, who can?'

'Star!' Barni interrupts.

'Shush!' Eliza clamps a hand over his mouth and then snatches it away quickly as his sharp teeth close over it.

'He bit me!' she wails.

'Barni! You sit under the bench.' Nyadena lifts him off the bench and plants him on the earth. 'Be good, or you will not see your father get his certificate.' The children settle down. Luko points as the flag opens in a breath of wind and streams out from the flagpole. Bands of black, red, and green, separated by narrow white stripes, flap, and dip in the wind. The blue triangle with the single yellow star in the centre hugs the flagpole, stretched out at top and bottom by the cords that raised it.

'All stand.' commands the bishop, an impressive sight in a flowing white robe and purple cape. The five drummers on the front row tap the palms of their hands on the leather skins of the drums and the choir, dressed in thin pink shifts, start the national anthem,

South Sudan Oyee. Oh God we praise and glorify you for your grace on South Sudan.

The children sing along with the catchy tune. Nyadena picks Barni up. Other mothers with small children are arrayed on the benches in front and behind her. They are to the left of the broad trunk of the cassia tree, so that any misdemeanours are partially hidden from the rest of the assembly. The trunk is three meters in diameter and branches arch over an area the size of half a football pitch. She feels safe under the dense canopy of small pinnate leaves, which provide shelter from the Equatorial sun. Two pods, missed in the community harvesting of beans, hang above her head, shaking slightly in the breeze as if echoing the drumbeats. The sweet cinnamon-like smell of the leaves and bark are slightly soporific to the fidgeting children. Behind the rows of benches, a bamboo fence encloses a family hut and Nyadena, singing loudly, admires the neat thatch and the shiny clay pot that tops the central pole, like a small minaret.

The anthem finishes with a roll of drums and the community sit in silence. The chaplains are ranged on plastic chairs to the right of Nyadena. In front of them are a row of dignitaries, the district commissioner, the commander and the local heads of the Police, Fire, and Ranger services. The bishop sits in a large wooden chair with high carved arms, facing the assembly. He fingers the metal cross that hangs round his neck and rests on his bony chest. He steps forward and grasps a wooden lectern with both hands, puts on his glasses and opens a Bible. The flag flaps softly above his head. There is a sense of anticipation amongst the townspeople, they rarely see dignitaries in this remote spot. Even the children are awed into silence.

'You have learned many things.' says the bishop in English. Families speak their tribal language at home but on formal occasions English or Arabic are used. 'This team have trained you.'

There is an outbreak of clapping, which the bishop halts with an upraised hand. We thank them later.' he says. 'First, we award certificates to those who have completed the course. You have received. Now you go. You teach your divisions and carry this learning on peace and reconciliation to others.' The crowd shifts uneasily. Memory of conflict is fresh in their minds. The brick buildings of the clinic, visible beyond the cassia tree, lie in ruins. Six years ago, tribal conflicts raged across the area, which lies to the south of the country's valuable oil reserves.

The bishop calls out names and men and women in uniform rise from their chairs in turn to receive their certificate. 'Reuben Thon.' As their father's name is called, his children sit up. Reuben shakes hands with the bishop and district commissioner and turns towards them. He raises the piece of paper above his head. He reads and speaks well, but this is his first certificate of achievement. His wife, and children clap vigorously, proud that their father is one of the privileged few who have received this training and a certificate to hang on the wall.

The district commissioner rises to add his congratulations. Nyadena and other women look anxiously around. The sky is darkening.

'It will rain?' she hisses to the woman next to her on the bench.

'We will take the children into the church?' They peer round the trunk to where a long mud walled, building crouches, its grass roof hanging low over the door and windows. Rain fails to penetrate the leaves of the cassia at first but, as it increases in intensity, large drops accumulate and fall to the ground pooling, between the tree roots. The damp earth smells of stagnant water and weed. The bishop and the district commissioner confer.

'We must go into the church.' the latter announces. Without further discussion, the women who have no children pick up the chairs of the district commissioner, and the commander, and carry them to the church, followed by the archdeacons and newly qualified chaplains carrying their own chairs. Two soldiers carry the bishop's imposing chair. Last come the women with small children, cramming into the open space at the back of the church and perching on simple log benches. The drumming of the rain on the roof is deafening. It is impossible to hear what is happening from the back of the packed building. Three narrow windows down one side allow shafts of light to penetrate the gloom. Children, faces invisible in the dark apart from their eyes, wriggle as they try to see past the adults, while the mothers strain to hear what is being said. The smell of tightly packed bodies, sweating in the humid air pervades the church, mingling with the smell of wet mud and trampled cassia leaves. Children who make a noise are pinched silently and warned with a finger to the lips to be quiet. Nyadena watches through the rear door as the rain pounds on the already saturated ground, until a large puddle forms in the doorway, blocking their exit.

'.......important announcement...........' an emphasized phrase penetrates to the back rows and Nyadena sits upright and listens intently as the commander steps forward.

'.......done well.' There is an outburst of

clapping. ' ……..posted to Juba.' Nyadena leans forward but there is a murmuring amongst the company that prevents her hearing what the commander is saying. The women look at each other and clutch the infants on their laps tightly. Who will be leaving? How long do they have?

The commander sits down. The bishop conducts a short service, but Nyadena's mind is in torment. Will she have to move with the children? Juba, the capital of South Sudan, is thousands of miles south of Pagak, on the main road to Uganda. She has no idea how they will reach there. Too late, the rain subsides, and the speakers become audible. The women sit through the prayers, but their thoughts are far away from the thanks being given for the team who have trained these newly fledged chaplains. Like anxious birds they cluster together on their branch, hoping any change will offer a good place to roost.

At last, the torment is over. Nyadena takes Barni firmly by the hand, tells Luko to take his other hand to help him over the puddle, and instructs Eliza to collect her father's chair and bring it back.

'When will they go? Is it everyone from this regiment?' The women speculate as they walk back but it is no good, no-one heard clearly, and they must wait till their husbands return.

Nyadena feels the rigid plastic of the chair beneath her as she sits with Reuben's hand in hers. The skin on his palm is dry and calloused but the back of his hand is smooth and dark, with raised veins that form a pattern like the divided channels of the river as it winds through the swamplands of the Sudd. The children have been fed and laid on the two single mattresses they share. Tired by the unusual activities of the day they sleep heavily, mouths open, breath coming in hot gasps that add to the humid atmosphere in the *tukul*. Reuben has confirmed that he is one of those chosen to go to Juba. The date is unclear, but it will be as soon as the floods subside and the road to Malakal is open.

'What about the children?' Nyadena asks. 'I pray and pray that their childhood is better than mine.'

'I know.' he says. 'Your family suffered because of the conflict, but we are at peace now. We are a new country.'

'It is peace to the government but not for the people. Why must you go to Juba? There might be fighting again, like three years ago. Even the President's Palace was not safe.'

'There has been no fighting in Juba recently.' he responds.

'I have friends here. There is a good school. There is the hospital across the border in Gambella but I cannot look after the children on my own.'

'Well, come to Juba with me. There will be the chance for secondary schooling. It is drier there.' The oil lamp flickers and highlights the dark creases on his face.

'I don't mind the rain.' she says. 'This land is fertile, and there is plenty of fish. We can plant crops. Have a good life. Besides, I hoped to join the police service again when Barni goes to school.'

'I'm sorry Nya. I must go where the commander says. It will be better for the children to have the opportunity of senior school.' He clasps her hands with both of his, rubbing her palm, roughened from washing muddied clothes.

'I love you.' he says.

Nyadena sighs. He has worked hard to win a place on the course and get his certificate. Now, as an army chaplain, he will have responsibility for the spiritual and mental welfare of his men. Perhaps there will be more money eventually. She wants to support him. He is a good father but to leave the place where she has been happy is unbearable. The children are doing well. The land can produce three crops a year. They could build the settled life she longed for as a child. She enjoyed her time in the police service, before she married Reuben, and had pinned her hopes on the favour of the local chief of police in getting her a job.

They wash in the last of the day's water from the kettle and go to bed, but Nyadena cannot sleep. There is a mosquito whining, and she slaps it away. The light cotton sheet that covers her is cool but the thin foam mattress beneath her feels like a furnace. Reuben snores rhythmically, worn out by the studies he completed this week. What can she do? Speak to the commander? He will not listen. Ask the pastor to pray, will God listen? She tries to make a plan. If she is organised it will not be so bad, but her mind refuses. She drifts off to sleep and tumbled images of the past jostle in front of her closed eyes, being held in her mother's arms as they fled west to escape renegades, hiding in a ditch while trucks rushed by on the dirt road, running into the bush as soldiers in tattered uniforms, many of them no more than boys, swarmed across the land. She was the baby of the family, her sister, Hannah, ten years older and her youngest brother an unpredictable youth. Her father left them at the Uganda border promising to find them when the fighting was over, but he never came. Many were killed in the decade and a half before peace was signed, probably her father and brothers were among them, she has never known for sure.

The following morning a group of women sit on mats under an acacia tree. The arch deacon's wife wears the blue and white fabric of the Mothers' Union, with its intertwined MU printed across a deep blue background. Two women wear the white robes and dog collars of a pastor but most wear a long brightly patterned cotton cloth looped around their shoulders and tied at the waist. Regardless of status or apparel they are united by their membership of their local Mothers' Union branch and bound to each other by ties of friendship, loyalty, and support. The group was formed at the bishop's suggestion after the fighting six years ago. Susana, wife of the bishop's secretary, is an able leader. She is a lean, agile woman with a long face and flared nostrils. Her wide mouth can speak sternly, in support of her ladies, but the kind eyes behind tortoiseshell glasses, gifted by a departing mission doctor, soften her angular jaw. She is a determined fighter for the rights of her group, in a culture that sees women as primarily for marriage and children. Her hair, though as tightly curled as the other women's is fine and escapes from the corn rows in which she keeps it. Wispy strands of hair stand up around her face like a halo. The women fear her and love her. Under her leadership they have become better managers of their homes, more confident mothers, and have been following a basic literacy programme using leaflets sent from the head office in Juba. Today the women are voluble, and Susana struggles to bring order.

'Mamas, please. Let us speak one at a time and listen to each other.' The hubbub subsides and Susana turns to a woman in a faded red cloth, who is often the spokesperson for the group.

'Betty,' she demands, 'explain why these ladies are upset.'

'Mama Susana, it is the words of the commander yesterday. These ladies do not know what will happen when their husbands leave. They wish to stay here and learn to read. They say they can grow crops now that there is peace.'

'Thank you, Betty.' Susana scans the circle of women.

'Raise your hand if your husband has been posted.' she tells them. Many hands are raised, and several women start speaking at once. Susana raises her voice to stop them.

'One person only to speak.' she commands. 'Leah, you are first.' A woman with a slender figure rises to her feet. She looks frail, but she is known throughout the village for her strength and stamina.

'The ladies are happy here, Mama. They wish to continue with the programme of reading. They fear that these lessons will end when their husbands leave.' She sits down.

'Thank you, Leah. Eunice next.' Eunice passes the baby she is holding to a neighbour and stands.

'We have planted tomato seeds and onions during

the rains. Will we keep our land when our husbands are gone? We want to gather our harvest.' There is a soft 'Mmmm. Mmmm.' of agreement from other women. Eunice sits.

'Joanna.' Susana signals the next speaker and a younger woman with soft delicate features and a gentle smile stands.

'Mama, our children learn well in school. The teachers are kind, they do not beat them. We are fearing the school will close.'

Nyadena rises, holding Barni firmly by the hand. 'Mama, it is far to Juba. How will our husbands send us money for the children?'

'Mmmm. Mmmm.' comes the murmur of agreement. 'That is well said.'

'Very well.' says Susana. 'I will speak with the commander. I will ask him about the land and the school. You can leave it to me. Now we will have a reading from the Bible and a song. Betty, please read Matthew chapter nineteen verses four to six.' Betty takes a small Bible out of the cloth bag on the ground beside Susana, and reads in a strong, clear voice. When she gets to the verse *'a man will leave his father and mother and be united to his wife and the two will become one flesh'* there is a sombre silence in the meeting. Nyadena glances round the circle and sees the women nodding. She can feel her passions rising. She does not want to leave Reuben, but it is he who is leaving her. She should go with him but that means taking the children from a place where they are doing well. They will have to start again and without the support of the older women in this sisterhood.

'Thank you, Betty. Leah, will you lead a song

for us?'

They stand, some with agility, older women more slowly. When all are ready Leah sings softly 'The Lord ees my shepherd I have all I want. He lead me by flat water. He keep me safe.' The women start to clap, softly at first but gradually louder. Leah's voice rises to a crescendo. 'He lead me along the right path for his name is great.' The clapping gets louder and all repeat at the top of their voices. 'He lead me along the right path, for His name is great.'

The shape of the notes is from the setting of Psalm 23 known as 'Crimond', but the tonality is that of the local culture and the rhythm is sharp and percussive with complex under rhythms that penetrate and fill the interstices of the melody in place of the harmony of the original. As the intensity of the clapping increases bodies move to the rhythm, swaying forward and back, sidestep and back, in unison.

Leah sings the verses, and the women repeat the refrain 'He lead me along the right path for his name is great.' The song climbs to a triumphant crescendo on the final verse and the refrain is repeated many times until the intensity diminishes and the singing fades to a slow murmur.

The anguish Nyadena felt during the discussion is gone and she takes comfort from the feeling of unity. When Susana raises her hand again and says a final prayer, she is content to leave with no further discussion. Susana will make her presentations to the commander. Nyadena will go with Reuben if she can find a way. She links hands with Joanna, and they walk back to their homes through the lush greenness of the village. Spotted butterflies, the size of a child's hand, rise ahead of them along the path. Vines hung with yellow speckled gourds ramble over the bamboo fences surrounding family compounds. The sun beats down and moisture rises from the damp mud, softening the outlines of the thatched roofs of their *tukuls* with their ceramic topknots. Loss and anxiety are buried deep in Nyadena's heart, but for now she is happy to walk home with her friend, hoping the future will be kind to her and her family.

3 CAPITAL JUBA

I arrived home from the conference in London yesterday afternoon and am resting on our balcony, which looks out over Juba city. My two-year-old daughter, named after my Aunt Roselyn, who looks after her when I am working, lies asleep beside me.

The morning sun has moved round so we are in shadow, but the temperature is still in the thirties. A red ant with bulging eyes is hurrying across the concrete floor. It is bigger than the ants that came into the kitchen of Avon View House, but it blends with the orange red soil of South Sudan. Here on the second floor, its colour flares against the yellow wall of our apartment. The ant might bite Rose, but thankfully it disappears into a crevice in the concrete.

Rose was excited when she saw me, shouting 'Mama, Mama.' I gave her the wooden Noah's Ark with carved and painted animals, which I bought in London. She has spent the morning fitting them through the animal shaped holes and opening and closing the red door at the back. Now she holds a zebra in one tightly curled fist, and her breath comes in faint, even sighs. Her eye lashes sweep over her beautiful dark cheeks. Her skin, which was glossy with exertion, now has the dusky smoothness of a deeply sleeping child.

I relax, and phone through an order for supplies for the salon. Later this afternoon we will walk there to check with my assistant how business has gone over the few days I have been away. I am tired from the flight and the long wait at Addis Ababa and start to doze but Rose is stirring. I was going to scan through my notes from the conference, but it is better that I have rested.

'Mmmm. Mmmm, Rosy. We are going to see Kaka.' I tell her. This is her name for the dog who moved into the room at the back of the salon during the conflict in 2016.

'Ka ka ka ka.' I wrap her in a cotton shawl and tie her securely onto my back. I can feel her body mould into mine, still soft and heavy with sleep. I am happy to be home. This is where I belong. Viewed from the plane, Juba is a green shawl tied around the red brown water of the Nile. Steep rounded hills form a necklace of teeth that protrude above the plateau and protect us from the desert winds. Here on the streets, beneath the canopy of leaves, the city is a cacophony of horns blaring, people shouting, goats bleating. Since the peace was signed in 2018, aid agencies have moved back, though many still base themselves in Nairobi. Chinese businesspeople are here on contract work. Their spouses come to the salon to have their hair cut but most of our income is from South Sudanese women wanting their hair straightened, and European women wanting their hair dyed. We are doing well enough to employ an assistant, Chika, who runs the salon when I am not there.

Rose is fully awake now and has started to wriggle.

'See, Rosy, big lorry!' She waves her fist in my peripheral vision and shrieks in delight when uniformed guards in the back of a pickup truck wave at her. A bicycle, so loaded with oranges that I cannot see the driver, swerves to avoid us. The pavement wide, uneven, and in places blocked by rubble is crowded with market stalls, their wooden sides leaning crazily against each other. They sell the same range of goods, bunches of several hundred small, sweet bananas from which customers select the ones they want, tins of oil, powdered milk, and small bottles of water, refilled from larger ones.

When Manny and I first viewed the shop space it was a dilapidated shell, sealed by metal doors. A flat roofed portico, held up by discoloured concrete pillars, links four premises. The only thriving shop was the nail bar next to our unit. The others were a general store selling little more than the street stalls, and a bike repair shop. Both went out of business when the row of shops was damaged in the clashes between the President and Vice President's forces in July 2016. It was heart breaking to see the salon we had just finished fractured by grenades and filled with dust, but we started again. Now there is a boutique at one end and a shop selling brightly coloured kitenge cloth imported from Uganda at the other. We have become a 'destination' for women with money to spend on themselves.

'How are you, Chika?'

'Mama Maria, I am fine. How was London?'

'It went fine, thank you. Has business been good?'

'Two new ladies have booked appointments, but Madam Wang has complained about the water again.

She does not like the smell.'

'Oh. I will talk to the water company; the tank needs cleaning out.'

'Ka! Ka! Ka!' Rose kicks her legs, thumping me in the lower spine so I untie the shawl and let her toddle across to greet her friend. Kaka is gentle and they will be fine together while I check the accounts. Chika brings the book and I sit at the reception desk and total the takings for the week. They have increased slightly on last week but if we have the roof tank drained that will be a heavy expense.

'Thank you, Chika, that all seems in order.' I hand the book back to her.

'Rose, you can walk, hold Mama's hand. Bye Chika. Have a good weekend.' Monday, Wednesday, and Thursday are my days for working at the salon, while my Aunt Rosalyn takes care of Rose. She says it gives her a rest from her cleaning job, and that the change is good for her. I doubt if she gets much rest with Rose, but we are thankful for her support.

We make slow progress; everything is fascinating to Rose. She traces the dry mortar in a pile of bricks by the side of the road with her chubby finger, shouts in delight as a lizard runs into a crack in the pavement and laughs at a stray goat eating a manioc plant. Eventually I persuade her to submit to being carried so that we can get home in time for tea.

Manny comes round the door while she is chewing on a slice of sorghum. His tall, strong figure looks exhausted, and his usual wide smile is replaced by a frown.

'There's boiled water in the flask.' I tell him. 'You look as though you need a cup of tea!'

'I need something stronger than that.'

'Have a shower and change.' I suggest. He moves to the door, taking off his jacket to reveal a sweat-soaked shirt. His office has a fan, but he will not relax his dress code to walk home so often arrives overheated.

'Come on, Rosy, let's get you ready for bed.'

When I return to the main room, Manny is slumped at the table, head on hands.

'What is it?' I ask him.

'Garang has disappeared.' I feel heat in my stomach and my hands clench. Garang is a close friend of Manny's, named after leader in the conflict with Khartoum in the nineties. He and Manny met in Pinjudu refugee camp in Ethiopia as children and travelled together through the bush. When Mengistu was ousted as leader of Ethiopia, the 'Lost Boys,' as they are called in the United States, were forced to leave. They walked to Kakuma Camp in Kenya and were eventually offered asylum in the USA. Garang came back to South Sudan in 2015, a year before we did, and works as a journalist for Al Jazeera, the Juba Monitor, and other papers. He and Manny both lost touch with their parents during the fighting in the 1990's. Manny first met him in the refugee camp he was determined to return to the battle but their teacher and pastor persuaded him to look for other ways to fight and he started to write In the USA he was able to train as a journalist. He, and Jacob, another friend, shared an apartment in the early chaotic days when they learned how to cope in a new continent and have remained close friends ever since.

'What's happened?'

'I don't know. He was on the TV last night reporting that the appointment of the Unity Government has been delayed again. There was no text from him this morning, so I contacted his office, and they told me he'd been arrested at dawn.'

'Why, Manny?'

'He sent me a piece he had written for the Askari Newsletter on corruption, here you can read it.' He searches in his email and then passes me his phone.

'Opinion: South Sudan leadership gets top marks for corruption.

The reputation of South Sudan's interim government reached its nadir this week when it was scored top in the Askari chart of corrupt African leaders. It is well known that the President and Vice President have luxury villas in adjacent residential roads in the exclusive Nairobi suburb of Lavington. It has now been revealed that both have extensive investments in Kenyan businesses, registered to family members.

Funding that should be invested in building the economy of South Sudan is being siphoned off into personal fortunes, leaving the people in acute poverty.'

The photo shows a large suburban villa. I remember meeting Jane at the Anglican Church guest house in the Ngong Road in Nairobi. We walked a few blocks one evening to a road full of large, shaded villas, their walls hung with bougainvillea, shrieks and splashes emanating from gardens as children swam or played tennis. A dream world compared to the dusty streets of

Juba and the hardship of people's lives here.

'Garang is careful, and his editor keeps tight control over what is published, but the Askari isn't circulated here so maybe he felt he could be freer.' Manny adds.

'It would only take one person to pass this on to the National Security Service.' I say as I pour myself a cup of tea and sit at the table beside him.

'Who would do that?'

'I don't know, Manny. People get desperate for money and tempted by bribes.'

'Maybe just commenting critically on the delay in appointments has put him under suspicion.' he surmises. 'The people at his office are making enquiries. I'll let the others know and see what else we can do.' He means the group of Lost Boys, who have returned to South Sudan. They keep in touch and help each other out.

Manny wanders out onto the balcony, and I prepare beans and rice for supper. There is a knock on the front door of our apartment and I open it to find Manny's friend, Jacob, there. He is a tall, slight Dinka, the quieter one of the three. but he is not to be underestimated. His influence can have an effect where their powers of communication fail. His calm and subtle spirit brings a more thoughtful approach to Manny's and Garang's energy.

'Jacob! Welcome.' I say, as I open the door.

'Hi Maria. I hope you don't mind me popping round. I've brought you some fruit from Uganda. Is Manny in?'

'Thank you.' I say, taking the box from him. 'You will stay to supper? How much do we owe you?'

'It's my gift, Maria. Thank you, I would like to join

47

you for supper.'

'Manny is on the balcony.' I hear Jacob ask if Manny has heard from Garang and Manny replies.

'No, he's not replying to his phone.'

'You don't think…...?' Jacob is asking as I carry a plate of fruit out and join them.

'His office people are trying to find out what's happened.' Manny replies. The same dread words are in all our minds 'The Blue House.' The National Security Forces have the power to arrest people. Their detention centre is known as the 'Blue House' because of its blue windows and roof. It is well known as a place of despair from which many do not emerge. They use torture to gain statements and South Sudan's weak judicial system provides no control over their activities.

'Garang has been more openly critical recently, not in the local paper but in the overseas press, perhaps someone leaked one of his reports.' Manny tells Jacob.

'If they have taken him, they'll hold him awaiting trial. One of the pastors was months there because he was heard criticising the government. He could not walk when they finally released him.' Jacob says.

'I'll see what I can find out at work, but people are unwilling to talk about anything to do with the 'Blue House.' The National Security Forces operate on their own.' Manny replies. We munch the fruit thoughtfully. We all love Garang's incisive wit and accurate summaries of the state of our country, the thought of him being held and questioned is horrifying.

'The mosquitoes are biting.' Manny breaks

the silence. He goes inside and fetches a couple of cool beers from the bucket of water in the corner of the main room. I close the balcony door.

'Do you need help dishing up, Princess?' Manny glances up at me.

'Yes, you can carry the plates through, put the greens on top and I'll bring the beans.'

The generator stutters into life and the lights come on, giving the apartment a yellow glow. The sturdy wooden table, made by one of Manny's friends as a wedding present, shines brown and gold in the dim light.

'What's your view on the latest postponement of appointments?' Jacob asks. 'Do you think we will ever get a Unity Government?'

'We have to.' Manny replies. 'Government offices are paralysed. Nothing has moved forward since the President increased the number of states from ten to twenty-eight in 2015. We do not have trained staff to cover all the ministries and states.'

'Are you sorry you came back here?' asks Jacob.

'Sometimes.' Manny replies. I don't like it when Manny speaks in this way. We knew it would not be easy.

'Jacob, please, help yourself.' I suggest. My distraction works and Manny passes him the dishes and then takes some himself.

'This is tasty, Maria.' Jacob says. 'It is a traditional dish, but I think you have added something?'

'There is English mustard in the tomato sauce,' I admit, 'and a dash of tabasco. Jane sends them out to us for Christmas.'

'Mmm. Very good.'

'How was your trip to Uganda?' I ask Jacob.

'It was sad. Many young people are stuck in the refugee camps near the South Sudanese border. They need education and activities to give them hope. We arranged some training to raise their spirits. The sooner we can bring them back the better, but people are frightened that there will be no peace until the Unity government is formed.'

Jacob works as the bishop's secretary, but I think he would like to have a government post.

'So, how are things with you?' he asks Manny.

'No change.' my husband replies.

'What's the problem, Man?'

'I've two areas of responsibility, ending child labour; and empowering and protecting women. I've been involved in writing plans, - the United Nations action on Women, Peace, and Security - but very little has changed. Some of the worst atrocities are committed by government officials. The police and security services are supposed to protect women and children, but they're sometimes the ones who are trafficking and abusing them.'

'It's seen as normal.' Jacob comments, his forehead creasing. 'People use the excuse of tribal customs, marrying young, taking on your brother's wife if he dies, that sort of thing, but they are operating outside the checks and balances of the tribal system. The chief's courts weigh cases and give judgement in the rural areas but, in the towns, there is no redress against brutality and injustice.'

I think of my sister, Rachel, who was forced into a marriage where she was brutalised by the 'aunt' who fostered her in Kakuma refugee camp. She is back with our family in Nimule now but is still recovering.

'Our state justice systems are too weak to protect women and children.' adds Manny, 'We still have no juvenile courts. Women lack the education to take a lawsuit or bring a case for rape or violence.'

'Come on.' I encourage them 'We must stay hopeful, things will improve.'

'You are always so strong and optimistic, Maria! You are right, of course!' responds Jacob, 'I must get going.' he adds, 'Will you be at the Cathedral for drumming practice on Wednesday?'

'Sorry.' says Manny. 'I'm flying to Malakal in the morning.'

'Where?'

'Upper Nile state in the northeast. I'm going to meet the FTR team, and then on to the Ethiopian border for a meeting with the district commissioner about refugees returning from Ethiopia.'

'FTR? What's that? Sounds painful!' asks Jacob.

'Family Tracing and Reunification.' Manny explains. 'They help families who have been separated to get back together again.'

'Well rather you than me, it's a long way.'

'No further than where you have come from!' expostulates Manny.

'Yes, but there are tarmacked roads in Uganda.'

'I'm going by light aircraft to Malakal and then by truck to Pagak. Kiki, my assistant, has just booked it.'

'Well, have a good trip.' Jacob responds. He turns to me:

'Maria, thank you for supper, it's been great.'

'Thanks for the fruit.' I tell him.

'Thanks, buddy.' says Manny. 'We'll keep in touch over Garang.' They clasp hands warmly.

We clear the dishes and then stand on the balcony gazing at the stars. The noise of the city has hushed, crickets chirp their nightly serenade from cracks in the walls. The air cools and a fresh breeze blows from the surrounding hills.

'We'd better get some sleep, Princess.' says Manny. 'My flight leaves at six thirty in the morning.'

'That's fine. I'll get up with you and go to the salon early. Aunt Roselyn can pick Rose up from there.'

'It'll be a small plane, so I should get a good view. I'll call you when I land if I've got a signal.'

'How long is the flight?'

'No more than a couple of hours.'

'There's no fighting in the northeast now?' I ask anxiously.

'There's still a substantial army presence but there is peace.' he reassures me.

'Why do you have to go?' I ask.

'People fled over the border during the unrest but now, with the fighting in Tigray Province in Ethiopia, they are returning. There is severe flooding and local populations are being overwhelmed by returnees and Tigrayan refugees. I'm meeting with the district commissioner to decide priorities for women and children, and then with the bishop to visit areas near the border where flooding is particularly severe, a place called Pagak. The main town is in Ethiopia, but I shall be meeting the community on the South Sudan side.'

Later, I lie in bed, listening to Manny breathing heavily. I am worried. Manny is flying to one of the most dangerous areas of South Sudan. The Upper Nile oilfields on the northern boundary with Sudan are a source of conflict. There are disputes over who should govern the state. It is a long flight in a small plane. I wish he did not have to go.

2nd December Pagak
Hey, Princess,
Great flight! It was misty but I could see the Nile twisting across the flood plain, which is bright green, quite different to the scrub around Juba. There was flooding as we flew north.
I met the district commissioner briefly and had a long talk with the member of his staff looking after children's welfare.
This afternoon we drove on to Pagak. The driver was skilled in negotiating flooded bridges and ruts in the road but about half a mile from the village he said it was not safe to continue, and we walked the rest of the way. The soil is black Nile silt, soft and sticky, my shoes are covered in mud, but the women who welcomed us have taken them away for cleaning. The village is primitive, with grass roofed huts with small pottery cones on top. Quite attractive. I am staying overnight in the 'conference centre.' This is four rectangular huts, poorly maintained. Locals were unpacking new mattresses when we arrived.
The bishop showed me round this afternoon. The medical centre is a ruin. It once had four wards and operating equipment but one building is left standing. The medical stores disappeared once the aid workers had left. The local wi-fi hub was looted and they rely on a signal from Ethiopia, which is erratic.
Give my rosebud a big hug from her dada.
Love
Manny

3rd December, Juba

Rose heard a plane go over this morning and pointed at it saying, 'Dada up!'

Aunt Roselyn is teaching her the old Dinka songs and stories about animals. She can mimic a monkey's chatter, which is cute!

See you soon,
Maria and Rose

4th December Juba

The eagle has landed! We flew back direct from Pagak. There is a good dirt runway there, maintained by the army.

A woman brought our breakfast this morning who looked exactly like my mother. She told me her name is Nyadena so it cannot be, though she is about the age my sister would be. Her husband is a chaplain in the Nuer regiment, so she must be from the local Nuer tribe, but it was strange.

Should be home in an hour depending on traffic.
M

He has put a picture of an American eagle at the bottom. I show it to Rose, who is in her highchair.

'Dada's home soon.' I tell her.

'Up!' she says, pointing to the picture.

'Down now. Finish your tea. We'll get you ready for bed and then there'll be time for a cuddle and a song with Dada.' She reaches her arms to me. I wipe her sticky fingers and face and lift her out.

As I bathe Rose, I chat and laugh with her but underneath my thoughts are churning over the woman Manny mentioned. The government post soldiers all over the country, sometimes stationed for many years in one place and then moved because of a new outbreak of fighting. Strange things happen in the turmoil that is South Sudan.

Later that evening Manny and I sit on the balcony to catch up.

'I was worried when you said the road was flooded.' I tell him.

'Yes, flying straight from Pagak on the return was much better. It's a beautiful place, but remote. The locals go to Gambella if they need hospitalisation.'

'In Ethiopia?'

'It's half an hour to walk, or if they are sick, they're taken on a wide tyred buggy.'

'That's awful. Imagine being bumped over the ground if you were really unwell.' I comment, and wonder what it would be like if you had complications giving birth? I guess it's better than most parts of rural South Sudan where there are no hospitals at all. 'Tell me about the woman who looked like your mother.' I ask him.

'Oh, well. It was just my imagination. Something about the eyes.'

'In what way?'

'Mama had slanting eyes, unusually close together. If she was frowning, she could look fierce! She was from the Bari tribe. Bor Dinka don't marry outside the tribe but my father was determined to have her. He paid a high bride price, but it was a source of tension with his family. This woman had a softer face but the same tight features.'

'Manny, you must find out more.'

'Leave it, Maria. It was just a coincidence.'

'How can you say that? Family likenesses are significant, particularly if she looked more like a Bari than a Nuer or Dinka. Surely you want to KNOW!' I am shouting now. I didn't mean to.

'THEY DIED, OKAY!' He is shouting too. He pushes his chair back hard, scraping it on the concrete wall, lurches upright, and blunders through the door into the main room. I hear the door slam and shortly afterwards I see him walking fast along the road outside. I should have waited. He is tired and stressed. He has always been convinced that his mother and sister died in the Uganda refugee camps. His father has moved back to Bor, but we have not been able to find any trace of those who were lost when the breakaway army attacked the town. Part of our reason for returning to South Sudan was to find proof that this is what had happened but none of the agencies have been able to help us. This is the first possible lead, and he will not follow it up. I fear that he will go back to Baltimore and his luxurious life there, and what would I do?

I tidy the kitchen, fold Rose's clean clothes and get ready for bed. I make a cup of tea and write up my notes but I cannot settle. I cradle the mug of tea and pray.

Manny returns hours later. His ebony skin is dry, his eyes stark and white, the pupils half covered by heavy lids. When his emotions are stirred, he retreats inside himself.

'I went to see Jacob.' he explains. 'One of the chaplains has confirmed that Garang is in the Blue House. This is bad news, very few journalists emerge from the Blue House without long term physical and emotional damage.'

'Oh. I'm sorry.' I can sense his tension and anxiety and go to hug him. He brushes me off and climbs wearily into bed. For the first time since we married there is no comfort between us. I dare not reach out to him and we lie rigidly side by side until I hear him snoring. I doze fitfully.

Too soon the sun is breaking through the curtains. Rose is burbling to herself in her cot. I can hear Manny showering. He enters the main room as I give Rose breakfast, comes across to her chair, gives her a kiss, but not me, and leaves for the office.

We go on like this for a week. There is a stone in my stomach, of anxiety about Garang, and the effect on Manny, but I dare not say anything. He goes round to Jacob several times, working out what they can do, but there is more than our fear about Garang between us. I can hear the voices of Manny's ancestors in my spirit and see their shadows sitting on his shoulders. Why will he not find out about the woman he saw? The soft spirit of our relationship has become sour and harsh.

The following Wednesday evening he comes home tense, angry and silent.

'Tell me what's wrong.' I plead with him.

'I'm okay.' He lifts Rose up and starts to throw her in the air, to her delight, but he ignores me. I can hear blood pounding in my ears. I am going to burst if I do not go out.

'I'm going for a walk.' I say quietly.

I stumble blindly along our street. The back of my head is pounding, and my eyes are full of tears. I don't know where I am going. The passing bikes and cars are a dusty haze. The smells of the city, diesel, gas, charcoal burners, ripe bananas, sour sweat, fill my nostrils. I wish I was back in the calm clean air of the UK. My steps have turned automatically to the Episcopal Church guest house, next to All Saints cathedral where Manny plays the drums on Sunday, and I help with the children. I will say 'hallo' to Anna, the manager, perhaps have a cup of tea with her. The shade of the trees is cool, with a promise of gentle night air as the sun sets behind them, leaving a dappled pattern on the ground.

'Maria, how is your famileee?' The voice is rich and dark, with a long drawn out eeee on the last syllable. It is Bishop Zak, who married us. He walks up the driveway beside me.

'We are fine. Rose is growing fast and talking now.'

'And Manny?' I want to answer positively but I say nothing. Pastor Zak's eyes search my face.

'I am on my way to meet a visitor here.' he says. 'You will have a cup of tea with me while I wait for him to arrive?' His voice rises in a question. His kind eyes compel me.

'Thank you. I'd like to.' We sit under a desert rose tree on the side of the driveway. The pink and yellow trumpet flowers cluster above us in the dark and the dense canopy creates a pool of cooler air. While Bishop Zak fetches two mugs of tea, I watch a lizard scurry up the wall to wherever he spends the night.

'Now tell me what is troubling you.' he commands gently.

'Manny has seen a person who reminded him of his mother. It might be one of his sisters, lost in the Bor conflict, but he does not want to do anything. This has put a bad spirit between us.'

'Mama Maria, you have a strong marriage, do not let this disturb you.'

'But why won't he find out?'

'People are different. He talks about his family?'

'No, never. He doesn't get on well with his father and brother, and he never talks of his mother and sister.'

'How old was he when the conflict came?' asks the bishop.

'He had seen eleven rains when the soldiers destroyed his village.' I reply.

'A young boy, perhaps he has put it behind him in order to grow up quickly.'

'He said it was tough to keep up with older boys.' I add.

'He had to become a man very early.' says Bishop Zak. He glances up as a car rumbles up the driveway, its headlights picking out first the tree branches, then the stony ground, as it bumps along the rough track. 'Give him time, Maria. He will find his own way. Here is the man I am waiting for. God, give you rest, Mama.' He rises swiftly from his chair, and follows the car, taking a route through the trees at the side of the drive, picking his way through piles of rubble where better accommodation is under construction. I stand and wave, but he has disappeared into the shadows of the newly constructed walls. I wrap my scarf round me to keep out the cool evening air and walk home.

I didn't see my family for twenty years, but I did have two fellow servants in the same household in Khartoum. We were from different parts of Sudan, but they looked after me, taught me and protected me. I suppose they were like a mother and father. Although he had more schooling, perhaps Manny had no-one to care for him.

I feel calmer. The beauty of the night wraps around me. The streets are quiet in the evening in this part of Juba. The daytime smells are fainter and overlain by the sweet earthy smell of desert rose and cassia flowers. Crickets scrape their evening serenade and a few fireflies dart above the walls of the bigger houses. I feel more at peace, the turmoil and anxiety of the last week stilled. It is Manny's choice if he does not want to find out about the woman in Pagak, and I must accept his decision.

I open the door of our apartment expecting to hear Rose, over excited from playing with her father. They are not in the main room and all her toys have been tidied away, the highchair stacked neatly in the corner. I tiptoe along to the bedroom. She is fast asleep in her cot, a light sheet tucked round her chubby body. Her face and feet are clean, her favourite zebra placed beside her. Manny is asleep on the bed, an untouched glass of beer beside him. I leave them and go back along the corridor to check on the kitchen, but all is neat and tidy. A plate of mixed beans and chopped tomato stands on the worktop, with a bowl of fresh ground peanut butter beside it. I feel ashamed that he has taken so much trouble at the end of a tough week and with all his anxiety about Garang. I make a cup of tea, add a spoonful of peanut butter to the bean mix and take it onto the balcony. The sky is blue black, dotted with pin pricks of light. A crescent moon is setting behind the government offices. The silhouette of the twin towers of All Saints cathedral are visible in the distance. I thank God for sending Bishop Zak. We will be all right, it will be tough, but with God's help we can cope.

'Princess!' Manny has woken and come to join me on the balcony.

'Manny! I should not have pushed you about your family. I'm sorry.'

'That's okay. Where did you go?'

'I walked to the guest house and had a chat with Bishop Zak.'

'I read Rose a bedtime story.'

'Did she settle alright?'

'I forgot the zebra, but once she had that she was fine.'

'Thank you for supper.' I say, looking into his dark face. How tired he is. I shall not mention his family until Garang is safe. If it is possible to rescue him from the grip of the National Security Forces. I find it difficult that he does not want to know for sure what happened to his mother, but it is Rose that matters, and how Manny and I are as her parents. Soon it will be Christmas, perhaps a short holiday will help.

'I'm sorry too, Princess. Garang is family to me more than anyone else can be. He and Jacob are the only ones who understand what it was like to run from our home and our families. Until I know he is safe, I can't concentrate on anything else.' He wraps his long arms around me from behind. A radio starts up in one of the adjacent apartments, playing a popular South Sudanese love song. I turn towards him. We dance close together, the darkness and the pinprick light of the stars making a perfect backdrop. The song changes tempo and Manny starts the ridiculous stick dance that we used to do as small children when he visited his aunt Nimule. We cling to each other, laughing. We are okay. No demons will trouble my sleep tonight.

Unseen, storm clouds are gathering, and spirits of fear, death, and loss will torment our friends in Europe, and test the hopes of every nation.

4 NYADENA'S JOURNEY

Nyadena's family celebrates Christmas in the way they have always done since they came to Pagak. She and Reuben have scraped together a few shillings to buy Eliza, Luko, and Barni new clothes. The local seamstress delivered shorts for the boys and a dress for Eliza made on her ancient hand operated sewing machine. It is hard without family nearby but Reuben's parents send fabric for new clothes and his father carves wooden toys for the children. It hurst that she is not in touch with her own family. She no longer hears from her mother and sister and her father and brothers were killed in the conflict years ago.

The children wake before sunrise and stare in wonder at the parcels, wrapped in fabric from old dresses, just visible in the pre-dawn light at the foot of their beds.

''It's Christmas.' whispers Luko.

'Shush.' Eliza hushes him, 'or you won't get the special breakfast.'

'Is it oranges?' wonders Luko.

'I'm not allowed to tell.' his elder sister says with an air of superiority. Luko stares at the parcels. Their mother enters through the door of the *tukul*.

'Time to get up. Sit nicely for your tea and there might be a treat!' The family sit on the ground around the brazier, warmed by its embers glowing in the cool of dawn. Nyadena passes round weak warm tea for the children and pours a mug, hot and dark, for herself and her husband. The children drink quietly in anticipation of the moment. Barni senses the excitement of his older siblings and waits in silence, for once. Reuben, squatting beside the fire, reaches behind him and brings out a brown bag. He rises to his feet in a single sinuous movement. The children sit up, alert, mesmerised by the mysterious crackle of the paper. He reaches into the bag. He pulls out an orange and hands one to each of his children, saying.

'Happy Christmas.'

Barni's face puckers as his infant teeth bite into the fruit and the juice squirts to the back of his throat. He gasps.

'Can I have some of Barni's?' Luko asks.

'No.' replies their father. 'He can eat it all.' Laughing, Nyadena says:

'Now rinse your hands and eat the porridge, then you can open the other packages.' Luko is always eager and assertive. His features are fine drawn, like hers but his sturdy limbs and soft padding gait are a stabbing reminder of her youngest brother, twelve years her senior and a teenager when she last saw him. They called him 'Kor,' meaning cat, because of his ability to creep up on silent feet and embrace his family unexpectedly. It was strange how that man that came from Juba reminded her of Kor. It could not be him. Her father and all her brothers died in the conflict. Her mother often told the story of how their father had seen her and Hannah to the

Ugandan border where they were within a few hours walk of her relatives and then turned back to fight the soldiers who had destroyed their town. Like many families in the camp, they had to build their own life, with whatever help relatives could give. It taught us resilience and how to make do on little, which had been helpful in the last few hard years in Pagak. She and her mother and sister had started again several times. She could do it once more.

Half an hour later they are ready to go to the Christmas parade, standing tall in new clothes. Eliza fingers the brightly coloured pattern of her dress. She feels older, prettier, than she did yesterday. She follows her family to the airstrip.

The sun lifts above the horizon. Misty indigo shapes of trees and bushes, change as golden light picks out each leaf and branch in turn. The translucent sky turns pink, then turquoise as the sun lifts above the horizon and the temperature climbs from the mid-twenties towards the thirties. Other family groups join them, youths clutching drums, girls in the pink tabards of the choir, mothers who have new scarves wrapped round their shoulders or tied in an elaborate turban on their heads.

Joanna comes alongside and she and Nyadena chat as they walk along.

'What have you done with your money from the big man? Did you spend it for Christmas.' she says in a low voice to Nyadena.

'No! I've hidden it in my old scarf.'

'Me too. It was a big gift; you never know when it might be useful.' Their heads move together as they delight in their secret bonus. Both women had been chosen to serve food to a man from the government who came to visit before Christmas. The Mothers' Union members provided the food and Nyadena and Joanna were the ones chosen to carry it across the compound from the cook fire to the bishop's guesthouse.

'He was a kind man.' Says Joanna. 'They are not usually like that the visitors in shiny suits and leather shoes.'

'He was from America.' suggests Nyadena. 'He spoke like those nurses who ran the clinic.'

'He would be a good dancer.' laughs Joanna. 'He moved like a leopard, although he was a heavy man.'

'You must not say such things.' chuckles Nyadena. In fact, the presence of the government man had unsettled her. His face had reminded her of the father, whose face she could not recall but whose presence she remembered as a powerful force that hefted her into his arms, a strong chin covered in bristly grey hairs that tickled her cheeks. The big man was clean shaven but there was something about his compact power, his strong features, dark skin, and wide smile that made something deep inside her vibrate like a drum skin.

The airstrip is swept clean, the sand with its ochre tints glistening in the sunlight. The army were out yesterday clearing the vegetation. Each side runs straight as an arrow to the far horizon, where the two parallel ditches disappear to a single point.

The families split and join their part of the parade. Nyadena hands Eliza her tabard and releases her to the choir. Reuben makes his way to the phalanx of army chaplains. Luko and Barni leap ahead of their mother, jumping from one side to the other of the ditch, their new shorts garish in the morning light. Nyadena joins the ranks of the Mothers' Union, holding Barni's hand tightly and indicating to Luko to join the other children at the front of their section. There is a ritual about these community gatherings that she finds comforting.

The choir lead the way, arranged in height order. They have been practicing for hours in the school compound and are word perfect on the song, and in total synchronisation on the forward and back dance step with which they lead the parade. The Mothers' Union members follow them, the few with the money to afford it wearing the bright blue cloth spattered with the intertwined M and U. Next come the youths, those who own them holding drums, ready to beat a steady rhythm. Behind them the leaders of the community march solemnly in step, heads held high, gazes fixed straight ahead. At the end of the procession the bishop in his mitre and cope, the thin rayon splaying out in the light breeze, appears as a daylight ghost, his crook held in his right hand and his left hand clutching his pectoral cross. The district commissioner, in his navy suit, face already shining with the heat, is a dark spectre. The church deacons and wardens, and the pastors, almost equal numbers of men and women, in grey suits or white robes and shiny white dog collars, form the tail of the procession. The armed forces are in a separate line-up of army units, police, rangers and the fire service, men and women marching together.

The last few stragglers find their places. The bishop raises his crozier and shouts a sonorous prayer. The youths start drumming, led by a young pastor, and the parade moves off, along the airstrip for half a mile, then left across a narrow wooden bridge over the ditch. They turn right along the path that leads to the church and circle the low, thatched building, crouched like a sleeping lioness among the trees. The drums stutter and stop. The district commissioner makes a speech, inaudible to most, but they know he is saying that it is Christmas Day, the birthday of the Lord Jesus, and a day of peace in war torn South Sudan.

Nyadena glances at the women around her, their faces eager, hopeful, but deeply etched with the anguish of six years ago when the armies came through the township, soldiers with rifles held high. She smells again the ammunition in the air, the hot acrid taste of it and the rat-a-tat of the gunfire. Eliza was a small child then, and Luko just toddling, they sheltered in the church with other terrified families, hearing the crash and rumble of the shops along the main street falling, feeling each other's sweat and fear as they lay touching, crushed together for comfort and safety, using their bodies to shelter their children. They remained there for days. When the wooden door was pushed open and sunlight poured into the dark church, they were silent, terrified until Reuben's voice rang out.

'The fighting is over! The rebel forces were driven away. You can come out.' Nyadena had run to him, Luko in her arms and Eliza clinging to her legs. He had hugged her briefly and then pushed them away saying:

'The clinic has been destroyed. I must help the nurses. Go straight to our compound and stay there. You will be safe this side of the river.'

Nyadena had been shocked by the devastation. Only one of the four concrete wards still standing, the rest a smoking ruin, a carved stone fountain in the centre untouched, a solemn sentinel watching over what had been a beautiful garden. She had hurried the children past, talking about what they would eat, and hoping that the sack of millet had not been looted.

The community worked together. Homes, schools, and churches were rebuilt, the clinic running out of the one remaining room, all the equipment stolen. The Red Cross still flies in supplies of drugs but for anything that cannot be treated with a pill they go to Gambella across the Ethiopian border. The brick rubble, all that remained of the shops, now forms a lumpy track from the clinic to the main square, lined by the hovels of those who lost their homes.

People from many tribes live in the area around Pagak. The aftermath of the conflict has been a deeply troubling time. Half Dinka, half Bari, married to a Nuer, local leaders viewed Nyadena with suspicion. The sense of betrayal over the looting and destruction from within their own community is deep. Most families lost a relative. The nightmares of Nyadena's childhood reawakened - running from the conflict in Bor in 1991, losing her father and brothers in the violence that followed, and fleeing with her mother and sister to Uganda. She lost touch with them before Barni was born. Reuben and the three children are her only family. Perhaps she should follow him, not flee to remote areas all her life. It is time to build a future for the children. Reuben is right, the capital is a better place for schooling, where they might continue to secondary level. How can it be done? Her husband will leave in the New Year with the rest of his platoon, but women are expected to stay with their extended family. Her mother and sister who are thousands of miles away in Congo. She does not know if they are still alive.

The problem is unresolved when she stands on the airstrip a couple of weeks later, with many women and their families, to wave off the soldiers posted to Juba. At the far end three army trucks are visible, faint in the morning haze, their huge tyres softening in the extreme heat, their exhaust pipes protruding vertically from the engine casing, a precaution against swollen rivers. Nyadena and Reuben walk together, Eliza ahead of them holding one handle of her father's kit bag while Luko holds the other. Barni, held tightly in his mother's arms waves his fists in excitement as girls walk past with baskets of lemons balanced on their heads. It will be an arduous journey on dirt roads that have deteriorated under the onslaught of rains. The silty soil is waterlogged, the ditches swollen and black with mud. There is a sense of unease in the crowd. The dark rain clouds echo the fear and uncertainty of losing the protection of these soldiers. To mask their feelings the women are animated.

'The frogs are singing in the pools for them.'

'The feast has given them strength.'

The commander had arranged for sheep to be slaughtered for a farewell celebration the previous day. The partying continued far into the night, becoming more energetic as the air cooled and the stars shone. It is clear from the staggering gait and erratic progress of some of the armed forces this morning that they are feeling the effects of a night of drinking.

'Barni walk.' demands her youngest.

'No, Barni, there are too many people. See

the trucks, you can walk when we get to those. Baba is going in one of the trucks. You can wave "Bye bye" can't you? Baba will find us a place to stay, and then we will go to Juba too.' Reuben's gait falters slightly in surprise, he has not been sure that she would follow him.

'Go, 'ooba.' mutters Barni experimentally.

'Yes. Baba will find a place for us, and we will go to Juba.' Their eyes meet over Barni's head and Reuben's mouth crinkles at the corners. There is no gesture, which would be unseemly in public, but their decision has been made.

'Baba will send a message to the commander when everything is ready.' he assures the little boy, who picking up the warmth in his parents' eyes, wriggles in excitement.

Nyadena stands at the end of the airstrip, watching as Reuben waits in line ready to be called to board one of the pickups. He looks handsome and confident in his camouflage. Barni plays at her feet, the others have gone off with their friends, bored by the long wait.

'Your children are enjoying the fun!' A sharp featured woman in police uniform stands beside her. Nyadena jumps in alarm.

'What are they doing?'

'Hey, it's fine, they're having a great time playing with my two sons.' Nyadena turns in the direction the policewoman indicates and sees Eliza and Luko, hot and breathless, running with a group of teenagers on the other side of the airstrip.

'They are not in trouble?'

'No, of course not. It's a long time waiting and it's better that they use their energy rather than bother us.' The woman laughs. 'How old are they?'

'Eliza has seen nine rains and Luko eight, and this is Barni.'

'Your husband is going to Juba?'

'Yes. And yours?'

'Yes. I should be working but my supervisor has let me come to see him off. I'm Miriam.'

'I'm Nyadena. You are in the Police Force?' Miriam's smile is warm and her eyes bright. Nyadena feels an instant bond with her.

'I was a police assistant before I had the children.' She says. 'I am hoping to return as soon as Barni is at school. How old are your boys?'

'Alek is sixteen and Yar fourteen. We are following their father to Juba. I want them to take their Certificate of Secondary Education.'

'I'm going too. I wasn't sure at first, but I have no family here. It's better for the children to be with their father.' Barni is bored with playing in the sand. He lets out a roar and Nyadena picks him up and points to the trucks.

'Baba is nearly there; he will be in the truck soon.'

'Ba-ba-ba-ba.' Barni waves his chubby fists in the direction of his father.

'How are you travelling?' asks Miriam.

'I don't know. I have only just decided.'

'There may be a police truck going to Pibor Post soon. They will take us, and we can get a bus from there to Bor, then take a river boat to Juba. I could see if there is a place for you. It's better to travel in a group.' Nyadena looks at her in amazement.

'How soon? Will they allow children?' she asks.

'Do you have a phone? Where do you live?' Miriam responds.

'No phone, but we live just off the airstrip, near the clinic. Ask for Reuben Thon's *tukul*.'

'We'd better round up the children; the trucks are ready to go.' Many women are calling and there is confusion as youths and children find their own family groups.

Nyadena gathers her children.

'Reuben!' she calls, and he looks across, face concerned, but apprehensive in case his family shames him in some way.

'We will come to Juba with Miriam, by boat.' Nyadena indicates her newfound friend.

'Tell the commander which boat.' he responds, and marches towards the next truck with his platoon.

Nyadena and Miriam stand together, Eliza and the four boys gathered around them. The engines roar into life, the men hold their guns vertically, like a picket fence around the inside of the truck and are gone in a cloud of dust.

'I will find you when I know the time.' Miriam says, and walks away, her tall sons trailing after her.

Nyadena's mind is in turmoil. Nothing is arranged. Supposing Reuben does not find accommodation for them? Will he take that quick glance over Barni's head seriously? Can she trust Miriam, and her boys?

She hears nothing for several weeks, then Miriam makes a visit.

'*Madho*! Nyadena, are you there?' Nyadena places the clothes she has been folding in a neat pile and goes to the door.

'Miriam, you are welcome.' Nyadena places a chair

for her and sits on the bed.

'The boss says there will be a truck going to Pibor Post at first light in two days to collect some recruits. There will be places on the outward journey. You will come?'

Nyadena has thought carefully about this over the last few weeks and asked her friends about Miriam's reputation. 'She is a good woman, that one.' Susana, the Mothers' Union lead, assures her. 'That one work hard and is respected.'

Nyadena takes a deep breath.

'We will come.' she replies. 'They know I have children?'

'You must bring food and water for them and wrap the little one well against the wind. It will be cold when the truck goes fast.'

'Yes. I will do that. They want money?'

'They want a hundred South Sudanese pounds per person and fifty for each child.'

'Where do I bring it?' Nyadena has the money Reuben left her and the funds she put aside from serving the government man. She can manage and have spare for the onward journey. He gave her dollars, which she will be able to exchange at a good rate.

'Come to the police post at first light next Thursday.'

So, it is decided. The family are on the move again and Nyadena, as a good army wife, must pack her belongings, move on, and make the best of whatever accommodation can be found for them in Juba.

'I am used to it.' Nyadena says to herself after she has seen the children to bed and sits outside planning in her head what needs to be packed up, and what can be given away. They cannot take much because everything must be carried by herself and the children, and Barni is only just old enough walk. It will be tough, but she has seen tougher times. Sitting alone in the soft darkness of the evening with the crickets playing their reedy song in the bushes she thinks of other journeys. The day her uncle Worro collected them from the refugee camp and took them on an interminable bus ride, she had been a child, unhappy at leaving her friends but excited at the promise of a new start in a big city. It had been harder for her mother and sister, she reflected, setting up a sewing business and earning money to build a house so that they were not dependent on uncle. It went well until Hannah's misfortune occurred. She was grateful for her uncle's help so that she could finish her education and apply for the job in the Police Force. He had given her the fare back to South Sudan, but it soured the relationship with her mother and sister.

'I was selfish,' she reflects, 'leaving Hannah, unmarried, pregnant by force, her reputation destroyed. I ought to let them know I am going to Juba. What if they try to contact me? I do not even have the same name.' Reuben had given her a nickname that sounded more appropriate for his Nuer relatives than the sibilant sound of her baptismal name. Since then, she has been Nyadena, wife of Reuben Thon, mother of his children. She chews on a blade of grass and wonders if she will ever reconnect with the woman she used to be before childbearing and army postings changed her life.

The rattle of the truck and the whistle of its

airstream passing the tall grass on either side of the track is deafening.

'Mama, will we see Baba tonight?' Luko leans towards her and whispers hoarsely in her ear.

'Not tonight, little monkey, we must get a taxi to Bor tonight, then a river boat to Juba. It will be two days before we see Baba. Look at the mangoes growing on those trees.' She tries to distract him but while the other children have been lulled into a state of stillness by the noise and motion of the truck, Luko is restless.

'Where will we sleep?'

'We will sleep with a relative of Miriam's in Bor tonight, then we will sleep at our new home tomorrow night.' She hopes this is correct. A message has been passed to Reuben through his commander, but there has been no response. It can take weeks for post to get to Pagak, and there is no mobile signal except from Ethiopia so if Reuben tries to get a message to her there is no guarantee that it will arrive. Nyadena's only hope is the directions to the barracks in Juba, written on a scrap of paper in her pocket.

'Will the place Baba finds be near a school?'

'I don't know, little monkey, we will have to wait and see.' He settles down and the two families doze as the movement of the truck becomes more familiar.

The wheels churn on the dirt road, causing the tall grasses to sway in their eddy, their yellowing stems, and brown seed heads, contrasting with the red brown of the sandy surface. Hamerkop birds feed peacefully on seeds and insects at the edge of the track, unperturbed by the passing vehicle.

There is a crash of gears and the truck skids to a halt. The driver climbs out and walks round to the back. A stream has burst its banks, the concrete parapet of a bridge visible between the swirling waters. The track leading down to the bridge has become a quagmire of dark red mud. On the other side of the swollen stream the track rises steeply, deeply rutted where other drivers have struggled to free themselves.

'Too deep. Everyone, get out.' He waves them to the side of the road. Nyadena eyes her bundle of their belongings, strapped to the roof, as he backs up the truck. The engine revs and the truck plunges forward at great speed, aquaplanes through the swollen water and ploughs up the other side carried by its own momentum. The driver stops at the top of the slope and waves them forward. Alek and Yar tread confidently along the top of the parapet, followed by their mother and Eliza, but Luko is scared and Nyadena is carrying Barni.

'I'm coming back.' yells Alek. He retraces his steps, takes Luko firmly by the hand and half leads, half drags him across, hands him over to Yar, and returns to Nyadena.

'I will take him.' he says. Nyadena hesitates, then hands the little boy over saying 'Barni, hold on like a monkey.' Alek crosses again and she follows. She is shaking when she reaches the other side but smiles confidently. She will not show her fear in front of this kind family. They climb back into the truck.

'This red mud bad.' says the driver as he shuts the tail gate. 'Pagak black mud is okay but red mud is hard, when it crack, then he ees soft. You hold on.'

There are no more ravines as steep as the one they

have just crossed but the rhythm of the day is set as the truck lurches from side to side, plunges down into valleys and accelerates out. The children find it exciting to begin with but soon tire of the endless bucking of their transport. There are few trees, and they rig an awning and lie under it. At noon they stop for samosas, water, and use of a pit latrine at a roadside bar, then jolt onwards, finally arriving at Pibor Post at four in the afternoon. The journey has taken longer than expected and they are hot and dehydrated.

'We must find a taxi soon,' says Miriam, 'or it will be too late to travel on to Bor. Nyadena can you buy some more water and biscuits and ask if there is a latrine we can use? Yar will help you. Alek, come with me and find a taxi.'

Nyadena pays for a crate of bottled water and use of a key to a latrine. When they have relieved themselves, Yar carries the crate to a large cassia tree, followed by Luko and Eliza. Nyadena holds Barni's hand and balances their bundle of belongings on her head with the other hand. A child approaches them, thin and dusty.

'Water.' he begs them.

'No.' says Yar, 'This is for our journey.'

'You give me, or he beat me.' says the boy.

'Who will beat you? Where are your parents?' asks Nyadena.

'No parents. Uncle beat me.'

'Well, you should ask your uncle to give you water.' says Yar angrily. The boy flinches as if expecting a blow. Miriam returns and at the sight of her police uniform the boy runs off.

'Nuisance.' mutters Yar.

'Well, he's gone now. Come on.' says Miriam. 'We have a taxi. Hurry, Alek is waiting just round the corner.' Yar picks up the water. Luko wants to help but is gently rebuffed.

'You can help later but we have to be quick now.' Barni starts to whine and Nyadena covers his head with her scarf to keep the sun off him and takes Luko by the hand.

'Eliza and Luko, I want you to hold hands and stay close.' she commands in a voice they know must be obeyed.

When they have all squeezed into the eight-seater and loaded their few bags on top it is full, but the driver pulls up a short distance out of town and opens the door to a large lady with two loaded shopping bags. She inserts herself beside them. Barni must sit on his mother's lap, where he grizzles softly. Eliza and Luko elbow each other until sharply reprimanded by Nyadena. The road is better maintained than the track from Pagak and straighter, but it is potholed in places and the dust seeps in through the open windows and covers their clothes, their hair, their faces. The large lady is deposited at an isolated compound about half an hour's drive from Pibor. The teenage boys, crammed into the child seats at the back get out and stretch their cramped legs. Barni is damp and Nyadena takes the opportunity to get a fresh pair of shorts out of the bag on the roof. Then on they go again.

Night falls. The road is becoming busier, and the truck must pause in passing places to allow oncoming vehicles through. The younger boys sleep but Eliza, seated at the far end of the rear seat with Yar and Alek, leans over them to speak with her mother.

'Mama? she asks. 'That boy who wanted water. He

said he had no Mama or Baba.'

'Yes, my butterfly, he was an orphan.'

'He said his uncle would beat him!'

'Who's this?' asks Miriam from the front seat.

'A boy who begged for water when we were waiting in Pibor. I wondered if he was *abid*, a slave.'

'Aie, aie, aie, the police know of many like that in Pibor. They train the children to be beggars and pickpockets and then sell them. It is a lucrative trade, but we do not have the staff to stop it. Even if we did there is no judiciary to bring these people to court.'

'We can do nothing, Eliza.' says her mother.

'I will alert the police post in Pibor,' says Miriam.

'I am going to pray for him every night.' Eliza says.

Several hours after nightfall the taxi drops them at the door of Miriam's relative. Alek carries the sleeping Luko to a mattress on the floor. Barni and Eliza share their mother's double mattress. After a welcome mug of tea, the weary families settle down for the night.

In the morning Eliza is persistent.

'What will happen to the boy?'

'Eliza, Miriam has let her colleagues know, there is nothing more we can do.' There is an edge of irritation in Nyadena's voice. It has been difficult to get this far with three children, without worrying about another one.

'He will go down the Nile to Khartoum.' adds Alek, unwisely.

'Will they beat him?'

'Eliza, that's enough. Eat your porridge. We must leave soon to get the boat. Say thank you.' Eliza abandons her worries for the moment and turns a wide smile on Miriam's relative. Her even white teeth split her heart shaped face and the tilted eyes she has inherited from her mother crinkle with the sincerity of her thanks. Nyadena prods her sons.

'Thank you.' Luko mumbles.

'Fankoo, fankoo' announces Barni banging his bowl on the table.

'Good. Now wash under the tap in the yard and make sure you use the latrine.' There is a scraping of chairs as the replete and rested party gather their belongings and the crate of water and take their leave.

'Thank you for your welcome. We will see you again.' The adults say goodbye with genuine warmth, but they know that meeting again is unlikely, in the turmoil of South Sudan.

The sun lifts above the horizon as they reach the water side. In the grey morning light, they can see dug-out canoes and small fishing vessels but there is no ferry. Miriam sets out with Yar this time, leaving Alek and Nyadena with the children. They watch as Miriam goes from person to person in the gloom.

'Ferry to Juba?'

'You want boat?'

'We want big boat, river ferry.'

'He come later, Mama.'

'How much later?'

'Soon, very soon.' Miriam and Yar return to the rest.

'They don't know.' concludes Miriam. 'Alek and Yar, go along the wharf and make sure we are in the right place. Check out those huts over there.' They shoot off together and Miriam joins Nyadena where she and the little ones are sitting on a tree trunk.

'When will the boat come?' asks Luko.

'Soon. Alek and Yar are finding out.' Says Nyadena. 'Why don't you find some stones and play fives, but stay away from the river, do you hear? There are bad spirits in the river. Eliza, please take Barni. And stay where I can see you.' Luko runs off, Eliza and Barni trailing behind.

'I checked with my aunt, there is a boat most days.' Miriam reassures Nyadena. 'Ferries are booked from Khartoum, so it depends how many want to travel, but she says it has been very crowded recently because of returning South Sudanese.'

A couple of men come up behind them.

'You ladies want nice hotel? We show you. Follow!' Miriam stands up and turns round.

'Scram, or I call my colleagues.' She waves her mobile and they vanish. 'Pests!' she comments. 'Where are the boys? They've been gone a long time.' For the first time Nyadena sees anxiety in her face. She tries to reassure Miriam.

'They are fine young men; you must be proud.'

'They are like their father, gentle but strong.' Nyadena checks on her children. They are playing together by a pile of rubble a hundred metres away. There is no-one around except a couple of fishermen mending their nets on the far side of the river. She shivers, though it is not cold. The morning sun is spreading golden light across the sky. The islands of water hyacinths floating in the river are a translucent green grey in the early light. Huge dragonflies hover over their blue flower spikes. On the near bank a clump of Egyptian papyrus waves in the slight breeze from the river. The frond fingers at the top of each tall stem cast strange shadows in the slanting light of early morning. 'What are we doing here?' she wonders. 'What if the boat does not come? I am mad to come on this journey. If Reuben is not at the wharf in Juba, how will we get to the barracks?'

Alek and Yar arrive panting for breath.

'We went to the nearby offices, but no-one knew.' says Alek. 'Then we ran to the big office near the centre of town. They said the boat has left Malakal and will be here by eleven.'

'It's very full. They say we can't have tickets till some people get off the boat.' adds Yar.

'Did they say where it comes in?' Miriam asks them.

'It comes to where those small offices are.' Alek waves a hand at the huts near the river's edge.

'Well done, both of you.' says their mother. 'We will wait by the huts. Maybe we can get some tea.' There is no-one there. The rusted metal doors are closed and bolted. One has a bench shaded by the steep corrugated iron roof, so they sit and wait. The temperature rises. The water reflects the blue sky and then becomes shimmering white as the sun dances off the ripples made by the floating islands. The bottles of water go down rapidly as one child after another complains of being thirsty. Nyadena tries to keep them in the shade, but they are bored and move off to play five stones in the dust. The sun is high in the sky before two men and a woman appear and open up the huts.

'You waitin' for ferry?' asks the older man. They nod. 'How many? Seven? Mmmm. You wait here.'

'Can we buy water?' asks Nyadena.

'Mama!' he calls to the woman. 'They askeeng for water.'   Nyadena gives Alek ten South Sudanese Pounds. He hurries to the hut and returns quickly. It's more than that for six bottles.' he says. Nyadena gives him another note. She checks her purse. She still has eighty shillings and the dollars but is not sure whether that will cover their fares. There is nothing to do but wait.

The sun is well past the zenith when the ferry finally appears. It has two decks. People are crammed around the railings and standing close together on the top deck. As far as they can see the lower deck is also packed. A rope is thrown, caught by the younger man on the shore and wound tightly round a bollard, as the ferry reverses engines and pulls into the wooden wharf with a gentle nudge. Splinters of wood show where other landings have not been so skilful. The younger children watch open mouthed as a gang plank is let down and men come ashore with sacks of grain over their shoulders. They are followed by a man driving ten goats in front of him. Finally, four women passengers disembark. Miriam and Nyadena look across to the older man, who stands with a clip board.

'Mail for Juba next.' he growls. A man carrying a large sack, staggers on board, followed by five boys, each with a live sheep tied across their shoulders. Two men carry a large wooden crate up the gang plank, straining to balance the weight. One plank bulges slightly.

'What's in there?' whispers Yar. 'Guns?' His mother glares at him and he is silenced. Nyadena's anxiety increases. What if there are guns on board? How safe is this journey?

The man with a clipboard beckons them. 'Room for four passengers.' he says. Then adds with a sly smile, holding up three fingers. 'Special arrangements for these.' He indicates the three younger ones.

'It's a bribe of course.' whispers Miriam. 'Can you pay?'

'Yes.' Nyadena feels the wad of money in her purse. She has enough with a little to spare for food until they get to Juba. What happens if Reuben is not there to meet them? She pushes the thought away. He must be there; she has no other resources.

Nyadena pulls out the notes she needs. Reuben will be angry that she has paid a bribe, but there is no other option. She places the money in the outstretched hand, picks up Barni, and tells Eliza and Luko to hold hands and follow Miriam, Alek, and Yar up the gang plank.

'Stay together.' says Miriam. But Alek and Yar push ahead, carrying the crate of water, and making for the top deck. Nyadena follows Miriam as closely as she can, carrying Barni and their bundle, but the boat is tightly packed; women balance baskets on their heads, youths shepherd goats to the foredeck, men lounge against the deck ropes. When they reach the rusty stairway Nyadena puts Barni down and tells Luko and Eliza to help him up the steps. A man standing at the foot of the stairs swings forward and flings an arm out to bar her way, then clasps his hand around her shoulder.

'Excuse me.' Nyadena asks.

'Hi Darlin, where you goin' my little ripe mango?' Shocked and frightened, aware of how vulnerable they are, Nyadena slaps him soundly on the jaw and pushes the children up the stairs ahead of her. Miriam, alerted by the slap, turns, and at the sight of her uniform the man glares at both women and moves away.

'Stay close.' Miriam repeats and they follow her to where the two teenage boys have found a small gap against the densely packed railings of the upper deck. Nyadena pushes Luko and Eliza in front of Alek and Yar and tells them to hold on tight to the railings. She places their bundle beside them and picks up Barni again.

'We do not move from here.' states Miriam firmly. 'Alek or Yar will go with Nyadena or me to buy food when we need it. How much water do we have?' There are two bottles in the crate, plus the ones purchased at the wharf.

'Make that last till we reach Juba.' says Miriam firmly.

'Thank you for your help back there.' Nyadena murmurs to Miriam.

'Slimy jackal.' she replies. 'Well done you for giving him what he deserved.' They chuckle about the incident but with an underlying note of hysteria.

'We're on our way!' says Nyadena as bare-chested men on the quay untie ropes, their skin gleaming in the afternoon sun. The engines start up emitting a smell of diesel. There is a violent lurch as the ropes are cast off and the ancient ferry leaves the wharf. The passengers on the upper deck stagger and slide. Nyadena gasps as the weight of many people falls towards the children but Alek and Yar have braced themselves against the railings to protect the younger ones. Nyadena holds Barni tight as the boat turns and heads into the slacker water at the edge of the current. The engines churn as they make their way upstream to Juba.

The world narrows to the rusted pillars of the ferry and the passengers crowded around them. Eliza and Luko lean over the lower bar of the deck railings, mesmerised by the islands of weed floating past and the waving fans of papyrus lining the banks. The upper deck has no shade and is hot despite the breeze created by the movement of the boat. Miriam and Nyadena rig up a shawl over the little ones and wrap their heads and shoulders. It is hard not to drink more than their ration of water allows. As the temperature rises further, women come round selling oranges and pancakes. Nyadena's money stretches enough to buy three pancakes to share between them.

The scent of oranges mingles with the sweat of many bodies packed together. There is no latrine for the passengers and the sharp odour of men relieving themselves over the side of the boat punctuates the late afternoon warmth. For the women and children discrete use of an empty jerrycan must suffice. It becomes stiflingly hot despite the movement of the boat. The children talk and giggle. Yar and Alek rest back-to-back. Miriam leans against the side of the boat, her legs glistening with sweat from the warmth of her dark uniform. Nyadena's thoughts flow freely with the current of the river. Her hand aches from her act of self-defence with the man who tried to grab her. A childhood memory, untapped for years stirs. A neighbour's warning that the Interahamwe rebels who had surged into Congo after the Rwandan genocide were spreading north to the forest area where she and her mother and sister were living. Women and girls should not go out. They were poor, her mother worked long hours as a seamstress. They needed water and it was the ten-year-old Nyadena's job to fetch it while her sister, Hannah, set the fire for breakfast. A rough voice behind her at the well. Strong arms pulling her back into the bushes, a heavy body covering her, fumbling with her dress, then a shout and the man ran off. She had staggered home without the bucket and been ticked off by Hannah. She had never told anyone what had happened but now sat silently shaking.

'Nyadena, are you ill? You're shivering.' Miriam speaks sharply concern in her voice.

'I was thinking of the man on the stairs. It reminded me of something that happened long ago.'

'Tell me.' So, for the first time Nyadena tells the childhood incident.

'If I had brothers or a father it wouldn't have happened, they would have protected me but we never heard from my father after he left us to fight. Mama has always said he was killed in the fighting, but we don't know really.'

Miriam puts a hand on hers. 'That beast! some men think it is their right!' Nyadena smiles and returns the pressure of her hand. They watch the sun sink towards the horizon. The boat creaks and groans but moves steadily upstream, belching diesel fumes from the narrow metal funnel rising through the centre of the deck. The prow carves a path through densely packed weeds, which close behind them as if no boat had passed. A feeling of calm seeps into Nyadena. She had been afraid of Miriam and her boys at first, but now they feel like family.

'Mama, he's looking at me!' Eliza breaks in on her peace.

'Who?'

'The boy who wanted water.' Nyadena follows her daughter's pointing finger to where a child sits alone, huddled into a space between the funnel and a pile of baggage. His eyes are desperate, pleading, the saddest she has ever seen. There is a sore on his arm, covered in flies. He looks weak and ill. She has some water left in her bottle. She lifts it up, and he slithers across the deck like a lizard, running between people's feet. In seconds he is squatting beside them draining the bottle with feverish haste.

'Where is your uncle?' asks Nyadena.

'Pibor. I run.' Nyadena turns to Miriam.

'This is the boy we saw in Pibor, the one who was begging.' Nyadena explains.

'What is your name?' Miriam asks.

'He call me "Boy".'

'How old are you?' The boy shakes his head, eyes down.

'Where are your parents?'

'They kill them. Soldiers did it.'

'How did you get on the boat.' Miriam presses him.

'Big box. I make open and get in.' He mimes taking the side off a box and squeezing in.

'He'd better stay with us.' says Miriam 'I'll call Pibor Post when we reach Juba.

'Let me see what I can do for that sore.' Nyadena offers. She cleans it as best she can with a rag and a little water, dries it and ties one of the clean rags she carries for Barni over it. The boy's eyes smart with the pain. Eliza sits beside him and Nyadena hears her soft voice reassuring him.

Darkness falls and the relentless thudding of the engine and the churn of the propellor through the water lulls the younger children to sleep. Eliza ceases her murmuring and lies down. Her eyes close. Her new friend lies wide-eyed and trembling beside her and then he too breathes deeply, twitching occasionally. Nyadena covers them both with her shawl.

The water tumbles and boils beneath the boat. Waves spread from the prow, lapping the banks, and creating gentle gurgling noises in the mud. Egyptian kites glide and swoop over the swamps beyond either bank, arched wings spread, wedge-shaped tails twisting, as they search for insects. In places the grassy slopes shimmer with fireflies, each tiny dot insignificant, but in their abundance creating a numinous light that makes even the rusted ferry seem ethereal. The decks fall quiet as passengers doze, dreaming of jobs, new lives, escape from danger, reunion with family. They arrive in Juba, where anything is possible, but little is certain.

5 MARIA'S FAMILY

My phone rings one afternoon as I am about to leave my Juba hair salon. It is my Peter, my brother, calling from Nimule. I have been worried about my mother since we visited at Christmas, where my mother and sisters live with my Uncle Amos and his family. Mama has suffered from a twisted back since the soldiers kicked her when I was taken as a slave but recently, she has not been eating.

'Maria, sister, I am sorry to trouble you when you are working.'

'It's fine, Peter, is everything alright?'

'Mama is getting weaker. She has stomach pains. We cannot move her. We have paid the doctor for the pills, but she is not getting better. Our sisters are taking good care of her, but she is weak.' Peter has seen many troubles in his work as a pastor in the camp for displaced persons in Nimule. He is a calm man. He would not ring if it was a minor problem.

'Maria? Can you hear me?'

'I hear you, my brother. I will come. Is there anything I can bring?'

'Can you buy pain killers?'

'Yes. I will do that.'

'Thank you. God go with you, Maria.'

'Bye, Peter.'

The thought of brave Mama, who has survived many dangers, being so ill, is unbearable. She was shot in the back in the 1990's conflict, trying to stop Khartoum soldiers taking Deborah, my older sister, and me as slaves. She has not walked upright since but has remained strong despite the pain. I will talk to the pharmacist and buy the best pain killers I can afford.

Manny comes home, after dropping Aunt Roselyn off, tired and with worries of his own. He kisses Rose 'Goodnight,' and we sit down to supper.

'A colleague of Garang's has disappeared.' he tells me. 'The new government is cracking down on anyone who writes about the delays and disagreements of our 'Unity' government. 'Discord' or 'Dishonesty' would be a better name.'

'Shush, Manny, don't speak so loudly, you don't know who may be listening in the street or through the walls. When did anyone last see this man?'

'He went to Garang's office four days ago. No-one has seen him since.'

'Aie, aie, aie, that's bad. I have sad news also; Mama is ill. Peter has asked me to buy pain killers and visit soon. Can we go this weekend?'

'Eeeer, yes, that is the right thing to do.' I can see from the deep creases that form across Manny's forehead that he is not comfortable.

'What have you planned for Saturday?' I ask.

'I arranged to meet with Jacob to discuss if there is anything else we can do about Garang, but I will rearrange that for next week.'

'Thank you.' I throw my arms around him

and then start to weep uncontrollably. For many years I did not see Mama when I was taken to the UK. We have visited frequently since we came to Juba four years ago. Now this time too may be snatched away.

At dawn on Saturday morning, we bundle a still sleepy Rose into her car seat. I sit with her in the back and give her breakfast. We stop briefly to change and dress her, then press on, arriving in Nimule just after noon. The huge metal gates of Uncle Amos's compound open as Manny sounds the horn and Amos is there to greet us. He is white haired, and his face is losing its roundness. His jaw is tense, and his eyes are dark with fatigue.

'Maria, we had hope you will come. Her breath is leaving her. Go straight to her. Manny, welcome, let me take little Rose.' Rose adores her great uncle and reaches her chubby arms towards him, nestling her dark head against his as he lifts her into his arms.

I make my way across the neatly swept yard to my mother's hut. Cotton cloths line the wooden beams that hold up the galvanised roof. The pattern of soft pink roses on a pale green background gives the light entering through the cracks in the metal window a soft glow. Mama is lying on a low bed, covered in a pale pink sheet embroidered in green and red. Her eyes are closed and one hand rests on the battered Bible beside her. I sit on the chair beside her bed and listen to her breathing. It comes in low rasps, as if she cannot find the energy to drag the air into her lungs. Her face is thin, the skin taut around her temples and brow, her eyes sunk deep in their sockets.

'Mama, it is Maria.' The hand not holding the Bible clutches mine. I cover it with my hand and enclose hers gently. 'I love you. I am glad we found each other, I say.' A faint smile crosses her lips, and she tries to reply. I bend my head close to hers.

'Not lost, always with us,' she says. I stroke her hand. 'You were always in my heart,' I tell her. She murmurs something I cannot catch but her breathing has eased. She seems deeply asleep now.

The door opens and Deborah places a bowl of soup on the table. We clasp hands briefly.

'She's sleeping,' I whisper. I place Mama's hand gently back on the bed, go to my older sister, and we hug for a long time. 'I brought the tablets Peter asked for.' I tell her.

'Thank you.' Deborah replies. 'She never complains but the pain is bad. We can tell from her face when we move her.'

'I wish I lived in Nimule.'

'You have brought the drugs and eased her suffering. Thank you.' says Deborah. Rachel appears at the door.

'Lunch is ready.' she says softly. I hug Rachel. Her body feels rounded and firm. I can feel the warmth of her, and the resurgence of her spirit. She is stronger compared with how she was when Manny and I brought her from Kakuma refugee camp but there is still a delicacy in her face and fine lines show the years of hardship.

We eat in a circle in the central yard of the compound. I am next to Manny with Rose perched on my lap, then Rachel, and her adult daughter, Adut, next to us. Amos, and his wife, are in an arc around the low table. Opposite us Deborah and her three daughters have arranged themselves in another arc, with Peter and a family friend, Samson, closing the gap at the end. The four tin-roofed, mud walled huts where we sleep are behind us. The room where the men sleep, storage huts, and the covered area where a large pot of stew steams over an open fire are on the opposite side, the double metal entrance gate between them. A cassia tree, cut many years ago so that several trunks spring from a single root system, spreads across the back wall of the compound, supplying shade over the circle of chairs. The front half is unshaded and bakes in the midday sun, the radiated heat trapped between the mud walls.

Lunch is a companionable meal. We are quiet of course, in respect for Mama, but the gentle flow of talk, catching up on news, is comforting. Rose enjoys the attention. Manny chats easily with Amos while I talk with Adut. She has been special to me since we found her, with Rachel, her mother, as a teenager in Kakuma refugee Camp. Rachel's husband would not tolerate Christian names, but Rachel named her after me, using my Dinka name, Adut. She lost her hearing as child due to her father's brutality, so I lean in close to speak to her.

'You have grown these greens?' I ask, pointing to the dishes. Her face lights up with a warm smile and she replies eagerly:

'A neighbour gave me some plants. They grew fast and I saved seeds to grow a second crop with the late rains. We have many rows of plants now.' Her hands are roughened from digging the sandy soil and the skin of her arms is flaking from working outside but her eyes are bright with enthusiasm. She attended a basic horticultural course in the camp and has built up a small business producing vegetables for the family and selling surplus to their neighbours.

'I will soon have onions and tomatoes to sell, and I have planted a lemon tree.'

'Well done!' I say. My attention is caught by a conversation between Manny and Samson. Jane introduced us to this man, when he was deported from the UK and returned to South Sudan. He was with my brother, Joel, in Libya when he died, took his papers, and impersonated him in order to cross into Europe. It caused distress but eventually he confessed and has helped our family ever since. He refurbished my salon when it was bombed and has helped Amos dig a new latrine and make a covered area for cooking. Manny is asking him what he is doing now.

'I am the local builder as well as barber.' Samson replies to Manny. 'Many Mamas are coming to Nimule with no husband or brother. If they have money, they pay me to build them a house, if they do not, I help them anyway.

We clear the dishes chatting as we do so. There is some teasing between my sisters about Samson's frequent presence and his readiness to help Rachel and Adut. Time flies as we laugh together. It is as if we had never been parted, yet our lives are very different. Deborah has lived most of her life in Nimule with the family. Rachel lived in Kakuma with Adut until a few years ago. I lived in England until Manny and I met and moved back here. The bond between us has remained strong through years of separation.

I wander back across the compound looking for Manny and Rose, perhaps they have gone off with Amos. The leaves of the cassia tree cast dark shadows on the ground. The air is hot and dry. I feel the sweat trickle down my back. I swat a couple of mosquitoes away. My city shoes leave deep footprints in the grey sand, and I can feel my feet burning as they chafe against the leather. I push open the door of Mama's hut and go in.

As my eyes adjust to the gloom, I see a figure already seated beside Mama's bed. It is Manny and his hand is held tightly in my mother's. I caress his shoulder and he turns to me.

'Where's Rose?' I whisper.

'Asleep in Deborah's hut. I came to see if Peninah needed anything.' Mama's breathing is shallow but even. She seems asleep but when Manny tries to withdraw his hand her fingers close, and he dare not pull away.

'I'll check on Rose.' I say and close the door gently, leaving him sitting in the dark with his mother-in-law.

On the drive home that night we climb slowly out of Nimule, queuing behind the trucks struggling up Gordon's Hill on their way to Juba and the north.

'I don't think it will be long, Princess, she is very weak.' he says. 'She is a brave woman, all those years of pain and crippled from her back injury but she never mentions it.'

'Did she speak at all?'

'I gave her some water while you were busy clearing. She thanked me but she was too weak to say more. I asked if she wanted the soup Deborah had left but she said she couldn't eat, just had a few sips of water. I helped her sit up.'

'Deborah and Rachel say she has not been able to

eat for the last two days.' I tell him. 'They have tried. She has taken a little milk, that's all.'

'I thought she'd gone to sleep but as I started to stand up, she grabbed my hand and just held it. She said I was a good husband for you. I try to be, Princess.'

'You are, you are.' He lapses into silence and is concentrating on the driving, but I can see the moisture at the corner of his eye, which he blinks away. Rose is asleep. I watch the bush flash by. Fireflies light up the grass at the side of the road for a few metres. Then we are back into total darkness again. The headlights occasionally pick up bright eyes watching us. The moon rises and the acacia trees cast long shadows across the bush.

'Manny?'

'Yes, Princess?'

'Do you ever wonder about your mother and sisters and what happened to them?'

'No. My father told me when I first made contact from Baltimore, that they had been lost for many years.'

'But don't you think they might be alive somewhere? My family thought Rachel and I were lost, and they would never have found us if it hadn't been for Jane and the Olaudah Trust. Maybe your mother and sisters are not in South Sudan.'

'We've tried the Red Cross, Save the Children, and many other routes. When Bor was overrun in the 1990s most of the women and children were killed, you know that.' he insists.

'There are people in Nimule and Torit who survived.'

'Not my people.' Manny's mouth shuts in a firm line. I know he is affected by Mama's death but he cannot speak of it. I have pressed him too far, and he has shut down.

Peter phones the following Tuesday to say that Mama died peacefully with the family around her. I am numb with grief. I was robbed of many years with my mother by the wicked men who seized me and kept me captive. I am thankful that we had these last few years close together. It has been a time of healing and love. Mama never stopped loving Rachel and me even when there was no evidence that we were alive. She never lost hope or showed bitterness. Her faith and trust in the Lord Jesus to rescue her children was absolute. She grieved over what happened to my brother, Joel. We found him too late to save him from deception and brutality. Then there was the chance remark from Samson that enabled us to find Rachel in Kakuma Refugee Camp and bring her home. Living through the darkness of South Sudan's continuing conflict will be harder without Mama's love for us all.

The funeral is arranged for the following Friday. We pick up Aunt Roselyn and drive to the New Jerusalem Church in Nimule, the place Manny and I first returned to, and where he asked me to marry him. The service is followed by an extended wake lasting several days when all our relatives and friends come to pay their respects. My brother, Aaron, and his family arrive from Bor, north of Juba, in a rented truck, bringing a cow for the wake with them. A grave is dug at the back of the family compound and the coffin lowered in. The cow is slaughtered and roasted, and a traditional Dinka party takes place with people from all over Nimule joining in. Women form one line of dancers and men another, but we are united in our grief for Mama, who was loved and respected by many. The dancing is a sign of grief, and of the honour in which Mama was held by her community. The pain is deep, but it is shared and acknowledged and that brings comfort.

'Your family do not have material possessions.' says Manny that evening as we share a beer before he drives back to Juba. 'But they are happy.'

'They live in the traditional way.' I say. They are cramped for space but that may change. Deborah thinks Rachel and Samson may marry.'

'He is a new man.' agrees Manny. 'They're all kind people.' he comments. 'Not like mine.' Manny never talks about his childhood and I'm holding my breath. He continues, 'Baba was strict, always had rules.'

'What rules?' I ask.

'It was about respect.' he replies. 'My father's sister married the son of the chief. He felt we didn't match up. We had to dress smart and be respectful. If we did badly at school, he beat us. If we fought, he locked us up. While my brothers were around, they took a lot of it but when they left for the army it all came on me. It got worse when Mom's family got involved.'

'What happened?'

'Mom was a Bari. My pop wanted to take a Dinka wife as well. When her people heard about it, they threatened to attack our village. Dad left, disappeared for several years till I was about nine. I went to my grandfather's compound. He was strict too, but he was fair. One day, after I was old enough to look after the goats and share a hut with the older men, my father came back. A few months later my little sister was born. I hated my father, Princess, he's brutal and unpredictable.'

'But you got in contact with him.'

'Only because I wanted to find out what happened to you.'

'What about when the Olaudah Trust flew us from the UK with Jane, and we were reunited with our families?'

'Well, there was a big crowd. Bishop Michael and Jane looking at us. My father and I are polite to each other but it's not like your family.'

Manny returns to Juba. Aunt, Rose, and I are staying for a couple of days.

He and Jacob are working with Garang's colleagues to gather evidence and lobby government officials to get him released. Aunt and I help my sisters wash Mama's sheets and the cloths which lined her room. We talk as we fold the cottons, reminiscing over Mama's life, learning from each other parts of her story that we did not know.

Amos, who has business in Juba, brings us home. I give Rose her tea and put her to bed, then prepare Manny's favourite dish of chicken, onion, and beans for supper. I place the bottle of wine that Jane left last time she visited in a bucket of water to cool. I have been totally absorbed in my family for the last few days, so I am going to make a fuss of Manny this evening, but it is past the time he usually comes in and there is no reply to my texts. Is it anything to do with Garang? I wish he would let me know.

I hear his key in the lock and turn towards the door with relief. He bursts through so fast that he nearly knocks me over.

'I've found her!'

'Manny, what are you talking about. Who?'

'The woman who resembled my sister. She's coming to Juba. I put a call through to the barracks.' His grin splits his face and his eyes crinkle with excitement, but I feel bemused, locked in grief over Mama's death.

'Have your shower and then tell me.' I try to slow him down. 'It's chicken and onions for supper and I've put Jane's bottle of wine to cool.'

'Yeehaw!' he yells, flinging his phone on the table and dancing down the corridor, leaving me torn between tears and laughter. American cowboy meets Dinka cattle herder. It amazes me that a man so tall, and thickset is so light on his feet. I take the wine out onto the balcony with a bowl of ground nuts. He joins me a few minutes later, running a hand over his wet hair and shrugging himself into a clean T shirt.

'Welcome back, Princess. How are the family?'

'They are doing okay. It was good to be together for a few days. I thought we would have a drink to remember Mama as they do in the UK.'

'Good idea.' he pours the wine.

'Here's to a brave lady.'

'Here's to Mama.' We touch glasses and sit quietly for a moment then I try to find out what has been going on.

'Who have you found? Is this about your family? I thought you had decided not to make contact.'

'I had.'

'So, what happened?'

'When I sat with your Mama, she was so fragile, but then she flung her hand out and held mine, it felt strong. I could feel the love in her for us all. I wondered if my Mama was lying somewhere alone, wanting to touch her family. While you were away, I contacted the commander in Pagak and asked about the women who had served the meals. I explained Mama was a Bari and that it was a woman who looked like her. He knew straight away the woman I meant because there are few Bari in Pagak. He told me her husband had been posted to Juba and she had left yesterday with their three children to join him.' He pauses, takes a sip of wine, and I wait, holding my breath. 'He told me the husband's name so I contacted the barracks here and asked for Reuben Thon. At first the administrator didn't recognise it, but I explained the platoon had only recently been posted and she found it.'

'Oh, Manny, they are here in Juba!'

'Well, no, Reuben Thon is here. His family are expected to arrive on the boat from Khartoum tomorrow evening.

'You think his wife is your sister?

'My youngest sister was a baby when Bor was attacked. She was only two, but everyone said how like my mother she was, and this woman was just as I remember my mother.'

'I hope it is her, but how would she be in Pagak? I thought your mother and sisters fled to Uganda?'

'I've got to see her, Maria. You were right, I have to try. I saw you with your sisters and your uncle, how you were comfortable with each other, even though you had been apart. You bring together the old ways and the new.'

'It's as much part of building South Sudan as our work.' I agree.

We fall silent. Manny is sitting on the edge of his chair twiddling the glass in his hand. I lean back and gaze at the constellations as they appear in the darkening sky. Orion, the hunter, as he is called in England. In Arabic he is Al Jawza, a woman. I wonder if the woman Manny saw, really is his sister, or if he has imagined the likeness. I thought I had found my brother, Joel, but when the time came, the man I met was a stranger, who had taken the identity of my brother. Samson was lost and confused. It was painful. Confession, and the message Samson brought from Joel's last hours healed the pain in time. It was through Samson's memories of being in Kakuma Camp that we found Rachel, but it has made Manny and I cautious about people's identity.

'Why don't we go to the wharf when the boat comes in? You could have a peep without them knowing.'

'Are you crazy, Maria? In the dark, in crowds of people!'

'Well, if the three children are with her, that should make it easier.' He shrugs his shoulders. He is upset and I fear a burst of anger. He eventually breaks the silence as I clear supper.

'What would we do about Rose if we go to the wharf?'

'Well, she's unlikely to wake up. I could ask Mama Abei, our neighbour, to pop across.' Mama Abei is delighted to be asked and says she will

104

bring her sheet and pillow.

'Don't you worry,' she says, 'I stay till you get back. That boat is always late.'

The moonless streets are dark and deserted when we leave the apartment the following evening. Manny drives along Lanya Street, swerving round the familiar potholes, south along Nimule Street, then straight ahead into an industrial area. The roads are gritty and pale in the car headlights. He pulls up next to a mountain of sacks and we walk across towards the river. There is no jetty, just a huge rectangle of cast iron beams dug into the bank of the river and covered with dusty metal plates painted with red oxide. A loading crane stands dejectedly at the water's edge, its lifting arm dropped flat against its main tower. It is a depressing place. There is no-one else here and no visible office. We wander aimlessly to the water's edge and stare downstream. The river is wide and towards the far bank water swirls past, dark and threatening. The west bank, where we stand is protected by a flat island of vegetation and the water is smooth and oily. Empty boats are hauled up at the side of the quay. Frayed ropes lie untidily at the water's edge. A Nile perch jumps, its spiky fins like steel. Bats flit overhead, their dark shapes chasing insects hovering over the water. We sit on a narrow bench. I lean against the metal support and draw my shawl round to cover my arms. I am wearing a tight-fitting rayon dress and regret that I am not in a looser cotton one. Manny strides over to the bushes at the edge of the quay and snaps off a couple of branches. He joins me on the bench, and we swat at the mosquitoes. There is silence apart from the splashing of the river, the occasional plop as a fish breaks the surface, and the whine of insects.

The scrunch of bicycle tyres on the gritty road ends our solitude. The wheels slide on the metal quay and screech to a stop. The man leans the bike against a corrugated iron shed and unlocks the door. We hear the whirr of a generator and overhead lights strung from long low sheds around the quay light up the shadows. The man reappears holding a clipboard from which pink and yellow papers protrude.

'Is the ferry coming?' Manny asks him.

'He come soon.' The reply reassures us that a boat is expected but this common South Sudanese reply means that it may be several hours before it appears.

The man retreats into a larger shed and can be heard on his mobile. Half an hour later several other figures appear and start to move a gangplank into position, bundle the ragged ropes to one side, and remove sacks from the large pile to reposition them near the ancient crane. There is still no sound from the river other than the murmur of the swirling current. I wish we had thought to bring water with us. The air is hot, despite the late hour, and I can feel my dress sticking to my back and shoulders. Three men in business suits appear, beer cans in their hands, and stand chatting beside the pile of sacks. My eyelids are heavy, and I drift into a semi asleep state. Manny's hands, typing rapidly into his phone are a comforting assurance of his presence. The rhythm changes and I wake, aware that Manny is no longer typing and that there is an increase in activity. The repositioned sacks now form a wall along the quayside that dwarfs the beer drinkers. But there is something else, below the rolling notes of the river current, a vibration, transmitted through the water to the metal girders, a slight shaking of the plates beneath us. Shadowy figures emerge from the streets around the dock and congregate in clusters at the edge of the wharf. The vibration increases in intensity. A speck of light appears in the distance, hugging the bank where the current flows less strongly.

There is a change in the vibration and a spurt of white water from the stern of the boat. It turns towards the quay. Dark figures move forward. Ropes are thrown, metal grinds against metal, the gangplank is dropped into position and the quay shudders. Manny and I stay in the shadows and watch as youths carrying heavy sacks stagger off the ferry and deposit their cargo on one side. The three businessmen hurry over eagerly. The sacks of grain on the bank are seized and a reverse procession of youths carries them onto the boat. The passengers must wait. Finally, looking weary and bemused, they shuffle down the gangplank. Lone single men melt into the darkness, hurrying home, or to whatever opportunity brought them here. Women and children are last, a dim kaleidoscope of shapes, clutching each other's hands, they step cautiously onto the quay, seeking a familiar face. Two women accompanied by two youths and several smaller children step onto the quay and stand under one of the lights strung across the quayside.

'That's her.' Manny whispers.

'She's got four children.'

'One of them must be from the other family, it's definitely the woman I saw in Pagak.' A figure detaches from the shadows and goes across to embrace them.

'Is that her husband?'

'I don't know. Let's go, Princess, we can't do anything tonight.'

We drive home and release Mama Abei with profuse thanks. It is past midnight.

'What will you do?' I ask Manny.

'I don't know. I'll think about it.' he replies. He falls instantly asleep, but my mind is tossing and turning. If the woman we saw is his sister, then this is the start of another long journey to find out where his mother and older sister are and what happened to them. Rose may have new cousins. If not, then we are duped as we were with my brother, when Samson was given his identity. I don't want Manny to go through that. It worked out well and led us to Rachel, but we must take care not to be tricked again.

6 NYADENA'S NEW HOME

Nyadena squats on the baked mud outside the front door of the *tukul* Reuben has built for his family, on the only piece of land he could afford. The plastic soles of her flip flops burn with hot sand scuffed up by passers-by. There is little privacy in this emergent suburb. Hastily built huts stand side by side, the galvanized roofs almost touching. She regrets the lack of a garden to grow crops, but the hut is sturdy, if cramped for six of them, and the roof is sound. Three palm trees provide an oasis of shade between neighbouring huts but otherwise the ground is bare sand, or mud.

Barni sits on a raffia mat under the palms playing with wooden 'soldiers,' bits of wood he has collected for himself. Nyadena finishes washing the children's clothes in a large plastic basin and drapes them on a washing line strung from the trunk of the nearest palm to a nail in the wall of their hut. She has laboured hard all morning, carrying water, rubbing the dirt stains out of the boys' shorts, and shaking out the creases in her own and Eliza's dresses. Later she will greet them as they come home from school, hear their triumphs and their struggles, and get their tea. It is a long and lonely day. Most people in this urban village, hanging on the skirt tails of Juba, have part-time jobs, or take work in, or both. It is a neighbourhood striving to carve out an existence in this conflict-ridden city. Most have family somewhere in the city but she and Reuben must make a way on their own.

Reuben's army pay covers food and a loan on the materials to build their hut, but it will not stretch to school fees, or clothes. She must make the effort to find employment. She should not have left Mama and Hannah so easily. If only her father had come for them, but he never did. She pauses for a moment, a pair of Barni's shorts in her hand. The butterfly motif on the label reminds her of washing clothes in Pagak, laying them out on the bushes to dry, and enjoying the black and white spotted butterflies resting before fluttering away to more nutritious flowers. Pagak! Not four weeks since she left, yet already it seems a lifetime away. She misses her friends in the Mothers' Union, the familiar crowds at church, the scent of the cassia tree that accompanied the long sermons. Pagak, however primitive had a sense of beauty, the houses with their ceramic topknots and the grass roofs trimmed in tight layers. Here there is no time for finesse, huts are inserted wherever there is a space, roofs are laid quickly to keep out the rain and families disperse at first light to school, to work, or to beg.

A bell rings and a neighbour bumps down the mud track in front of the house, jolting over the deep ruts, balancing a pile of laundry from his working neighbours for his wife to deal with.

'Shalom, Mama.' He raises a hand in brisk greeting. She returns the salute, and he wheels to an abrupt halt.

'Pastor says you want work?' he says.

'Yes.'

'You like washing?' Nyadena thinks quickly. She loathes washing but this could be the opening she needs.

'Yes, I am skilled at washing clothes.' she responds, turning to gesture at the neat line of shorts. Well, it is true, she has been doing it for years.

'You visit with Mama Nyango. She need a helper.' He gesticulates towards a hut at the far end of the street.

'Thank you.'

'You follow.' He pedals off again, one hand balancing the load of clothing and bed linen. Nyadena picks up Barni, who protests vigorously. She closes the door of the hut, and sprints after him. Half an hour later the deal is agreed; she will collect washing at noon each day and return it clean, dry, and folded at sunrise the following morning. There is a slight breeze under the palms and with the high afternoon temperatures it should be possible to meet the requirement, if Reuben strings up more lines. The pay is a few shillings a week, but it will help towards the school fees and perhaps if she can find something else as well, they will be able to cope. It is a start and a way to feel part of this community.

It has been a bewildering few weeks since Reuben met them off the ferry. Her relief at seeing him was immeasurable. She loves him and trusts him but fear almost overwhelmed her on the journey up the Nile. He would not be there. They would be alone in the unfamiliar city. She had dragged her children into a situation where their survival was at stake, but he was there and had found them a home, and a school. She had parted from Miriam with gratitude for her company and protection, and with assurances that they would meet again, though how and when this might be possible, she could not imagine.

Reuben had greeted his family with hugs and kisses, lifting the children off their feet with delight. Then, a shout:

'Aargh, go! Get back on the boat!' Eliza had grabbed his arm, a tigress in the face of his clenched fist.

'No, Baba, he is my friend. He is Isaac.' Reuben looked across at his wife in disbelief but seeing her pleading eyes asked:

'He is with us?' Eliza had quailed at an undertone in his voice she had never heard before but stood her ground. Isaac had shrunk back against one of the posts on the jetty. Nyadena had taken his hand and pulled him forward, saying:

'His uncle beat him and gave him no food and no name. Eliza felt sorry for him.' Miriam is finding his parents. It will just be for a short time.' Reuben had seemed mollified and led them through the dark streets to their new home.

Later that night, after the weary children had been shown the mattress they were to share and lain down with a thin cotton sheet covering them to keep the flies off, Nyadena had sat with her husband on their own mattress.

'The boy.......He was asking for water when we stopped at Pibor Post; you can see he is starving and scared. You know how Eliza likes to help people.'

'She has a compassionate heart,' Reuben had

agreed, 'but she should not interfere.'

'We ignored him in Pibor, but he was on the boat. He'd run away. He seems to have pulled the side panel off a wooden crate and climbed in. Eliza recognised him. He was scared and weak. We had to feed him. Miriam has reported it.'

'But for now, we have to fill another belly.' Reuben had responded wearily.

'We can shelter him till she finds them.'

'The house is not big but the best I could afford.' Reuben apologised.

'It's a fine home.' she had reassured him. 'We can make a start. I will take the children to register for school in the morning. Then I will look for work. I am thankful, my husband, for your provision for us.'

'The school is next to the church, run by the pastor's brother.' he tells her, then adds 'The *tukul* is small, I was not expecting we would be six.' Nyadena had quailed inwardly at the accusation in his face, but she was brought up to believe that if you do the right thing, by the will of God, it will turn out for the best.

'Eliza always has to have someone to care for.' She had pointed out. Reuben recognised the quality of his daughter's compassion but had added. 'She does not think how we're going to manage with an extra mouth to feed.'

'I told her not to talk to people on the boat and she obeyed but she collected several bags of food from people who saw what happened.' Reuben had laughed and said:

'We'll manage somehow.'

The next morning, he returned to the barracks for the week and Nyadena was left to cope with settling the children into school and persuading the head teacher to take an extra child. She explained the situation to the pastor's wife, who urged her:

'We expect good behaviour and obedience, Mama.'

Isaac is silent for long spells, eats ravenously, and has not learned to wait for others. Nyadena is gradually instructing him in the rules of family life, share, wait your turn, ask politely, say sorry. He tries hard, she can see that, but the tension builds in his undernourished body, and erupts in bursts of wildness. He has run away several times, to Eliza's distress, and then crept back at night and in the morning is huddled in a corner of the hut, terrified that they will send him away. He becomes over excited in games of football, grabbing the badly scuffed ball and hurling it into the trees, or throwing it under the tyres of a passing bicycle, then going into a frenzy of biting and kicking when the others complain. Dealing with Isaac is time consuming, and the unpredictable nature of his behaviour sets her nerves on edge. She worries that he will be sent away from school, and she will have him with her all day.

The children will be back soon and there is supper to prepare. She lights her small brazier and leaves it to build up heat while she fetches the rice and fish skins for supper. They cannot afford meat, but fish is plentiful, and the local shop sells heads, tails, and skin cheaply. Nyadena nods politely at neighbours on either side, working at the same task.

'You are helping Mama Nyango.' says one. News travels fast in this cramped space.

'Mr Odiengo needs help, I hear.' says another,

adding, 'Too hot for my liking.'

They are talking about the local bakery, which produces batches of long white rolls every morning. Nyadena cannot afford them but perhaps if she worked there, she would be able to get some. It would help feed the growing appetites of the children.

'Where do I find him?' she asks shyly.

'Old Odiengo? I'll take you in the morning. You'll need hands made of crocodile skin!' They laugh, but not unkindly, and Nyadena is glad to feel that she is being accepted.

The following morning, a Friday, she asks for directions to Odiengo's shop and walks there with Barni. She could start on Monday if she gets the children's clothes and meals organised over the weekend. It is only ten minutes away, but the road is unmade up and deeply rutted. There are few cars in this area but those who do venture into the settlement are used to dirt roads and travel too fast, stirring up mud and stones. Nyadena protects Barni's face with her scarf, but he grizzles. The sight of the baker's shop cheers him. There are neat rows of baskets filled with white rolls and the smell of freshly baked bread from the back of the shack is delicious. Barni's eyes widen, and he is quiet. A wizened man, once tall but now stooped into a question mark, steps forward from the shadows of the timber hut.

'Yes, Mama? Fine bread. How many?'

'*Kudual*, good day.' responds Nyadena. 'A neighbour says you need help in the morning. I am a good cook.'

'Sorry, Mama, my sons are the ones for the oven and the rolls. You can deliver? At sunrise to all the customers in this section.' Nyadena shakes her head.

'No, *sayyid*. I cannot. I have to get the children ready for school.'

'Aie, Mama, if you have many children then it is not a job for you.' She turns away to hide her disappointment.

'Mama, some rolls for your little boy.' He hands her half a dozen fresh rolls in a paper bag.

'Thank you.' She breaks a piece off one and gives it to Barni, who smiles happily and waves.

'Say 'thank you, Barni.' He mumbles something but his mouth is full of bread and the adults laugh. Nyadena waves her thanks, turns, and sets out along the rutted track. Barni is happy now and she sets him down and, holding his hand, adjusts her steps to his small ones. She has more time for her surroundings. They pass a concrete church with a tin roof and a large wooden cross on the front, its wooden doors stand wide open, but there is no-one inside and it looks badly neglected. She and Reuben take the children to a church of traditional mud and timber build, with a grass roof. It is dark and cool, like a cave, close to their street and the hub of the community.

Four open fronted wooden stalls are selling oranges and bananas. Nyadena eyes the fruit carefully. The produce on the last stall is fresh and not over ripe, she marks it down for the future, when she hopes there will be money to spend on fruit. Further on a woman sits out on the street, a basket of material beside her and a battered sewing machine on a table in front of her. She turns the handle skilfully and a pair of shorts emerges under her guiding fingers. Nyadena's mother taught her to embroider as a child. She joined the police partly to escape from her mother's sewing business, but it would be a useful source of income now. She hesitates. Barni's faltering steps gain new energy and he stares at the machine. The woman pauses and smiles at him.

'Aie, little cub. You like to turn the handle?' She finishes the pair of shorts and cuts the thread, then inserts an oddment of cloth under the needle and invites Barni to turn. He is slow and tentative to begin with but soon gets the idea and laughs with glee as the wheel spins and the needle bobs up and down.

'Stop!' cries the women, 'No more cloth, there will be a knot.'

'Thank you,' says Nyadena. 'My mother has a machine like this, but she is far away.'

'Any clothes you need, Mama, you come to Mama Mabal. I am best in this area.' Nyadena smiles and continues up the street.

Reuben comes home for the weekend and the children are happy and excited. He has brought a bag of groundnuts with him, from a sack that split when it was unloaded at the barracks. Nyadena puts them aside gratefully. She serves a supper of fish skin stew and then watches as Reuben plays running games through the palms until the children are tired, and ready for bed. Then husband and wife sit outside the *tukul*, watching smoke rise from the homes around them and listening to snatches of music on neighbour's radios.

'A big man came to the barracks on Wednesday.' Reuben tells her, 'Says he knows you from Pagak. His name is Manny Deng. He is a lawyer in the department of Gender, Child, and Social Welfare.'

'What did he want?'

'He is looking for his family. He saw you when he visited Pagak and noticed that you had a look of his mother. Could he be your brother?'

'My brothers were killed in the fighting in 2013.' she replies.

'You didn't see this man when he came to Pagak?'

'I served food to a visitor. He was tall, very dark.'

'Yes, that's the man.' Reuben encourages her.

'They called him Mr Deng, but it is a common name.'

'He was asking about a sister named Esther. He said he was the youngest brother.'

'Oh.' Nyadena trembles slightly at this use of her childhood name. 'Kor was thirteen when I last saw him. He rarely came to Mama's compound. He was in the bush with the goats.'

'He has asked us to lunch tomorrow at their apartment in the centre of the city.' Nyadena is tired and overwhelmed by this unusual invitation.

'Who has?' she queries.

'Manny Deng and his wife, Maria. They have a baby daughter, Rose.'

Nyadena calculates. To get the children ready for a visit will be time consuming and exhausting but there would be lunch provided. She would not have to beg for left over vegetables to give the family a decent meal.

'Well, we could go and greet them.' she agrees. 'It cannot do any harm.' She is thinking how it could help, to have a relative in government, someone to go to for advice in this bewildering city. The invitation is a welcome chance to leave this slum for a day and see the city centre.

'How will we get there?' she asks.

'It's less than an hour to walk, nearer than the barracks.'

'The older ones will do it; Barni will have to be carried.' Two men are coming towards them from the neighbouring huts.

'Coming to the meeting?' they ask. Reuben is about to decline but Nyadena nods vigorously. It will be good for him to have local friends.

'You go.' She urges. She watches him walk with the men towards the open ground at the top end of their street. Then she checks on the sleeping children, picks up the bag of ground nuts and sits down outside to shell them.

The air is heavy with wood smoke, and redolent with onion. Voices mingle, odd snatches of conversation waft on the air currents, formed as the heat of the day ebbs. On one side a Kenyan channel is playing popular songs while on the other side a radio blares out the national news. She crushes each groundnut with a thumb and then prises it apart to reveal the two russet skinned beans inside. She will grind them to make peanut butter to spread on the rolls the baker gave her. It is a repetitive task, sometimes revealing three beans, occasionally four. The pile diminishes slowly and Nyadena's fingers become roughened and red with the husky pods, but her mother taught her there is high food value in these peanuts.

'These are the same as a meat stew and the oil is very good for you.' her mother's voice repeats in her head, instructing her older sister, while she eagerly watched. That was when they were in northern Uganda with families she knew, the friends that she grew up with. There was plenty of food at first. They could collect bags of beans and rice every month and each family had a *shamba*, a garden, where they could grow vegetables. Mama had money so they could buy groundnuts, tomatoes, onions. More families kept arriving. The *fundi* made benches to seat all the new children under the tree where they had school. It was fun. Pastor Ezra taught them. They giggled about his bent back and stiff hands, but he was strict, used a cane occasionally, and expected their best.

'You practice your letters and read your Bible' he would say, 'and you will do well.' Few families had books, but the youngsters tried hard for him. She had learned to read and write in English and Arabic during those lessons under the trees. The learning continued but the supplies of rice and beans dwindled, and the pupils became lethargic. She did not like to think of those years when there was not enough food and her stomach ached with emptiness. That must not happen to her children. Luko's appetite was already a challenge and now there was Isaac, until they could find a home for him. The washing of clothes will not be enough. She must find more work. She places the last nut in the thick pottery bowl and goes inside to fetch the stone she uses for grinding. It is a messy but satisfying job as the oil oozes out of the nuts and it becomes a smooth rich slurry. She covers the bowl with a cloth, licking her fingers with pleasure.

She thinks back over the conversation with Reuben about the tall man. Kor, she did not remember much about him. He was eleven years older than her, younger than Hannah. He slept in the men's space, near the goats; she was in her mother's hut like all young children. She tried to remember his face, but nothing came. She had a fleeting memory of a heavy boned youth, taller than his friends but with a cat like way of walking on the balls of his feet that gave rise to his family nickname. Kor meaning big cat. She had been singing a song about a bird that the grand mamas had taught the children. She was dancing and twirling. Kor had come soft footed through the gate, grabbed her hands, and swung her round, joining in the song. She had been terrified and exhilarated and had hung round the door giggling as he spoke with their mother. Then he left, as softly as he came. She recalls his rounded fingers and broad wrists, a wide grin, and the bump in his neck going up and down when he sang. He had been like a god to her, this big brother, who whirled her up in his arms. Twenty-nine rains ago.

Nyadena gathers up the groundnut husks and adds them to the brazier. They will help her to get the wood burning in the morning. There is still a faint smell of rice, overheated oil, and charred wood but the smoke has dispersed. The neighbouring huts are quiet, music from a bar a couple of streets away is audible through the humid air. Raucous singing pierces the quiet. It is late. She begins to worry. Her husband is a good man, he does not drink or treat her roughly. She waits. He returns when the stars have moved far in their overhead dance.

'Sorry, Nyadena. They wanted help with the school porch. We patched the wall but there is more to do. We went for a beer afterwards.'

He staggers inside and collapses on their mattress.

She watches his chest rise and fall, his strong arms limp across his belly, legs, usually so straight and controlled, sprawled across her side of the mattress. Nyadena washes, exchanges her dress for a loose shift, gives one leg a push and lies down beside him. She does not sleep. The church elders are strict on no alcohol because of the damage it brings to family members. What prompted this lapse? Is he regretting letting his family join him in Juba? The risks of making a livelihood in this busy urban environment threaten to overwhelm them. She lies staring at the tin roof of the hut, its rafters laced together with sisal. She tells herself they are lucky to have a home, to have neighbours who help, to have each other. The power of giving thanks for what is good is a lesson that her mother instilled in her.

Her mother's face appears above Nyadena's, her slanting cheek bones and bronze skin so close that Nyadena can feel its softness, the caress of her hair as they ran through the bush, jolted in her mother's arms, clinging on by instinct. Tears trickle down her cheeks, and the wetness brings her fully awake. There is no sound apart from Reuben's heavy breathing and the soft random snorts of the children. No cock crows. No light. A rustle in the rafters, mice, or lizards. She has not seen her mother for twelve years, had no word from her for seven years. Their parting was not cordial and Nyadena blocked from her mind her decision to leave, rather than stay and help her mother and sister. There was no future for her. Her sister's disgrace and shame followed wherever they went, Hannah's child a permanent reminder, but she missed them and regretted the harsh words. Her mother had worked long hours to pay for her schooling to general certificate level. She had learned in French, another language she could master. The administrative post in the Police Service had been fun, and her rapid promotion an encouragement. They had promised they would have her back when she spoke with the Pagak police post, but Juba might be different. Until Barni was old enough for school, she would have to do her best to earn enough to pay for the older ones. Now there was Isaac as well. She worries how she will find enough food for the days ahead. The lunch tomorrow will help.

A cock crows. There are faint noises from adjacent huts. Nyadena gets up, fills a bowl with water, quickly washes and dresses while the children and Reuben sleep on. She fills two jerry cans from the standpipe at the end of the street and staggers back, knees bending, and shoulders braced for the heavy load. She fills the brazier with charcoal, lights it and places a kettle on to boil. Luko appears at the door.

'Wake Eliza and Isaac, and wash.' she says. 'All over, including your necks. I will do Barni here.' She hears them splashing and giggling at the standpipe as she washes Barni. They come back with the underpants they have worn in bed wet through, but it saves washing.

'Put clean pants and T shirts on and come and have breakfast.' she tells them.

'Mmmm groundnut butter.' says Luko.

'Bread!' shouts Barni. She gives him half a roll. Reuben appears at the door. His dark skin has a grey undertone, and his eyes are heavy with sleep.

'Sorry, Nya, I drank more than I meant to last night.'

'It's fine. You work hard. Help me get the food inside and we'll get going.'

'Going?' he echoes.

'To this man who's asked us to his house.'

'By my father's cow, I'd forgotten! I'll have a wash and be back soon.'

He runs down the street, sluices his head, face, and torso thoroughly and returns. Nyadena has tidied the dishes, but Barni is still seated on the ground finishing his roll. Reuben strokes his black wiry hair, lifts him into his arms and carries him indoors.

'You are looking sporty, this morning.' comments their neighbour when the family pass her hut twenty minutes later.

'We have been invited to lunch with an important man.' replies Nyadena. The neighbour's eyes narrow and she watches them as they pass her door. Reuben with Luko and Isaac, one on either side, followed by Eliza and Nyadena, holding one of Barni's hands. '

We look okay.' thinks Nyadena. 'They are impressed that we are going to see a man who wears a suit.' She breathes deeply and admires her family, the boys with their hair neatly combed. Isaac for the moment at peace and walking quietly. Eliza is pretty in her best frock, much washed and a little short. Barni is striding out on his short legs, determined to keep up with the older ones. What will he be like, this man they are going to meet, and his wife? If it is Kor, he will not be the soft footed youth she remembers. Will he look like their father? She barely remembers him either, she was only two when they fled. Baba was a presence, who occasionally came to her mother's hut and caused her to hide behind Mama's robe. How can will this man be able to recognise her in the toddler who fled in her mother's arms? She clutches a small cotton bag that hangs over one shoulder. It contains her police discharge papers, the only official document she possesses. It gives her married name, and her age but not her place of birth. She has been told many times that she resembles her mother but how will she know him?

'Do you think you'll recognise him?' Reuben echoes her thoughts.

'I don't know. He lived with the men. I did not see him often.'

'He's working for the government, Nya. We must make a good impression.'

'That is what I think.' she agrees. They regard Isaac. He is generally quiet and obedient but they fear his outbreaks of anger, unpredictable and difficult to manage.

'We must be calm.' she says. Their eyes meet over the children's heads. They will be courageous and dignified. The strength they give each other has been built through their transfer to Pagak, and the hardship of life in a town demolished by conflict, as well as the separation of their recent journeys to Juba. Whatever the future holds Reuben and Nyadena are committed to facing it together and teaching their children to be respectful and resilient.

7 DIFFICULT CONVERSATIONS

Manny and I overslept this morning and were woken by a roar from Rose. It is a cross sound rather than distressed and I blunder over to her cot to find her gesticulating at the precious zebra, which has fallen through the bars of her cot. With zebra restored she is sunny tempered and ready to chat.

Manny has showered and is grabbing his tie and bag. He has meetings with Jacob and an official from the Justice Department today about Garang's case.

'Bye.' I blow him a kiss, my arms filled with wriggling infant.

'Ba ba,' Rose burbles as I prepare her bowl of millet porridge. The sound sometimes refers to her father but is more often a generic term for anything she wants, in this case food. I lift her into her highchair and join her at the table with a cup of tea and two tiny ladies' fingers bananas.

'Ba,' she waves a chubby fist at the bananas.

While she is busy with a peeled banana, I settle down with my phone to scan the news. There are clashes in Jonglei State between the South Sudan Defence Forces and soldiers aligned to Riek Machar's government in opposition. Thousands have been forced to flee. Once again, our country is failing to find a peaceful path. Scrolling down photographs show ambulances lined up outside a hospital in Europe and a corridor crammed with people on stretchers. The disease that Manny spoke about, and that Jane was worried might cause our conference to be cancelled has overwhelmed Italy. Thousands are dying. I cannot believe what I am reading. They are calling it coronavirus and it is spreading across Europe.

There are footsteps outside and I open the door to Aunt Roselyn.

'Hi, Aunty, there's tea in the pot.'

'How's my little cub?'

'She's had her breakfast and is ready to play.'

The bedroom becomes my office during the day. I have a metal table in the corner by the window. The mango trees, which line our street, give welcome shade. I open the laptop the Olaudah Trust have provided for me and start to deal with emails from anti-slavery contacts in Nairobi and London. Amongst them is a worrying one from Jane:

Bristol 4th March

Hi Maria

I hope all is well with you and Manny.

We have had more response to the talk you gave in January and a partnership with another anti-slavery charity as a result.

We are worried that the virus causing so many deaths in China and Italy has spread to the UK. Cases are spreading and there is talk about special measures to prevent an epidemic. We have to postpone the conference.

Jane

Jane sounds worried but London has many big hospitals, and the doctors are skilled. It will be okay. I go through to the main room.

'Maria, you heard me put the kettle on.'

'No, I didn't, Aunty, but I'm ready for a cup of tea.' We sit on the floor with Rose and help her make a tower of plastic tubs, which she knocks down as fast as we can build it, with shrieks of delight.

'They are talking at my church about this disease in China and now Europe,' Aunt Roselyn says.

'Yes, my conference is cancelled.'

'Sorry, you are disappointed, but it is better not to take risks. You know how it was with Ebola.' My aunt is always so calm and sensible. She never gets agitated. She has a cleaning job and has to be careful of disease during the ebola crisis.

'Yes, I know.' I give Rose a kiss and return to my work.

Manny drives Roselyn back to her apartment after he finishes work. We are still eating when we hear a knock on the door.

'Manny, open up, it's Jacob!' We open the door, and he rushes in grabbing our hands and pumping them up and down.

'Garang is being released!' he tells us.

'When?'

'Later today, we think.'

'Is he okay?' Manny asks.

'His colleague says he has burns on his hands and one leg is twisted, possibly broken. The worst is that he may have internal damage. We're trying to raise funds to get him treated in Nairobi. Can you help?' Manny and I exchange looks. We have a savings account where we put a little aside each month for a bigger flat, or even a house, but as fast as we put money away, it is needed. The drugs for my mother were expensive but we cannot refuse. Garang is like a brother to Manny.

'Of course.' Manny replies. 'I'll bring something round to you tomorrow.'

'Where is Garang staying, will we be able to see him?' I ask.

'They're taking him to the house of a journalist friend. We must get him to safety soon. He has acute pain in the groin. It's not safe for him to stay here. The paper will pay his fare to Nairobi.'

'We'll do what we can.' Manny promises. Jacob shakes our hands warmly and leaves. He has others to visit. Manny and I clear the dishes in silence. Garang has survived the treatment of the National Security Service. We know from the Lost Boys network in America that other journalists have not. It is upsetting to think that he has been hurt in his body and in his spirit.

'We are lucky to have a flat with water and a bathroom.' Manny comments.

'Yes, we are fortunate.' I agree, but it is hard at these times to think of how life might have been if we had not chosen to come back to our country. Manny would have continued his job as a family lawyer in Baltimore in the US, and I would be with him. We would be able to afford a house with a garden, and a school where Rose would have the chance of a good education and perhaps go to university, as Manny did.

'Things will change.' he says. 'We must trust God for better times.'

I barely see Manny for the next few days as the Lost Boys and Garang's colleagues work to get him to safety. Finally in the second week in March he is on a plane to Nairobi where he will be met by Jonas, Jane's father-in-law, and taken for treatment. There is a profound sense of relief.

I have been exchanging emails with Jane about the situation in the UK. People here are frightened that this disease they are now calling Covid 19 will come to us. Each night our chairs and sofa are filled as one by one neighbours drop by to check the truth of the rumours they have been hearing. There are thousands of cases and many people dying. The hospitals are running out of oxygen to save them. It is spreading in the UK. Manny phoned his sponsor, Kenny, last night. There are no cases in Baltimore. Even in the US there is no treatment for this coronavirus. What will happen if it comes here?

The following evening, Manny arrives home tired but exhilarated.

'I've spoken to him.' he announces.

'Who?' I ask more sharply than I intended.

'What's wrong?' he asks.

'Rose wouldn't go to sleep and supper isn't ready.'

'Would you like me to fry the leftover chicken and make some chips.' I nod my relief. In many ways Manny has become a typical African man, but I am fortunate that he learned to cook for himself when he was working in Baltimore. I tidy Rose's toys and relax on the sofa.

Manny tucks a tea towel into his shorts and starts to cut the sweet potatoes into neat chips.

'So, who is this "him"?' I ask.

'I went to the barracks at lunchtime and asked for Reuben Thon.' He pauses, places the chips beside the pan, turns the ring on, and then goes to the fridge for the chicken. I turn and curl my knees under me on the sofa so that I can see his face clearly. He starts to slice the chicken thighs and pile them up next to the chips. He is absorbed in the task. I wait until he is ready to tell his story. He places the chicken beside the chips, checks the temperature of the oil and turns to me.

'Do you mean the husband of the woman we saw get off the boat?' I prompt him.

'Yeah.' He sounds very American. 'I was worried I wouldn't get through the sentry post, but I picked up a file from my car and showed them my business card. When they saw I was from a government department they asked who I was meeting so I said the safeguarding officer and they directed me to the gun depot! I walked about looking important and asking anyone I saw for chaplain Thon. The first few men I spoke to just said he would be there soon but after a while I found someone who knew him and said he had just come from the parade ground. The drill was over, but the chaplain was directing the men to pile up sacks.

'I asked if I could have a word. I showed him my badge and explained that I was baptised Manny. I told him my sister was very young when we fled the fighting. I explained that his wife resembled my mother, but the name was not the same. I felt an idiot, but he smiled and asked:

'What is your sister's name' I told him. Then

he was silent. He seemed to be thinking deeply. Chaplain Thon raised his head and said:

'It may be. Many people lost their families in the conflict. I will tell her we met.' I have invited them here on Saturday afternoon. He will text me when he has spoken to his wife.'

'Oh, Manny, do you think it is her?'

'I don't know.'

'What about the virus? Is it safe to have people round?' I ask.

'There are no cases here yet.'

We wait anxiously for a text for the next two days. Rose and I go to the market and buy a live chicken and keep it tied up on the balcony with water and some millet. Rose loves feeding it and soon learns to be careful of the sharp beak. On Friday evening Manny receives a message from Reuben Thon.

We thank you for the invitation to lunch. Mama Thon wishes to greet you.

'When will they arrive?' I ask. 'Are the children coming?'

'I don't know.' he replies. 'We can manage, even if they are. We don't want to offend them.' I sigh in exasperation at this loose planning.

'Well,' I say, 'you can kill the chicken early tomorrow morning and I will pluck it and cook a pot of stew and rice ready for midday. Rose can have some for her lunch and we'll warm it up again when they arrive.'

'We could take them to the river after lunch, so the children can run around.' suggests Manny.

Just after noon on Saturday, Rose is waving a spoonful of chicken in the approximate direction of her mouth. Manny is filling a bowl of water to cool the beers and I am piling plates and cutlery on the worktop, ready to serve, whilst keeping an eye on Rose and her dinner. The spoon stops in mid-air and gobbets of chicken and vegetable drip on the floor.

'Bang!' she announces with a flourish of the spoon. Manny and I glance at each other. I go to the front door and open it wide. They are standing together against the opposite wall of the corridor. The children's eyes are huge, their faces nearly invisible in the gloom. A man steps out from the shadows while the woman holds two boys against her skirt. A girl not much older carries a young child, drooping under the weight.

'Chaplain Thon?' I greet him. 'Welcome! I am Maria, Manny's wife.' Manny has come to stand beside me, and we shake hands.

'This must be your family.' I say.

'Nyadena, my wife, with Eliza, Adam, Barni, and a friend of Eliza's. We call him Isaac.'

'Come in and meet Rose.' I lead the way to where Rose is banging her spoon on the tray of the highchair. Manny hands Reuben a beer while I pile some of Rose's toys on the mat and show Barni how the doors on Noah's ark opens. I gesture to Nyadena to sit down and she and the other children perch on the sofa, their backs very straight. Nyadena holds the hand of each of the two boys while the girl sits alone at the end, her knees pressed tightly together. She has the same slanting eyes and heart shaped face as her mother, though the nose is still the rounded nose of childhood. I wipe Rose's hands and sit her on the floor by Barni.

'Eliza, you could help them fit the animals into the Noah's ark.' I suggest. She moves swiftly onto the floor and is soon supervising the play of the other two. Now the boys, what can I arrange for them? None of Rose's toys are suitable. I glance across at Manny, who is pouring a glass of water for Nyadena and placing the empty plastic bottle in the box for return to the store. Aha!

'Luko and Isaac, please choose two empty bottles each and take them through there.' I point to the balcony door. 'I'll show you a game.'

I follow them out, seizing a pair of Manny's pants drying on the rail, and roll them into a ball. I show them how to roll it at the bottles, taking it in turns to knock them all over.

'When you can do it, you can collect more bottles.' I tell them, 'And see who can knock down the most with one throw.' They are going to lose the 'ball,' so I open out the cardboard box I have been using for dry laundry and tear it into strips to go around the edge of the railings. Luko quickly gets the idea, and I leave them to finish making their 'skittle alley' and return to the adults to hear Reuben describing their accommodation:

'I've rented a small plot in Lologo district, near the parish church. I had the offer of the remainder of a big delivery of corrugated iron, so we have a watertight roof. We have our own space and a roof over our heads.' He speaks proudly, and I think of the many families in this city who share accommodation.

'Is there a school for the children?' I ask.

'They're attending the local school.' he replies. Nyadena has not yet spoken but sits with her hands in her lap.

'Do you like Juba?' I ask her.

'Yes, we do.' she responds.

'How old are the children?'

'Eliza is the girl, she is eight, Luko is six. Barni is three.'

'And Isaac?' I ask.

'We don't know.' Reuben responds. 'He attached himself to my wife and daughter on the boat. A friend contacted the police.'

'His 'uncle' beat him.' says Eliza.

'Eliza, wait until you are called to speak.' chides her mother.

'Yes, it is true.' adds Nyadena. 'He was begging at Pibor. Later he was on the boat alone. Eliza, you may tell us now.' Eliza kneels bolt upright and holds her arms straight on either side of her torso.

'His 'uncle' gave him no food or water,' she states, 'and was beating him if he did not bring money each day. He ran away to the boat. He hid in a crate with goats. We named him Isaac because God gave him an animal to save him. He doesn't remember his name.'

'His master was a bad man.' Nyadena adds. 'His back has wounds. He has bad dreams.' Manny and I glance at each other. This is a family with many needs.

'Let's have some food.' I suggest. 'We can talk later when the children are fed.' Nyadena looks relieved. 'We only have four chairs,' I continue, 'but we can move the table over and two of the children can sit on the arm of the sofa.' I put my head through the door onto the balcony.

'Please bring the plastic chairs and come and have lunch.' I tell the two boys. I lift Rose up from the floor and carry her towards the bedroom for a nap. Manny moves the highchair to one side to make room for the chairs the boys are carrying.

We are squashed with eight round the table. I just have room to bring the casserole and place it on the table with a large bowl of rice. Soon the plates are cleared. I bring in a hand of bananas and the children eagerly take one. Nyadena tells them to say thank you for their meal.

'Thank you for my dinner.' they chorus, except for Isaac, who looks blankly around.

'Take the chairs back to where they came from.' says Reuben. The sun has moved round but a narrow shaft of light falls across the table, and a fly buzzes lazily. Eliza is on the floor with Barni, lining up the animals up for him to pop into the ark. Now is the moment, while the children are busy. There is a fly in the kitchen and Manny jumps up in exasperation to swat at it. He misses, of course, and sits down looking agitated. There is a long silence. He must say something.

'Well,' he continues, 'as you know, when I went to Pagak, I was struck by the resemblance of Nyadena to my mother. But I expect it is an embarrassing mistake. I haven't seen my little sister for over thirty years. My father always thought she and my older sister were killed in the fighting in 1991.' He stumbles to a halt and there is silence again.

'Why don't you tell them what happened to you?' I suggest. 'Then we can hear how Nyadena and Reuben came to be in Pagak.' Manny wipes his forehead with the tea towel on the table beside him:

'I was a boy; it was before I'd passed through the initiation rites to be an adult. I was taking care of the goats, out in the bush, near Bor, with the rest of my age cohort. We heard gunfire in the town. We could see fires and hear screams. The older boys started running past. They told us to run for our lives.

'We walked across the bush for days to reach Ethiopia. They said we would train there to be soldiers and revenge our village. We never did. We were moved on and ended up in a camp in Kenya. I was one of the lucky ones chosen to go to the US. I never knew about any of my family till I contacted my father in 2014. He told me my mother and sisters died in the Bor massacre. I checked but I could never find any record of them.' Manny's words falter to a halt, and he wipes his forehead with the tea towel again. There is a crash on the balcony and Isaac's head appears round the door.'

'Luko hurt.' he states baldly. Reuben jumps up and goes out. Nyadena watches anxiously.

'It's okay.' Reuben says as he returns to the table. It was just an accident.' he explains. I wonder what the smile of relief that crosses Nyadena's face indicates. Whatever is going on with Isaac will have to wait until we all know each other better. I smile with as much encouragement as I can muster and say:

'It's your turn to tell your story, Mama Nyadena.' She shifts her position and glances round at Eliza and Barni, who are absorbed in their play with the wooden animals.

'I was a small girl. I had seen two rains. I do

not remember my brothers. Even littlest brother is too old to live with Mama. The soldiers are coming. Mama carries me. The thorn bushes grabbing my hair. My father run with us but then he go back to fight. He tell Mama to go to Kaya in Uganda, where there is uncle.

'We sleep in the bush for many days. There is no water. Young children get sick from drinking from pools, but Mama is nursing me, so I am fine. We stay in Achol-Pii refugee camp for four years. Mama's uncle bring us timber and tin to build a shack and we have a small garden. Then the drums say there is danger because of Joseph Kuony. You know this man?'

'Yes,' I say.

'Lord's Resistance Army.' adds Manny.

'They take children for soldiers so Mama's uncle say we must go away from the area.'

There is a loud wail from the bedroom. Rose is awake. I excuse myself and go to lift her out of her cot. I hope she will play with Barni and Eliza but as I set her down Luko stumbles over the patio door sill and starts nudging his father's knee. Isaac lurks behind him, eyes flashing dark glances at the adults.

'Shall we go to the river?' I suggest. 'We could all fit in Manny's car.'

'Let's go!' exclaims Manny. 'Can you pack some water and snacks, Princess?' He adds brightly. 'Follow me.'

We load the three older children in the rear facing seat. Nyadena and I sit Rose and Barni between us in the middle and Reuben sits in the passenger seat. I smile to see the way we travel here. In the UK there is always so much concern over safety, and seat belts, and expensive new cars. In Juba, any car is a luxury and those who have one are expected to help their friends and family. Nyadena is uneasy, glancing anxiously at the children in the back seat.

'It's okay.' I reassure her. 'The door has a child lock.'

'They will make your car dirty.' she says.

'That's fine. We can soon clean it.' I reassure her.

Manny parks near the old girder bridge. The children race down to the water's edge and start throwing stones. Nyadena and I place Barni and Rose on a blanket well back from the river and give them each a plastic beaker to dig with.

'You were telling us about going east.' Reuben reminds Nyadena and she continues:

'There is an uncle in Goma who wants seamstress, my uncle Worro. Mama is good for sewing and embroidery. He say they will find people to buy.'

'Goma? Where is that?' I ask.

'On lake Kivu in Congo.' Reuben replies.

'We are poor.' Nyadena continues. 'We live on the black soil near the mountain they call Nyiragongo. There is a demon inside that mountain spits fire and turns the soil black.' Manny and I exchange glances. What can she mean?

'Mama works and pays for us to go to school. Then she start training other ladies in sewing and my sister helps. I do not like that work. I join the police force. I am posted to Ezo. Reuben is there, we marry. Eliza come soon.' She speaks hesitantly but I see beneath the shyness a strong and determined woman. I meet Manny's eyes. They are dark pools of grief. The loss of his family, and the loneliness has been buried for years, deep in his spirit.

'What are your mother and your sister's names?' I ask.

'Mama Elizabeth is my mother. My sister is Hannah. She has one son, his name is Adam.' Manny has never mentioned his mother's name.

'And brothers?' I press in, feeling uneasy but we must find out if this is the same family.

'I have three big brothers; they are killed in the fighting.' Manny shifts uncomfortably on the log; he is not meeting our eyes.

Reuben steps in.

'Sir,' he says, 'You mentioned that you were enquiring after a sister, Esther. My wife was given the name at baptism. You are brother and sister?'

Manny stands up and starts to pace up and down the sand. He spins round to face us.

'I don't know.' he says. 'I remember a kid sister, called Esther but it was a common name in our town.' I'm shocked. Surely, he wants to talk with Nyadena and try to find their common memories. Then I remember how Samson tricked us by pretending to be my brother. It was painful to forgive, even when I realised that Samson had been Joel's friend and looked after him when he died. Joel gave him his own documents so that he could get to the UK and find me. Manny has not come to terms with the need to forgive and trust God.

'I have my police papers here.' Nyadena says, pulling a cloth wallet out of her bag and hands them to him.

'That proves your name, but not your family.' is Manny's surly reply.

Nyadena pushes the wallet back into her bag.

'Are you in touch with your mother?' I ask gently.

'Not since Pagak' she replies. 'I send a letter, but Pagak is very far.'

'We have to know for sure.' Manny responds. 'We need evidence.' His tone is harsh. He is upset. Nyadena's eyes are downcast. Reuben is standing straight, as only a soldier can, and but his eyes flick with anger.

'Let's give these children a snack and then we will run you home.' I suggest.

I open the packet of biscuits, and the children appear, running up the beach. Luko is holding a tin box with a pile of stones that he has collected. I give Eliza one her and one for Barni and Rose adding:

'Thank you taking care of them.' A smile lights up her face. 'Thank you to bring us to the river.' she replies. I am touched by her charm.

Isaac hangs back while Luko and Barni take their biscuit, then he grabs one and devours it in a single mouthful.

'Isaac! Eat slowly.' says Nyadena. I can see that he is trying but his eyes dart anxiously from the biscuits to Nyadena's face. His hands clench, and he thrusts them into his stomach as if to fill the craving inside him.

Manny picks up the water, used cups, and biscuits and leads the way back to the car. It is not far to their new home on the edge of Juba. The streets are rough tracks between rows of mud huts. Most have tin roofs, but a few have grass roofs. Timber built latrine sheds lean at awkward angles alongside each house. There is little space between them. We pass a mud walled church. The wooden cross at one end of the roof trembles with the vibration of the car. Reuben indicates a narrow track to the right and then points to a large palm tree. We leave them at the door of a small mud walled shack.

'Goodbye. Thank you for lunch' Reuben says formally. He waits as if he expects us to say something more. It is for Manny to make it easier for them, but he says nothing.

'Goodbye may God bless your family. We will let you know.' I say. I feel unbearably sad to see them so dejected.

We return home and I put Rose to bed and tidy up. At last, we sit down together.

'You were rude this afternoon.' I tell him.

'I wasn't.' he sounds surprised. 'We must be sure, Maria. Remember how upset you were that Samson pretended to be your brother.'

'But I knew from the start that he wasn't. Don't you feel deep down whether Nyadena is your sister or not?'

'Esther was a baby when Bor was destroyed. I don't feel anything. She seemed less like my mother today. How can I be sure they are telling the truth.'

'Is your mother called Elizabeth?'

'No, Lada. My father did not like Christian names. She insisted on having us baptised but he would not use those names, that's why I was known as Kor.'

'Reuben is a good man.' I assure him. 'Nyadena was shy, but the children obey her.' I watch him drain the beer. 'She was describing the same events as you.'

'Two thousand died and many thousands fled. We have to be careful, Maria, we can't afford to support more people.'

'We can't just leave it. They are a kind family; we must be open with them.'

'We shouldn't have started,' is his unhappy response, 'not knowing has made it worse than thinking they were dead.'

'If we could go to Goma, perhaps we could find out more.'

'Maybe.' he replies.

We are tired. It has been a long day. I decide to say no more tonight but I am turning over, deep in my spirit, how we can resolve this painful situation.

8 NYADENA'S VISITOR

The road that runs past the Thon's home is no more than a mud track. Vehicles have churned the surface into deep ruts. The air is thick with smoke as families ready themselves for the day, making tea, washing children, eating porridge. Rusty bicycles bump past, loaded with goods for sale, or jerrycans of water.

It is seven in the morning. Nyadena is brushing the mud around a small brazier and tipping pieces of charcoal back onto the glowing embers. School children are setting out for their first lessons before breakfast, a few with pancakes or rolls clutched in their fists. Others have no food, perhaps they have already eaten, or must wait for the evening for their meal of the day. A tall woman with a child tied on her back with a shawl pauses cautiously in front of the palm trees beside the Thon's *tukul*.

'Good morning, Mama Thon. The Lord spared you this night.' She gives a common greeting.

'Mama Maria! Yes, praise the Lord.' Nyadena responds.

'Luko left behind the stones that he collected by the river. I thought he might miss them.'

'You are good, Mama. Luko was upset. He is careless. You have come far. Sorry.'

'Manny brought me to the market at the top of the

145

road in the car. He had business this way.'

'You will have some tea?'

'You are busy?'

'You are welcome.'

'Thank you. I would like that.' Nyadena places her dented kettle on the brazier and blows softly on the embers, still glowing red from early morning tea, they fan into flames. It is strange that the lady has come. She and Reuben no longer speak about their lunch with the man and his wife. Reuben had chided her that she could not remember anything that might have triggered a memory but the only response she could give was that she had been too small to remember. She knew he was troubled by the expense of being in Juba and the addition of Isaac to the family, which had not been part of his calculations. Isaac was a troubled boy. Nyadena admired the way Reuben handled him, giving him love but a firm instruction to help him adjust, but it was not easy.

'Do you like being in Juba?' her visitor asks as Nyadena brings a mug of tea over.

'I do not see much, this area only, and the visit to your apartment. Thank you for the meal, and for taking us out. The children are very happy to see the river. They like it on our journey here on the boat.'

'You were brave to travel alone.' is the response.

'I am with a friend, Miriam. She is in the Police Force.'

'Oh. I see.'

'Please.' Nyadena gestures to a chair by the palm trees and pulls another alongside. She waits while Maria settles Rose on the shawl and gives her one of the painted wooden animals that Barni loved to play with, then passes the mug of tea, made strong and sweet with plenty of dried milk powder.

'Where is Barni?' Maria asks.

'He is with a Mama,' she replies and adds 'He is near.'

'I mustn't keep you.'

'It is fine.' responds Nyadena, but in truth she is anxious. She has a sheet to embroider for Mama Mabal and washing to hang out, which must be dry and ready to return this afternoon.

'Are the older children at school?'

'Yes,' she replies, 'Reuben ask for them to start when we reach here.' She adds, 'Now we have Isaac it is difficult. He does not like school. He is good in his heart, but his mind is not quiet. Eliza must make her father happy over this bad thing.'

'Rose can make her dada do anything she wants.' Maria says and laughs.

'Mama Maria, I like to talk but I have to sew a thing by this afternoon. I fetch it?'

'Oh. I am sorry, Nyadena. I didn't think. Yes, of course. Would you like me to leave?'

'Please stay. I can sew and we talk. It is fine.'

She retreats into the tukul and brings out a carefully folded cloth, grey with age, unwraps it, and draws out a bright green sheet with a half-completed design of flowers and twisting stems.

'It's beautiful.' Maria comments. Nyadena picks up the needle and slips it skilfully in and out of the design.

'I work with my Mama and sister in their sewing business. My uncle help me work for the police but now I must do the sewing.'

'And you met Reuben in the Police Force?'

'Yes. The Lord's Resistance Army come to South Sudan from Uganda. Reuben's troops come to Ezo. The LRA is running all over western Equatoria. The police forces have to help. I work with Reuben. We marry, then Eliza and Luko come and I leave my work. There is fighting over oil near Pagak. We have to go there.'

'And you lost touch with your mother and sister?'

'In Ezo, my uncle call my mother every month. In Pagak the phone signal is from Ethiopia. It cost many South Sudanese Pounds to call. No-one will do it.' Nyadena ties off the purple cotton she is using, rethreads the needle with pink and starts another flower.

'What was your father like? Do you remember him?'

'He come to the *tukul* from time to time. He bring me sugar cane, or an orange. Mama say I am too young for this but I like it. He pick me up and swing me round. Mama say 'Leave that child alone, Sahib, you make her dizzy.' Maria laughs.

'What was the rest of your family like?' she asks. Nyadena sticks the needle into the cotton and pulls it through as she tries to remember.

'Hannah say my father is an angry man. He argue with mama's family and leave. Kor stay with my grandfather. Father come back in the dry season before I am born. My big brothers live with him in the men's huts. Kor, he live with my grandfather. He is too young to go with the men and the cattle.

148

Hannah say Baba is strict with Kor. He beat him. My father is a proud man, for his cattle. Each child has a special cow. Kor has the white cow with a mark like a K. Mine is the red cow. My father make me see it but I do not like the long horns. It is my bride price. Mama say we must stay pure for our marriage. Now with Hannah's shame we have to make our own way. '

'Surely your father would not reject you because of what happened to Hannah! That is unfair.'

'She is not pure. We are scorned.' Nyadena bends her head and her needle darts in and out of the green cloth. Maria retrieves one of Rose's wooden animals that has strayed into the dust. She places the child on her lap and plays with her for a moment:

'Hannah is older than you?' she asks.

'Kor is the firstborn to my mother, then Hannah. I am the small one.'

'Is Eliza named after your mother?' The visitor asks gently.

'Yes, of course.'

'Does your mother have an African name?'

'My uncle sometimes call her *Lada*.' She responds.

Maria hugs her child tightly and nuzzles her face into the wiry head. She seems moved, Nyadena notes as she stitches away, there are tears in her eyes.

'Do you still have a number for your relative, perhaps we could contact him?' Mama Maria suggests.

'Yes, of course.' Nyadena replies. She ties off a thread. 'I get it now?' She jumps up and goes to the *tukul*. As she returns Mama Maria is giving Rose a drink of water from a plastic bottle. Nyadena hands her a grubby slip of paper with the number, and watches as she taps it into the phone. Mama Maria hands her the phone.

'Hallo? Uncle? This is Esther. God has spared you?'

'Esther! Praise God. You are well.' a warm familiar, voice replies.

'Yes, uncle. I am in Juba. Reuben's platoon is posted here. He is an army chaplain now.'

'Is he? God is good. And Eliza and Luko?'

'They are at school. We have a third child, a boy.' She pauses, wondering when to mention Isaac. It is too complicated to explain.

'You have a fine family.'

'Yes, uncle. My aunt? She is well?'

'We are well, thank God.'

'Uncle, how is my mother? They are still in Goma?' Nyadena's hands are shaking as she holds the phone. She is aware of Maria near her, Rose held in her arms.

'Ah, Hannah and Adam are in Goma but your Mama is a counsellor for the Guérir les Gens Hospital? Do you remember the big hospital in Goma near Lake Kivu?

'Yes, I remember. Can I reach her there?

'I will send you her number.'

'Thank you, Uncle.'

'I can call on this one?'

'It is the phone of a friend, uncle. She is married to a man who remembers my mother. It is okay to give the number?'

'Yes, yes. The friend?'

'A man who came from Bor. He works for the government.

'Ah, that is good.'

'Thank you, uncle. We will speak soon.'

'Goodbye, Esther.' Nyadena hands the phone back to Maria who closes the call. Nyadena turns to Maria.

'Mama is a counsellor.' she explains. 'At the Guérir les Gens hospital. My sister is running the sewing business now. They are fine.' Nyadena covers her face with her hands, as tears squeeze from her eyes. She feels Maria's hand on her shoulder. Maria says:

'It is hard when you are far from your family. I didn't see my mother or sisters for many years.'

'He say they love us.'

'I am sure they do.'

Nyadena wipes her eyes with her fingertips and looks up at her new friend. They smile at each other; Maria's eyes too are full of tears. Nyadena senses that her visitor shares the heaviness of heart that she carries deep inside, an ache for loved ones that she cannot see.

Rose starts to wail. 'Rose needs her lunch and nap soon.' Says her mother. 'We must go. It is alright if Manny and I call this number?'

'Yes, yes. Thank you. We will meet soon if God spares us?'

'Yes, I will visit soon. May the Lord bring your family together.' Mama Maria says. 'Goodbye, Nyadena.'

'Goodbye, goodbye Rose.'

'Bye, bye, bye.' Rose waves a chubby fist as they set off down the track. Nyadena picks up the embroidery. She finishes the blue flower and starts on the last piece of the design, a small bird flying above the flowers. She chooses a vibrant turquoise shade that clashes with the green of the sheet, and sews as fast as she can, occasionally dashing tears from her eyes so that they do not fall on the cloth. Mama and Hannah, and Adam, they were so close. Hannah was a second mother when mama was working the land, they were given in the Uganda camp to grow crops. Then, when they moved to Goma, it was Hannah who made her breakfast and saw her to school, while her mother toiled on the rusted sewing machine that had been her first purchase. Gradually life had become easier and they had acquired a small house and surrounding garden. How could she have left them? Her foolish ambition and pride! But it led her to Reuben and a family of her own, a family to be proud of. If the Lord is willing, I would like Mama to see my family, and for my children to know her. And Hannah. Everyone said how close they were. Nyadena fills in one wing of the bird and starts on the other. She too is flying with one wing. The half of her life when she was Esther is in Goma. Adam! Her children have a cousin. How many rains have there been since she left? She has not counted, but he must be a youth by now. And if Manny Deng is her brother, then Baba too is alive. Nyadena stitches carefully round the beak of the bird and threads a small length of brown to make its eye. 'Trust the Lord for one thing at a time.' Her mother often said. It would be good to see her mama and sister again if they still love her. Nyadena sews steadily until the sun is at its zenith, and then fetches Barni from her neighbour and starts on the washing. It is a hot day and the clothes will dry in time. It was good to see Maria. There was a reason for her visit, Nyadena reflects.

She and Reuben did their best, it is up to Mama Maria's husband to decide what to do. If no more troubles come, they might make something of this new life.

For Nyadena, and many others, there are troubles around the corner, which must be endured before they can find a secure place in the bustle and growth of Juba.

9 JUBA CURFEW

'How did it go?' Manny asks that evening.

'Well.' I reassure him. 'Nyadena opens up more easily in her own place. She made tea and talked about how she came to Juba, on the boat with a friend.'

'Did you find out anything else?' He is eager, - and apprehensive. I understand why now. His family were not united even before the conflict split them apart. He was pushed out to his grandfather. His memories are painful.

'Yes, I did. She has an uncle who helped them. He sometimes refers to her mother as 'Lada.' Oh Manny, it must be your mother. They kept in touch till she moved to Pagak. She still has the phone number so I offered to call for her. She spoke to the uncle. Your mother is working in a hospital in Goma, and her sister, Hannah, is running the sewing business.'

Manny is pacing the floor of our apartment. He is sweating and wipes his brow with a tea towel.

'Manny, we have to follow this up. There are too many coincidences. The uncle referred to Nyadena as Esther. I am sure it is the same person as your sister. You must remember!' He stops his pacing and sits on the sofa, head in hands. Manny never cries, but a deep sigh escapes him and his face is glistening with moisture. I sit beside him.

155

'Oh, Manny. We must see them. It's your mother and sister!'

'I was sure they were dead. I tried everything to find them but there was no trace. My father said that he had checked the refugee camps but he didn't know that they had gone to Congo. I should have checked. I feel real bad.'

'It's not your fault, Manny. Many people's lives have been disrupted but now we can go to Goma and find them. It will be expensive but our new home can wait. We must do this.'

'Yes. I will ask for some time off and for permission to take the car. How soon can we go?'

'I will ask my family to look after Rose, perhaps we should take Nyadena too.' We start to make plans and it is much later that we catch up with the news, and all our planning is curtailed.

President Kiir today issued Republican order 08/2020. Under this order a High-Level Task Force Committee has been formed to take extra measures in combating Covid 19. The Committee is conducting a risk assessment of information provided by the Ministry of Health. The Committee will ensure that quarantine centres are set up and well equipped with personnel and medicine to prevent the spread of Covid 19 infection. Vice President Hussein Abdelbagi has suspended all physical learning at all levels for 30 days. All gatherings whether for sport, political, religious, or social purposes remain suspended.' President Kiir appears on the screen of Manny's phone, instantly recognisable by his large hat, long face, and small beard, smiling, and greeting the Vice President. They are not shaking hands but bumping elbows. The footage goes on to show them inspecting a store of face masks, and hand sanitisers. Manny's eyes are narrowed, and his brow lined. He looks weary and anxious.

'Where's all the equipment for the quarantine centres coming from?' I ask him.

'There is no equipment.' he says savagely. 'It's an exercise in calming the people. The only quarantine centre is in the Presidential Palace. There's no money in the health budget, all our oil money has gone on guns.

'So, it will be for us to do what we can?'

'That's the reality.' he replies.

'Why are we taking these precautions when the UK is not?'

'We've had pandemics before. HIV, Ebola. We can't rely on our health system; our only hope is to lock down early and keep it out.'

'We'll have to postpone any plans to go to Goma, won't we?'

'Yes, Princess, I'm afraid we will. We won't be able to travel outside the country until this plague is over.'

That Sunday the mood in church is sombre. We have our usual opening songs with church leaders, the choir, the Mothers' Union, and the Youth processing but now people become still, their eyes white in dark faces. It is so quiet that we can hear the crows on the roof and the buzz of traffic bumping along the main road. My nostrils tighten against the smell of baked dust, sweat, and something else, the acrid smell of fear.

Bishop Zak rises and crosses to the wooden lectern, which he grasps with both hands.

'In the name of the Father, the Son, and the Holy Spirit. Amen.' he prays, and we echo his words, but the usually joyful 'Amen' is subdued.

'We must protect ourselves from this disease.' he continues, 'We do not have the hospitals and medical staff to save people. Already many in Europe have died. Mama Lydia will share a plan with us later but first we pray.' He leads us in a lengthy and fervent prayer. One by one people speak their own prayers aloud. I pray for my friends in the UK and Manny prays for Kenny and Mary in Baltimore. Others pray for family members scattered across the world, the South Sudanese diaspora in Norway, Australia, South Africa, the UK, Khartoum. We pray for the people in Italy where so many are dying. We pray for protection for South Sudan that the disease will not spread here. After an hour, the bishop ends the prayers with a loud.

'Amen.'

He invites Mama Lydia to the front and explains that she will be training those who are willing as coronavirus advisers, who will handing out masks and hand gel, supplied by some of the aid agencies. When she finishes Bishop Zak nods to the band to start the final song. Manny is playing the drums as usual, but he seems tired and listless. His usual ebullient energy is gone, and his drumming is languorous, his face thoughtful.

I wish for a moment I was still in the UK. The big hospitals will keep them safe. In South Sudan we must protect ourselves from a disease we have no way of fighting. We did not imagine that a few weeks later the wave of disease would crash over the UK with such force that we feared for the lives of our friends.

My legs ache. My feet are burning as the sand of the street penetrates the soles of my shoes. The medical mask I am wearing feels hot and moist, its fibres loosening in the intense heat of midday. My arms cannot bear to lift another bottle but still the queue lengthens in front of us.

News of the pandemic in Europe has spread rapidly through the city. Each evening the South Sudan network shows videos of hospitals across Europe and America in crisis and there is great fear in the city. We are prepared, thanks to Mama Lydia's training. Jessica, who is alongside me, has a daughter the same age as Rose. Her husband, Dut, is at home with Manny, keeping an eye on the two little girls, and probably sharing a beer. Our job is to hand out small bottles of antiseptic handwash, which we replace from the boxes under the table, and to give out masks. We are explaining to people what they must do to protect themselves.

'Mama, you take this and place it over your ears. It must cover your mouth and nose, then pinch here to fit. You must wash your hands thoroughly with this soap. It will kill the germs. You sing our national anthem all the way through while you do that, then your hands will be clean. And teach your children to do this. How many in your family?'

'Thank you, thank you. I will do eet.' The stout mama puts on her mask, picks up the antibacterial soap and six more masks and hurries away.' A young man eagerly takes her place.

'Sahid, you take this, and place it over your ears, like this. How many in your family? For your mother and younger brothers and sisters? Eight – here you are.

And you must take this special soap and sing the national anthem while you wash your hands. That will kill all the germs.' He bows slightly and walks away.

A woman steps forward leaning on a stick. I start again.

'Mama, you take this and place it......' She struggles to place the mask round her ears and peers anxiously at the soap when I hand her the bottle. She is elderly and frail.

'Mama,' I add, 'this disease is dangerous for the respected elders of our community. Do you have someone who can bring you food?'

'I have one son left to me, in Nairobi.' Her voice shakes with fear.

'May I write your name and where you live? We will send someone to help you.' I pick up a clipboard from the table and add her name to a list of vulnerable people who will need help. She thanks me repeatedly and I have to ask her to step away. And so it goes on. There is no time to glance across to Jessica. I hear her repeating the same phrases. Sometimes our voices synchronise, but mostly we are speaking across each other. We are on duty till three. There has been no time for food. One of Mama Lydia's team brings a cup of sweet tea in a plastic mug occasionally to help us keep going.

The piles of hand sanitiser and masks are diminishing. The discarded boxes and plastic covers accumulate behind our table. The queue is building and now snakes round the corner at the end of the street. People have been waiting over two hours and tempers are rising. One of the pastors pulls up in the bishop's car and unloads more boxes.

'Pastor, can you help us? They are pushing.' Jessica says anxiously. We unload the boxes. The pastor walks along the queue. The site of his dog collar reassures people, and the anxious murmuring subsides.

'We should put out a notice to say that there will be no more handouts today, otherwise the queue will just get longer.' I suggest.

'I will see what I can arrange.' he assures us and returns up the drive. I glance at Jessica. It is going to be a long and difficult afternoon. We open the boxes and start the repetitive task again.

'You must place the mask over your mouth and nose. If you sneeze or cough you must wash your hands, also before you are cooking food…..' I say, as Jessica starts at the same moment:

'You must wash your hands and sing the national anthem, make sure you wash thoroughly including your nails…' We sound like two videos played simultaneously, a cacophony of instructions, but people are eager to hear and strain to catch every word. An hour later Pastor Mark returns with the last batch of boxes and a blackboard, easel, and chalk.

'Where do you want this?' he asks.

'I need to calculate.' I tell him. 'We have twenty boxes and there are sanitisers for thirty-six people in each box. Pastor, can you count off one hundred and eighty people and ask the last person to move the easel forward with them?'

I write on the board in large letters. 'No more masks or soap today, please return tomorrow.'

'We need to write in Arabic as well.' suggests Jessica. I rub out the first sentence and ask Pastor Mark to write. 'Please return tomorrow.' in Arabic. He picks up the board and moves along the queue. He seems to have gone no distance at all when he gives an older couple responsibility for the board and places it in front of them. Voices are raised. An argument breaks out in Arabic, but the pastor stands his ground and reluctantly people drift away.

'They are afraid.' he says when he reaches us. 'They have heard the news from Europe and are worried about their older people and their children. I told them there is no Covid in South Sudan and the closure of schools is just a precaution. Some do not have anyone to take care of their children and are worried about how they will do their jobs and feed their family. I will speak with the bishop to see what else we can do to help.'

'Thank you, Pastor Mark.' we say in unison, and laugh at ourselves. It is a brief light moment in a long afternoon of explaining and repeating till we have given out all the masks and bottles we have. Pastor Mark was accurate in his counting and the couple responsible for the board hand it over and receive our thanks. There is enough sanitiser for several people who had hung on behind them but no masks.

'Very sorry.' says Jessica.

'Come back tomorrow.' I reassure them.

'That was a loooong day.' comments Jessica.

'Yes,' I agree. 'Let's pack up and get a cup of tea.' We haul the table up the drive taking one end each. I have the easel, and Jessica the board in our other hands. We drop them outside the dining area and collapse exhausted onto plastic chairs while someone kindly fetches tea.

'Well done, both of you.' says Mama Lydia. 'I will see you next week.'

Handing out the masks and bottles of antibacterial hand-wash becomes the highlight of my week. Manny has stopped going to band practice and his trips to bars or football matches with colleagues have ceased. He exchanges texts with Jacob and other lost boys for news of Garang. We know from Rory's father that he has been admitted to hospital in Nairobi but there has been no further news. We take it in turns to look after Rose. Aunt Roselyn cannot come because of the curfew. She phones sometimes and plays with Rose over her phone, singing songs and telling her stories. It is funny to see Rose stomp about to the songs and listen quietly to the stories, but she soon gets distracted and loses interest in this disembodied 'aun'y Rslyn.' My aunt misses her, and with her own work ended because of the curfew she spends too much time alone.

I am fortunate because I still have my work for the Olaudah Trust. Jane sends me the link and then I can join the meetings in the UK. It has been strange to see Jane and Paul and others in their rooms, the trees visible through their windows are bare and damp, while I sit on the balcony with the sun baking the walls.

Manny is frustrated with the lack of progress on child safety. It is difficult to work remotely from Kiki, his assistant. The initiatives to set up children's hostels and build an embryonic juvenile court are halted. There has been further fighting in Jonglei province and thousands have been displaced including children. Women have been raped. All his work for the last few months has stalled. He is concerned about the food shortages affecting the refugee camps. He gets home just before the curfew comes into effect and is almost silent during supper, however much I try to interest him in what Rose and I have been doing. After we have eaten, he sits on the sofa playing short snatches of music on his phone. He is engrossed in a new social media app that he tells me is for musicians but when I glance at what he is playing I see scantily clad girls. He is using it to distract him from worries, and I cannot break into his thoughts.

I answer a phone call and am relieved to hear from Peter that my family are well, though sad, and worried. Long queues are building up at the border with Uganda because of the checks on lorries coming into the country and the fear that the drivers may bring Covid in. The delays are causing food shortages, but my family are managing with what Adut is growing along with basic supplies of rice and beans. I send them all my love and close the call. Manny is still on his phone and the tinny sounds, which are all that reaches me, are irritating. I decide to take a break on the balcony. Music no longer fills the Juba nights, but silence is better than the distorted noises from Manny's phone. There is a knock on the door and when I answer it, Jacob is standing well back, his face covered with a mask.

'Would Manny like a walk? he asks. I open the door and point wordlessly at my morose husband.

'Hey, Man, come on, time for some exercise.' he says. Manny does not react at first, then shakes his head, like a lion roused from slumber.

'Hey. Come on. You need a walk.' persists Jacob. Manny reluctantly puts his shoes on and goes off with his friend. I watch them pass out of the door and head off round the block. Jacob is quick and eager, turning his head to speak with Manny, who lopes along beside him, silent and lethargic. He has not been out much. One day a week he goes to his office as soon as the curfew lifts at eight in the morning and returns as it starts at six in the evening. Some days he sits at his computer at home with scarcely a break. I go out with Rose for some fresh air each day, but he rarely joins us. Whereas I have my video calls with my colleagues in the UK, and my sessions handing out masks and sanitisers, he has had nothing except work. A walk with Jacob will do him good.

We used to go out once a week for a romantic evening, often to the Eastern Plaza Hotel near the airport, where a friend is the receptionist and there is good Chinese food. Sometimes we would take samosas to the river and sit and eat them or drive out into the hills around Juba. After Rose was born my aunt stayed late occasionally so that we could go out. Recently we have lost the habit, my mother's frailty, the funeral and now the curfew has made it impossible. I should have realised how hard Manny is taking it. Everyone is finding the curfew tough in different ways.

Bristol 18 May 2020
Hi Maria,
I hope you, Manny, and Rose are well.
Rory has Covid and is seriously ill. They have taken him to the Bristol Royal Infirmary for tests. I am having a few days off so that I can visit him and give attention to Camarg and Carlye. Camarg is preparing for school exams and Carlye is too

little to understand why her dad is not here. Paul will be on the video call.

Stay safe!

Jane

My hands shake as I reply to her message. Jane's husband is a fit man. The hospital will know what to do but news shows the numbers dying in the UK is even higher than Italy. Poor Jane.

I go to check my child. Rose is breathing deeply, and her body is soft and relaxed in sleep. It does not seem possible that this terrible disease is having such an effect. Over a thousand deaths a day in the UK and we have four cases. I am a strong person. I have survived being taken from my family and abandoned in the UK. I have never given up on them and now we can see each other again but the problems we have in this country, and the worry about bringing Rose up here are overwhelming. I must dig deep inside myself to find the strength for all these matters. I will ask the Lord Jesus for peace to continue, to care for my family, to do my work, to help our community through this time. The air is heavy, the rains are late. The weight of unshed tears is locked behind the clouds, waiting for the pressure to reach a point where drops must fall.

The door to the apartment bangs shut and Manny calls out:

'Maria?'

'On the balcony.' I reply. He comes round the glass door. He has a can of beer in his hand.

'We walked to the old bridge. It was good to be out but there is sad news of Garang.'

'Oh?'

'He has permanent damage to his groin. They have operated but he will not be able to have children.'

'Oh, Manny, that is sad. Is there nothing they can do?'

'They've tried but there is too much damage.'

He drains the beer and retreats to the sitting room. He is upset and I cannot reach him. I go indoors and find him listening to songs on his phone again and staring at the screen. I glance at it as I go past and there are half naked figures dancing. He seems completely absorbed in their antics.

'Come,' I say, 'We must get to bed. Rose will be awake in a few hours.'

'You go ahead.' is all he says. I wash my mug out, hurt, and shocked.

The days merge into one, a round of looking after Rose, video calls, and giving out sanitisers. We have no masks to give now and perhaps it is as well. People fear that those who wear masks are bringing the 'western disease' into Juba. To begin with having a mask was a status symbol, now people do not want to wear them.

The feeling among our church leaders is that food supply, not Covid, is our biggest problem. Supplies of food from aid agencies and through Uganda no longer reach us. Many people do not have money unless they work. There are already reports of parts of Juba not having enough food. I worry about Nyadena and her family, but I cannot visit because of the curfew, and she does not have a phone.

Manny is tense and reluctant to talk. Most nights he sits on the sofa listening to this music app and watching the videos, which he tries to hide from me. Tonight, is the anniversary of the day he came to find me in the UK. He is finishing work early and going for a walk with Jacob again. I doubt if he even remembered our special day. He finally appears around eight.

'Sorry, Princess. I went back to Jacob's place and then had to come back through the side streets to avoid the curfew.'

'What if you'd been caught? You could lose your job.' I am delighted because it is the first time he has called me 'Princess' in weeks.

'Jacob's been on at me to call my father to ask about my mother and sisters, and I thought I'd better do it before he got mad at me. My father confirmed that they fled towards Uganda. He left them near the Ugandan border and turned back to join the army. He said my mother was heading for relatives in Uganda and confirmed that there was a branch of her family in Eastern Congo.'

'Oh, that's good.'

'Jacob offered to come here tomorrow, and we'll ring that hospital in Goma.' I feel hurt that he wants Jacob not me. I bite my feelings back and ask:

'How was your father?'

'Okay. More relaxed than I expected. We spoke about the time before the massacre. He talked about my favourite cow with a spot on its coat like a K. He remembers you from visits to Nimule. He said you were a determined little girl. He was pleased when we married. He's never told me that before!' After all the bitterness and tension of the last few weeks, Manny seems released, able to share again. We sleep wrapped in each other's arms for the first time in weeks.

The following afternoon the doorbell rings just after we have finished lunch and there is Jacob.

'Come in.' I say. 'I'm going to put Rose down for a nap and take a walk.'

'I'm always happy to have children around, as long as they're asleep!' jokes Jacob.

Usually, I walk to the salon or seek the cool shade of the cathedral compound, but we have closed the salon, and the compound will be busy with the daily routine of handing out hand gel. There are no street sellers or bars open, so I wander aimlessly seeking shade and holding my scarf over my head and mouth to keep out the dust. I pray continually as I walk, that they will be able to get through to the Guérir les Gens hospital and find Mama Elizabeth. After half an hour I wander back, taking my time as I linger in the entrance to check for post and slowly climb the stairs. I listen at the door and hear the low murmur of their voices.

Jacob leaps up as soon as I enter.

'I must go. I've got to be at the cathedral in ten minutes. Manny, remember you promised.' Jacob leaves us, closing the front door gently behind him.

'Did you get through?' I ask.

'Yes, but we were not able to speak with Mama Elizabeth. They confirmed that she works for Guérir Les Gens but is not based there. They gave me a number but it does not connect.'

'We should have gone to Goma while we still could…'

'Yeah, yeah. You always know best.' He replies. I am pushing him too hard again.

'What did you promise Jacob?' I ask. He looks away and then says slowly:

'My father. I didn't want to contact him because

last time we talked he told me he had a new wife. He has married again and has three young children.'

'Oh, I see. It would not be convenient to have his other family get in touch.' I am not sure what this has to do with the promise he made to Jacob, but he is talking about his family, and I am eager to listen.

'My grandfather had four wives.'

'Well, it was our custom then.' I try to comfort him.

'But you see…. Jacob says…' Manny stares at the concrete floor. 'I started looking at that music app. I was ashamed but I couldn't stop. I've promised Jacob that I will delete it.'

'Delete it, but why?'

'Bad things can pass through the family line, like physical characteristics. My grandfather and father both have a desire for many women, and now I've started to look at these online women. He says I can inherit the tendency, but I don't have to let it take over my life. 'Cut it out' that's what he told me.'

'But Manny, you like the music.'

'There are other ways to find music that don't involve such… flaunting.' I am not sure what to say. There is a place deep inside where I feel heat like midday sun on dry sand, burning and rough between the toes, blistering the soles of the feet. Manny has not been open with me. He has shut himself away and found comfort in these videos of girls flaunting themselves. Does he take after his father and grandfather? Have I married someone who does not keep his commitments?

Others seek Manny out for advice. He has held me up many times and helped me work through difficult situations. The stresses of his government post, the isolation of the curfew and his uncertainty over getting in touch with his family have brought him to a low point.

'I'm sorry.' he continues, head bowed, and shoulders rounded. I put my arms around him.

'It's okay.' I tell him. 'We're all frightened of what this pandemic might do, and you have many worries. It's a sign of strength to recognise and deal with things.' We rest in each other's arms.

'I promised Jacob that I would let him know when I had deleted the app. '

'Then you must do it.' I give him a kiss and turn towards the bedroom. 'Manny?'

'Yeah?'

'You are not like your father. You are an honourable husband and a good father to Rose.'

We must find the strength between us to be honest with each other and stay strong for whatever lies ahead.

10 ISAAC

Nyadena heaves a sigh of relief and arches her tired back. Sheets and pillowcases hang limply from lines strung between the palm trees. Their colours, some bright, others faded to soft greens, browns, and blues, make a vivid bunting against the dark grey of the ground. No time for a cup of tea, the sun will soon be dropping behind the trees, and she must make supper for the children.

The shouts of Luko, Eliza, and Isaac are audible at the end of the street where they play football with other children, kicking an ancient ball across a hard baked area of mud. She collects Barni from the enclosed space between several huts where an elderly widow looks after him and three other small children. Her kindly face is carved into deep wrinkles by hardship. In return the children's mothers cook the old lady her meals. Food supply is daily becoming more difficult. Fresh fruit and vegetables are less available and too expensive for most families. Fish skin stew is a rare treat because fewer people are fishing. Most survive on a basic diet of millet, beans, and rice. Local markets do not hold much stock and Nyadena and her children sometimes visit several locations to buy enough to feed them all. It is a necessary exchange for the elderly to watch over the young in return for their food. Nyadena is glad that she did not take the job with the baker. He has had to close because no-one locally can afford his fresh bread.

'What did you do today?' Nyadena asks her youngest.

'Stories.' replies Barni. Nyadena smiles, Mama Mary has a stock of myths, fables, and songs, that the children love.

'Which story?' she asks him.

'How the Dinka got the cow.'

'Oh, that is a fine story.' Nyadena thinks sadly of the times her mother told her that story, how the cow had avenged the killing of its mother by submitting to humans so that they became dependent on her milk. There was more fighting over cows than any other beast. She sometimes feels a deep anger inside that their move to Juba has deprived Barni of the morning milk that he still really needs. When this curfew is over, she must renew her efforts to find a cow. Somewhere in this sprawling warren of huts there must be space for pasture. Perhaps she should try further out, but there is no spare time to fetch milk. She holds Barni's sweaty palm tightly and tries to think of the good things here.

'Did you play games?'

'Bottle 'ill.' he responds. The older children collect plastic bottles for the younger ones to build with. 'My one was big!' he adds proudly as they reach their own hut. Nyadena gives him a drink of tepid water and collects what she needs for supper. It is not much; beans again, and some dried pepper, carried from Pagak. She chops greens, given her by the lady she sews for. It is not much for four hungry children, but she is grateful.

The sewing work has reduced because many are too scared of the pandemic to work and so have no cash. Nyadena tries not to worry about this coronavirus. Reuben says it will not come to hot countries and that it is a disease that takes the elderly not the young, but many people listen on their radios, or hear news from friends in the USA or Europe. Rumours abound and there are days when Nyadena finds herself caught up in the web of fear that entangles the township. The church is her only bastion against panic, the outdoor prayer meeting on Friday evenings, when the men working away return, her only comfort.

'Luko runnin'.' Barni announces suddenly. Nyadena stands, putting the greens on the chair behind her and goes to meet him. He hurls himself into her arms.

'Isaac! He's fightin' with the big boys. They're kickin' him.'

'Stay with Barni. Where's Eliza?'

'She's shoutin' at them to stop but they won't.' Nyadena lifts her skirt and runs up the street, jumping the ruts and potholes with a skill born of familiarity. Round the corner, a cloud of dust rises from an open area of mud, partially concealing flailing arms and legs. Her daughter stands at the corner shouting and crying.

'Stay back.' Nyadena yells to her. Deep in the recesses of her heart, drawn to the surface by adrenaline, lie skills acquired in the police.

'Break it up.' she shouts in the deepest voice she can manage. 'Do you want me to tell your fathers? Or shall we talk before they take a cane to you?' Her strong words penetrate the swirl of grey dust. Three pairs of eyes survey her warily.

'You won't, Mama?'

'Not if you tell me truthfully what this is about.' They glance furtively at one another and the tallest boy, hair tousled into tight knots in the fight, steps forward.

'He's cheating, Mama. We tell him. See those cans? They're goals. They don't move.' he finishes firmly. Nyadena recognises the truth in this description of typical behaviour. Isaac has spent years developing survival skills of cunning and sleight of hand. She watches him like a dog watches a troublesome pup, but he can filch extra food, or remove other people's belongings in broad daylight. Already she is aware that he has scuttled away like a crab and gone to Eliza. She turns.

'Isaac, Eliza, come here please.' She knows Eliza will not have been involved but will protect Isaac. Nyadena hates the role of minder that her daughter has taken on. Experience has taught her it is best to involve both of them.

'Isaac, did these boys explain that the cans were goals?' Isaac's eyes shift rapidly from one face to the next, but Eliza is standing there, and he knows she is a straight witness.

'Yes, Mammm.' He mumbles.

'And you understood?' Isaac's eyes swerve sideways, seeking a convenient answer but Eliza is there looking straight at him.

'Yes, Mama.'

'You will say sorry to these boys now.'

'Sorry.' he mumbles.

'No.' says the woman who has become his mother. 'Look at them and show that you mean it.' Isaac swallows hard but Nyadena's face is stern, and Eliza's gaze is unflinching.

'Sorry.' he says again. The faces of the three older boys relax.

'You're quick.' One of them offers. 'Be a good goalie one of these days.'

'Well done.' Nyadena tells them. 'Come, Eliza, Isaac, tea is nearly ready.'

While they eat their tea, Nyadena ponders how to deal with Isaac. He is better when Reuben is around, but it is Tuesday, three more days before Friday evening. The closure of schools and the lack of a structure to his day makes Isaac more difficult. It is time to contact Miriam and see if there is any hope of a long-term solution. Isaac needs time and patience to work through all the problems of his cruel childhood.

'Luko, Barni, you will clear tea please. Eliza, fetch water in the bowl and wash up. Isaac, help me fold the sheets.' She walks over to the trees, not checking whether Isaac is following. She needs him to know that she trusts him. She walks into the triangular space between the drying sheets where they are secluded, though still in earshot of surrounding homes.

'Isaac?' she asks quietly looking him in the eyes. 'What happened? How did you get into a fight with those boys?'

'They said I was cheating?'

'And were you?' Isaac's eyes flick sideways and back again. 'Were you?' she repeats.

'Yes, Mama.' He stares at the floor and his words are so soft she can scarcely hear them. Nyadena waits. There have been scenes like this before and she has learnt not to hurry him.

He seems so small, although he is older than Luko.

He is tough, wiry, and fast, with a pent-up anger that escapes uncontrollably. His soft brown eyes peep up at her. 'That big one grab me.' he says. There is another long pause. The boy starts to shake as if he was having a fit. Nyadena hugs him. 'He was taking me, like **they** did.' he sobs. She holds him tightly as the tears escape from eyes squeezed shut, and form runnels through the dirt on his face. When at last the rivulets dry up, she reassures him. 'They were not taking you, they wanted to play with you, but you must play by the rules and not change things.'

'Yes, Mama.'

'Isaac, I know it's hard.' She waits while he calms down. His head comes up and he steps away from her. 'Is that what happened to you? Big boys captured you?'

'At the market, with Mama. She want some cloth. They grab my arms, and put a shirt in my mouth, they ran. I had to run too. I did not see because of the shirt. I heard Mama calling but we were too far. They hid me and the master came and beat me.'

'Oh, your poor mama! How old were you?'

'I seen six rains. I stayed with the master. He told me to steal from people. I'm good at begging. I must take everything to him, or he beat me. I was hungry. I steal when he not watching.' Poor child, thinks Nyadena, no wonder he is so quick and deft, it was the only way he survived. Perhaps his parents are still searching for him.

'Help me fold the sheets.' she tells him, and the child obediently holds the corners, and follows her instructions as they fold in half, stretch the sheet straight and fold again.

'What was your Mama's name, and your Baba?' she asks. 'My Baba was not there; I don't know his name. My Mama was Nyadhial, my grandfather was Gat Wich.'

'You are Nuer?'

'Yes.' Nyadena and Reuben had wondered if he was from the Zande tribe because of his smaller frame and bronze skin but maybe that is just the effects of malnutrition. She places the sheet on her scarf on the ground and starts on the next one. The pile is starting to tilt by the time she has folded the last one She picks it up and places it in his outstretched arms. The pillowcases follow and Isaac can hardly stagger under the load as they walk the short distance back to the hut but he walks proudly. He does not have to do this, but his new mother, who cares about him, has asked him to.

Reuben is one of the few who still goes in to work in the curfew. When he returns that Friday evening Nyadena can see that he is tense. She lets him play with the children and gives him his tea. Then she sends them to bed and sits outside the hut until the scrabbling and giggles die down. She cautiously puts her head round the door. Luko, and Isaac lie head to toe on one side of their double mattress, Luko sprawls across his end in an untidy mass of arms and legs, he breathes rapidly as if running. Isaac is curled into a tight ball, his thin frame wound in on itself like a snail in its shell. His breathing comes in short irregular jerks, he often wakes in the night and occasionally seeks the comfort of the marital bed. Eliza, on the other half of the mattress, sleeps tidily on her side, arms tucked into her body, hands folded round each other, breath almost silent. Barni still sleeps in his parent's bed. He lies on his stomach, bottom hunched in the air, snorts and snuffles coming from his flattened nose. Nyadena smiles and gently shuts the door. They seem so beautiful in sleep, but she must talk to Reuben about Isaac. First, she must encourage him to talk about his own week.

'They're asleep.' she tells him. 'The older ones wore themselves out playing football at the end of the street. Barni had a busy time with Mama Mary. I've finished the washing, there is just embroidery to do. I will fetch it later, tell me about your week.'

'Juba is calm. We chaplains have another training session next month.'

'In Juba?' she asks. If he is away at the weekend dealing with the children becomes a relentless task.

'Yes, at the prison with the other uniformed forces. It may not go ahead.'

'Oh?'

'There's been a counterattack by the Murle tribe in Jonglei Province. Do you remember the Nuer attack in March? Several hundred people killed, women raped, thousands fled. There is talk that we may get posted.'

'Why, why has it happened?'

'Revenge. The state government is not in place yet. Local army commanders and spiritual leaders are working against a cycle of attack and counterattack. It's reported as "cattle raiding," but it is a fight for power and control. Nyadena takes his hand, knowing that his desire is to bring peace through his work as an army chaplain. A vision of a united army fills the politician's rhetoric, but the reality is deeply discouraging. One of our neighbours walks past and glances our way:

'Coming for a drink, Rube?'

'Not tonight. Family first.' He turns towards Nyadena, brown cheeks flushed red. The church pastor left him in no doubt that drunken behaviour was not tolerated, and he'd been ashamed that his lapse was known. He constantly warns his men of the dangers of drunkenness and its association with keeping company with prostitutes. Nyadena had laughed and teased him, but it was a serious slur on his character, which must never happen again.

'Have the kids been better than their dad?' he asks wryly.

'Mixed. Isaac got into a fight when some of the older boys grabbed him to stop him cheating at football. A demon of anger rose up in him. He fights like a devil. He has said sorry, but I cannot go on, he needs so much attention. And there is fallen mud on the back wall.'

'I'll look at the wall later. We can't make up for Isaac's capture.'

'No, but he needs someone who can give him the time to work through it. I have our own children to think of. We didn't plan it like this,' she laments, 'but we cannot abandon him. Eliza would stay with him if we did.'

'What do you suggest?'

'Isaac told me his mother's and grandfather's name today. The demons have kept them hidden from his mind till now. I would like to call Miriam and see if she can have another search now that we have names.'

'There is disruption in Pibor Post because of

people fleeing but we can try.' He hands her the phone and heads round the back to investigate the mud that has fallen from the wall of their hut. Nyadena dials carefully, unused to the strange device.

'Hallo, Nyadena, you are safe?'

'We are fine, thank you. And you? How is your new job?'

'It is good.'

'Did you hear anything from Pibor Post about the boy's family?'

'Nothing. It is usual.'

'I have a name now, will that help?' She gives the names, but Miriam can offer little reassurance. The fighting in Jonglei has caused many families to flee and there is confusion across the region. The call ends warmly, with a promise to see each other once the curfew is over and it is safe to do so.

Reuben decides to walk to the stream to fetch mud so that he can repair the hut. It is a clear night with a full moon. Nyadena fetches the pillowcases to embroider. If she sews the orange cottons, on this bright green it should be clear enough to see. She can hear shouts and music from nearby bars, and over towards the church the youth are having a drumming practice but otherwise all is quiet, and she enjoys a moment of peace. Cooling smells have cleared and there is a scent of cassia from the tree at the end of the street. The palm trees next to their hut rustle softly in the breeze from the river.

'Aarrch.' The evening quiet is shattered by a cry of pain from one of the huts close by.

Nyadena's hands clench, the needle emerges at the wrong point. Aieeee, she will have to redo it. She knows the cause of the shout and waits tensely for what will inevitably follow.

'No, no, you are drunk!' There is a sharp crack, and a thud. Anxious faces appear from neighbouring huts. No one says a word but wide eyes, dark cheekbones picked out by moonlight, glance towards each other and away. Sobs can be heard and a burly man swings past the huts replacing his belt in the loops of his trousers. The neighbours exchange glances but Nyadena's steps out from her home with a bowl of water and a towel over her arm. It is a common sight on a Friday night. Most families are loving and respectful of each other, but tensions rise in the hardship of daily life and for some men the right to beat their wife is part of their marriage code. She bathes the woman's head, presses the damp towel to it to bring out the bruise, and gently helps her to the torn mattress.

Nyadena returns to the chair outside her own *tukul* and corrects the stitch she misplaced. She closes her eyes for a moment to rest them and hears again the cries of her mother years ago, when Hannah's body, bleeding and broken, was brought home by the girls she had gone to market with several hours earlier. Five girls, all in their early twenties, attacked and raped in the open by a group of soldiers. The other girls had been able to walk home but Hannah had been savagely beaten and assaulted multiple times. She had lost consciousness. They were never able to find out whether it was the Rwandan mercenaries or soldiers from the rebel forces under General Nkunda. Who had done it did not matter, fighters on all sides terrorised the people living in eastern Congo.

Nyadena had thought her sister was dead. She had watched appalled as her mother washed her twisted body, fetching bowls of water repeatedly and putting the stained cloths to soak. Shocked and frightened she had held back her tears and kept calm as she helped her mother. Then in the long recovery that followed she had sat by Hannah, making sure she drank plenty.

She had listened to the voices of the uncles as they sat outside in the evening discussing what should be done. She feared that they would be on the move again, seeking another new home, returning to the refugee camp in Uganda. The uncles raised their voices, and her mother became silent and withdrawn, retreating into the business she had built up and calling on Nyadena to take Hannah's place in turning the handle of the ancient sewing machine. How she loathed sewing! With a start she opens her eyes and searches for the needle that has dropped from her fingers. The moon is setting behind the palm trees. She folds the sheet away to finish next day.

'Come to bed, Nya.' Reuben comes round the side of the hut, his hands grey with mud.

'Sorry, husband, dealing with Isaac tires me.' He takes her hand and pulls her to her feet.

An hour later Reuben is stretched out on his stomach on the mattress beside her, snoring loudly, exhausted by the week's work and the walk to the stream for mud. The children's breath comes in steady low murmurs, except for Barni, who snorts loudly on each indrawn breath. Isaac turns and cries out softly, his breath coming in rapid gasps. Nyadena sits up, ready to comfort him, but he turns over and breathes easily. The burden of caring for him and helping him come to terms with the brutality of his life is exhausting. He needs more help than she has time to give, and it is taking her attention away from her own three children.

'If Miriam cannot find the parents, perhaps we could ask this new relative for help.' She murmurs.

'Mmmm.' Reuben agrees, but he is fast asleep. If Manny is a relative, it is his duty to help. When she searched the face and actions of this well-fed government official with his shiny suit, his American accent, and his well-groomed wife she could find no resemblance to the wiry youth, smelling comfortingly of goat and sweat. It was kind of Mama Maria to bring the stones. She stares up at the ceiling wondering if Maria and Manny Deng have rung the number her uncle gave. Perhaps she and Reuben should try to call. She could at least write to her mother at the Guérir les Gens hospital. The three had been so close when Nyadena was young. Despite the nine-year age gap, she and Hannah had been each other's constant companions. Nyadena had sat by her for weeks until she was able to eat a little. One day she saw Hannah's stomach jump while she was asleep. She ran to tell her mother, afraid that a demon had taken up residence. Elizabeth had calmed her anxious fears.

'We need a midwife, not a witch doctor.' she had said. By the time the rains came their little family had gained a new member. They called him Adam. He was beautiful. Nyadena remembered that perfect little red brown body, delicate fingers tightly curled around her own dark one. When the neighbours started calling

Hannah a loose woman, Nyadena was indignant, it was not her sister's fault. Her uncles refused to have any more contact with them, saying that Hannah was 'spoiled,' they would never get a bride price for her now.

'You are tainted too.' they told her 'No-one will want you.' The hurt of this was as sharp as the pain caused by the attack on Hannah. Her sister's body had healed but her reputation was gone for ever. Hot tears squeezed down Nyadena's face as she remembered the shame, the humiliation of being no longer wanted in the community that had welcomed them. She had moved away as soon as she had the chance, delighted to work in the Police Service.

She was ashamed that her letters had gradually petered out, though her mother's letters continued to reach her once a month all the time they were in Ezo, but Pagak was too remote, and no word came. Mama did not even know about Barni. She feels the sharp sting on her eyelids as tears of regret escape from deep within and trickle onto the pillow.

'Hannah, Adam, where are you?' she sobs. 'Mama, I'm sorry. I didn't mean it to be so long. I have offended our ancestors.' She tries to breathe calmly and turns over. Reuben flings out an arm, and she holds his hand for comfort. He rolls towards her, still fast asleep. He had been so different from other men, kind, courteous, determined to build respect and tolerance among his soldiers. Eliza was like him. 'We can talk in the morning.' she told herself. 'I can do more sewing and save up to send a letter.'

At dawn, the air is hot and humid.

'Rains will come today.' comments Reuben. There are jobs to be done, checking the roof, making sure there are no other weak spots, planting a few seeds in the small area of space around their hut. Nyadena gets her household organised.

'Eliza and Isaac, take the clean sheets back. Luko, help your father. Barni you can help Mama grind millet. At noon, the clouds darken, and a few raindrops fall. The wind picks up, blowing litter across the street. The air feels thick and oily. Suddenly the clouds spill over, and huge drops splash onto the mud. They fall faster until there is a sheet of water around each hut. Adults stand in the doorways, savouring the smell of damp earth. The gullies in the street become torrents, the hard packed paths turn to grey ooze. Children dance in the deluge, splashing each other with mud. Rain is a blessed release from heat and anxiety about food supplies.

It is not possible to light the brazier for cooking, so Nyadena gives her family dried fish skins and chopped greens. It is nutritious but not filling and there are complaints at bedtime. It is late before she and Reuben have a chance to talk. The rain continues to pound on the roof. To open the door is to confront a sheet of water pouring down. The floor is tacky. They sit at the other end of the hut from the sleeping children. The temperature has dropped with the rain and, while western aid workers mop the sweat from their faces, locals put on knitted caps and cardigans. Reuben and Nyadena huddle round a small tallow lamp for comfort. The coal in the brazier is damp. There is no hot tea until the rain ceases.

'I dreamed of my mother and sister.' she confides. Reuben is alert, listening. Dreams remembered on waking are from the spirit world and significant. 'They were calling me. I dreamed I was a child playing in the woods. Other children were wanting me to run with them but I was sitting on a branch of a tree and a demon held me back against the thick trunk so I could not move. My sister was calling me, and I shouted to show her where I was, but my voice made no sound. Then I heard my mother calling. I tried to grab the demon but when my hand reached there was just dust.' Reuben has not moved, and he does not speak. She watches his face anxiously in the flickering yellow lamp light. Their shadows loom over them, softened by the smoke from the lamp.

'It is time to write to them.' he says slowly. 'They are your family.'

'If I can find extra sewing work, I could save up for the letter.'

'You work hard enough.' he says. 'I have a better idea. The big man called my phone today. He has contacted the hospital your uncle spoke of and confirmed that your mother works there, but he was unable to speak with her. Her work is not on the wards but with the people of the town. He is planning to visit the hospital as soon as the travel restrictions are lifted. He asked if you would go with him and Mama Maria.'

'To Goma? It is far.'

'Over one thousand kilometres. It will take many days.'

'I cannot go, what about the children? Who would look after them, and what about Isaac?'

'Yes, it would be difficult.' he agrees. 'Perhaps it is better that you stay.'

He reaches for her hand and the shadows leap on the walls as if in agreement.

'There is a place for Isaac. I am sure of it.' he says, gently pressing the hand held in his own. 'God has given him into our care. We ask for a home for him one day soon.

,

11 GOMA, CONGO

We have stopped Manny's car at Karuma Falls on the road from Nimule to Gulu in Uganda. Torrents of water swirl around us, pouring through a narrow gap between dense forest, cascading over rocks, churning, and tumbling as cross currents collide and retreat. The noise is a storm in my head wiping out all other thoughts. The White Nile, smooth and dark in the distance, becomes a raging turmoil as water boils over the band of rocks across its path.

I peer over the guardrail into the cauldron of foam beneath. Waves break as if on a beach, but their nemesis is not solid ground but treacherous whirlpools. Birds swoop and glide unperturbed by the boiling torrent beneath them. Manny and I hold hands and glance at each other, pointless to try to speak above the thunderous sound of the water. Eventually, sated by noise, and disorientated by the roaring energy, we retreat to the car and perch on the bonnet to eat breakfast. The air smells moist, cooler, and fresher than the air in Juba.

We started from Nimule at first light this morning, leaving Rose with my sister, Deborah, and my nieces. She will be spoiled and over mothered, but it was hard to say goodbye. She was so sweet yesterday playing with her older cousins, her little black head bobbing back and forth, as she followed them round, a willing helper, while they prepared the evening meal. When we left this morning, she was curled in her travel cot, bottom rounded and padded by her nappy, her fluffy monkey, currently her favourite toy, clutched in her hand, fingers curled into its soft fur. It is the first time we have not taken her with us since she was born and for Manny's sake, I must let go of my anxiety and enjoy this time together.

We never had a honeymoon; all our savings went on buying, and furnishing, our apartment. This trip has taken many months of planning. We called the Guérir les Gens hospital several times. We have spoken to people who confirmed that Elizabeth Deng is listed as a counsellor, but it has not been possible to speak to her, or to find out her address or a mobile number. Nyadena has given us the last address she has for her mother, and we have decided to drive to find her. South Sudan opened its borders in July and Congo in August, but we must travel through this northwest corner of Uganda and the border was closed until October. At last, we are on our way to find Nyadena's mother, and Manny's, their sister, and the child born through an act of war, now sixteen years old. There have been many delays, trying to find hotels that would take a pre-booking, getting permission to travel and arranging Covid tests. When we leave Goma, we will have to pay for another test for the return journey. Garang wants to introduce us to the fiancée he has met in Nairobi. It is not safe for him to enter South

Sudan, so we are staying at a lakeside hotel in Entebbe on the way back.

We shall be away for ten days and travel thousands of miles, but Manny seems excited by this. He used to drive from Baltimore across the eastern States for holidays. It is costing us thousands of dollars. We have postponed our plan to buy a small house and are using the money we had saved. Manny's sponsor, Kenny, has made a generous transfer of dollars into Manny's account to help him find Mama Elizabeth.

'Feeling rested, Princess?'

'Exhilarated rather than rested.'

'Yeah, quite a spectacle. Ready to go on?'

'How many hours to Fort Portal?'

'Six, if we get a clear road. We'll stop for lunch. Kiki recommended Nguse River Camp. It's a stopover between Murchison Falls and the Gorilla safari camps.'

We clamber reluctantly back into the car, thankful for air conditioning and good suspension. Manny has special permission to take his government vehicle on this long journey. I sink back into the seat and enjoy the rich greens of the Karuma Forest to the right of us. South Sudan is a predominantly dry country, where the red sandy soil is part of the landscape. Here the soil is invisible, cloaked in forest on one side and a patchwork of small, cultivated fields on the other. The road is well maintained. Manny seems relaxed, happy to be venturing beyond the confines of Juba.

My mind wanders, lulled by the steady drone of the engine, the blur of Uganda's lush vegetation, and the clear blue sky above. Manny's hands rest lightly on the steering wheel, and I am content that we are on this quest, with time to talk and enjoy being alone together.

'Manny, why did you come to the UK to look for

me?' I ask him. 'You hadn't seen me since we were children. How did you know I was there?'

'I didn't. Garang, Jacob and I were discussing whether to settle in the US or repatriate. There was a US government scheme to encourage repatriation.' Manny continues, 'Boys who were already married wanted to stay in the US. I didn't know which way to jump. I'd had girlfriends but it never worked out. I was confident that as a lawyer I could get a job in Juba, but I knew I'd come too far to settle back into a traditional marriage. I needed a South Sudanese girl with an understanding of the west. One of the guys was talking about the diaspora in the UK. I thought you might have gone there. It sounds crazy, but I remembered how we always were in step.'

'All the time I was stuck in the UK I remembered those visits to Nimule.' I tell him. 'It was a miracle when you emailed Jane. I was afraid of you when we met you at the station in Bristol. You seemed so, well, American!'

'Me too. You were a confident woman managing Avon View House and looked up to by everyone.'

'Then we went to that gig where Rory was playing.'

'And danced.' Manny chuckles.

'None of it mattered, we were back in Nimule!'

'And all the years in between were pounded away by the beat of the drums.' He drops a hand from the steering wheel and clasps mine.'

'Are you glad we came back, Princess?'

'Yes, it's tough. We would have a better life

in Bristol or Baltimore, but I would always feel I was missing the most important things to me – family, customs.' He falls silent and his hand returns to the steering wheel.

We have left the forest behind and are travelling through an area of grassland and thorn trees. I relax into the steady motion of the car and watch the landscape unfolding through the window. This adventure is a welcome change from our limited routine of online work, playtimes with Rose, and calls from family, friends, asking anxiously 'How are you?' Rory has made a full recovery but many in the UK have not. It has been a sad time.

'Oh, you're awake?' says Manny.

'I haven't been asleep, just thinking.' I reply.

'About?' he prompts.

'How difficult life has been recently with nothing much happening.'

'There's been plenty going on,' he counters, 'the fighting in Bor and Warrap state, that appalling business in Yei. There's been more reports of abuse, child abduction, and trafficking than ever before.'

'Will we never be at peace?'

'Well, some things have improved, at least my pay comes through each month. Though more of it seems to go on helping Esther and Reuben.'

'It's not their fault. Nyadena works hard but she struggles to cope with Isaac and her own children. We need to find a better place for Isaac, then Nyadena and Reuben will manage without help.' Manny makes an American noise deep in his throat that sounds like 'iergh,' as though he is about to wring a chicken's neck, something I doubt he has ever done. What he feared has happened and Nyadena's little family have become dependent on him. It is the South Sudan way. You are expected to help your family when your life goes well. There is no government money for families as there is in the UK.

The scenery has changed. We have left the forests behind and are passing through a more open area of grassland and scattered trees, like an English parkland, except that these are acacias and thorn trees. Every few miles we pass a village with cultivated land, banana palms and fruit trees around it. The houses have blue corrugated iron roofs that glint in the sun and the crops are tall and green from regular rainfall.

Thoughts of Nyadena fill my mind. I have visited several times and can see her life is getting tough. With the borders closed there is little food coming from Uganda. The older children are wire thin. Little Barni has a rounded belly, but his legs are stick thin and he grizzles. The situation has worsened because people have fled from the fighting in Warrap and squeezed into the overflowing refugee camps around Juba. They are fed by the United Nations and aid agencies, but basic foodstuffs are in short supply and prices are rising constantly. We discussed the cost of this journey for many hours, but in the end, it was the urging of Manny's sponsor that decided us. We need to resolve this issue of Manny's family and I can see already that the feeling of an open road and a break from routine is doing him good.

The Nguse River Camp is a neat wooden structure, open sided. They are only serving vegetable curry and rice because of Covid, but it is freshly cooked, and the dining area is cool and pleasant. Usually, it is packed with safari buses, they tell us, on their way to Murchison Falls, or Kibale Forest but no tours come now, and they are struggling to keep going.

It is another five hours before we arrive at Fort Portal. We are staying at the Dreamland Hotel, recently opened by a relative of one of Manny's colleagues. Individual rooms with an ensuite shower open into a courtyard. Lines of yellow bricks at head height break up the brightness of the orange brick walls. We are made very welcome and sleep soundly. We linger over our breakfast of tea, millet porridge, mango, and bananas.

'How long have you been open?' Manny asks.

'For two year.' The owner replies. At first, we are busy, and I think soon I will pay for the roof but since March there has been nothing. You are the first visitors this week.'

'What do people come for?' I ask.

'Oh, lady, they come to see the gorillas in Kibale Forest. People walk in the mountains. It is very beautiful. You must stay and enjoy.'

'Sorry, we are on our way to meet someone in Goma.'

'Goma! It is far.'

'Ready for another long day, Princess.'

'Yes. I'm ready. And you?'

'Let's go.' he says.

The scenery changes again as we drive south. In the distance a smooth line of mountains, with an occasional sharp peak are visible across the parklike savanna. In the early morning they are misty, with a lilac hue, but as the sun rises, they become darker and more clearly defined.

'The Great Rift Valley escarpment,' comments Manny, 'runs through Kenya too, like a great embrace encircling East Africa.'

'We've sometimes seen it when I've flown to Nairobi with Jane.' I respond. 'There is a chain of lakes in the floor of the valley on the east side that are visible on a clear day.'

The road winds through low hills with the Rift Valley escarpment sometimes visible on the horizon, at other times hidden by forest. After four hours we stop for lunch near the Queen Elizabeth National Park. We have passed several safari lodges and once seen elephant in the distance. Manny pulls in to where there are a line of shacks selling samosas at the roadside. We eat them enjoying the view east across an area of swamp to a lake beyond. Behind us the mountains are closer, their peaks softened by the midday haze. I would like to stay here but we must travel on. The surface is not as good, and Manny must negotiate ruts and sandy areas.

'We should be able to see Lake Edward soon.' he says but nothing is visible apart from the endless tall grass and scattered thorn trees. We reach a sign to Kekenki and a track branching off to the right, which Manny takes.

'I need a break.' he says, 'Let's see if we can get a cup of tea.'

The village is beautiful, the lake visible beyond it, vast like a sea. There are fishing canoes drawn up on the shoreline but no shops. We ask a fisherman if there are any bars. His wife will make us tea, he says. She brings a pot of chai, tea made in the kettle with milk and sugar.

'How far to Goma?' I ask. He shrugs.

'To Congo, two hours walking. Goma is very far.'

'I'll drive for a bit.' I say firmly and to my surprise Manny acquiesces. I drive more slowly than he does, and I can feel his irritation at first, but his breathing slows, and he sleeps. At the border we change time zones, Congo is two hours behind Uganda, and it is now four instead of six in the evening. There is another long delay while our documents and Covid certificates are checked. We set off again as the sun is setting. Manny takes over the driving and I try to keep him awake for this final leg of the journey.

'Tell me about your Mama.' He does not respond, and I wonder if he will ever break his silence about her. I wait. He drums his fingers on the steering wheel.

'She was the driving force behind our family.' he says at last. 'Her father was a chief, a good judge, and greatly respected. He led our villages well. When Khartoum started to impose sharia law and Arabic in schools he met with other local chiefs and made an agreement that we would form a local militia. My brothers signed up, but I was too young. That militia became part of the South Sudan People's Liberation Army. Mama organised the women to make caps, shirts, and shorts, so they had a uniform. She was the Mother's Union leader and organised training for the women. She was always busy when I was little, organising projects, cooking food, bringing the women together to sew uniforms, making sure they had support when their children were born.'

'What about when your sisters were born, who supported her?'

'There was almost a competition to see who could

do most. They loved her, I guess. When Esther was born there were gifts on the doorstep, people offering to help with the chores.'

'What about your father?'

'He's always been focussed on the animals. He doesn't think about anything else. He would spend hours studying our cattle, naming them, and mating them to produce the strongest animals. He was away at a cattle camp for most of the dry season taking them to the swamp areas where they could feed.'

'Your mama didn't go?'

'No, she stayed in our compound with the baby. I was due to go for the first time. Then we heard news from villages to the north that the government was paying the mujahedeen to fight for them so we did not go to cattle camp that last year, 1991 it would have been. The men stayed in the village, in their uniforms, ready to fight. People started to arrive from the north with tales of bombs falling from planes and women and children taken as slaves by the mujahedeen.'

'Was your village bombed, like Torit?'

'No, that's what we feared but it was the Sudan People's Liberation Army who turned on us. The Nuer forces, led by Riek Machar signed a peace agreement with the Khartoum government and sided with their forces to attack us.'

'My brother Peter has always said that the Nuer forces betrayed us.'

'It was a confusing time, and some disagreed with the policy of fighting for independence. My father talked about making terms with the Khartoum government so that we could continue with our traditional way of life. My mother was adamant that we should make a stand against sharia law. There were arguments. I was too young to understand at the time. We pieced it together later from what we each knew and what we could read in the news.' I know from his tone of voice that he is talking about the other Lost Boys. They are a family to him in a way that his parents never seemed to be.

'How did your Mama and Baba meet?'

'Their parents arranged the marriage. My grandfather had many cows. He could afford to pay the bride price for a chief's daughter. My mother was young, she was beautiful and strong in her spirit.'

'But it wasn't a love marriage?' I suggest.

'To begin with. She gave him the sons he needed to look after the herd. When the conflict between north and south increased I don't think my parents' feelings for each other survived the tensions. Baba just wanted a quiet life. He wanted me to take as much interest in the cattle as he did, but I'd already started studying with my uncle, the pastor. I knew I wanted to learn from books. It took longer than I was expecting!'

'But you made it!' Manny's habit of being taciturn over family matters, his reluctance to recognise Nyadena and his withdrawal into online entertainment have made our relationship difficult recently but he does persevere through whatever life throws at him. Conflict, separation, flight, famine, transport to another continent and an unfamiliar way of life have not prevented him from achieving the dream he had to study books not cattle. I watch his hands on the steering wheel, his grip light but firm, head erect, alert, ready for the unexpected. He can be difficult, but I love him. I watch the shadows of the bush flash past us.

Dust cakes the car windows, and the outlines are softened and distorted. I can see a few stars, but the murky windows filter out the full glory of the African night. The engine drones on, the car headlights pick out the ribbon of road, grey against the surrounding darkness.

'Wake up, Princess, we're on the outskirts of Goma. I need your help to find the hostel.' I try to make sense of what is visible in the dark. In the distance strange cone shaped hills rise above the town. The ground in front of the homes is dark and twisted like rope. We wind through backstreets. We cannot afford another luxury hotel so are booked into a local hostel, Maison Matu. It is gone eight in the evening local time; we have been travelling for over twelve hours.

Our room is basic, a wooden bed with a foam mattress, brightly coloured sheets and pillowcases and a mosquito net, clean but grey with age. The concrete floor is painted dark red, and the walls are mustard yellow. There is a single square window, with a wooden shutter, closed by a metal bolt. We lift our suitcases, and a small crate of water bottles that we bought in Fort Portal, onto the long low table and unpack the minimum we need for the night, including face masks, which we must wear outside our own room. We have supper at an adjacent bar. The conversation is in a language I do not understand, perhaps because the tables are widely spaced, and I am too tired to hear clearly.

'They speak French here.' says Manny. 'I had a few colleagues who spoke this language when I was working in Baltimore, but I never got far with it. Maison Matu means House of Matu.' The conversation at other tables is animated with unfamiliar gestures and shrugs of the shoulder. It feels strange after our long journey.

'Toilet flushes but the shower is cold.' Manny reports, returning from the bathroom. 'And there's no light. The security guard said the generator's gone off for the night. At least there's water.'

I have a quick refreshing shower and return to our room. Manny is already asleep. I drink from one of the bottles of water, and join him in bed, but I cannot relax. Tomorrow, we have allowed ourselves the morning to rest and orientate ourselves. Then we go to the Guérir les Gens hospital to find Elizabeth Deng. What if she is not here and we have come all this way for nothing? I try to forget the length of the journey and focus on the good things, our rest by the Karuma Falls, the views of the Rift Valley escarpment. There are new sights to see in Goma too, but first we must find Elizabeth.

Neither of us wakes till gone eight o' clock. Slivers of gold show around the wooden shutter but the room is cold. I struggle out of bed and fetch a shawl from my bag. There is a moan, and Manny turns towards me.

'What are you doing?' he asks.

'I'm cold. The sun is up but the air is cool.' Manny reaches for his phone.

'It's twenty-seven degrees, Princess, warm in Baltimore or Bristol but we are used to temperatures in the thirties.'

'I suppose so. I'm glad I brought one of my UK cardigans.'

Dressed in thicker clothes than we are used to, we

venture out to find breakfast. There is a small park at the end of the road with a shack selling tea and pancakes. We sit on a bench outside. The streets resemble parts of Juba, concrete houses with corrugated iron roofs and small plots around them where people are growing vegetables. The scenery is different. A mountain rises above the city, swathed in cloud. The slopes are bright green but with dark patches slithering down them like snakes. Manny goes over to the shack.

'*Le nom de cette montagne*?' he asks.

'*Nyiragongo volcan. Très dangereux*!' Manny returns to his seat and searches on his phone.

'It's a volcano.' he announces. 'An active one called Nyiragongo. It erupted in 2002 and is expected to erupt again. There is a lava pool within the crater. Those black areas are where lava has flowed down the mountain.' He shows me a picture.

'It is fire, moving down the mountain?'

'It is from deep within the earth where it is so hot the rock has melted. The pressure builds and the volcano explodes, and the molten rock pours out. That is what Esther meant when she said there was a demon in the mountain.'

'Well, it seems we are in the right place.' I shiver as I remember Nyadena, Esther as I should think of her, I suppose, and her account of her childhood here. What a strange place, a place where men feel free to attack women, and where mountains send out fire.

We chose Maison Matu because it is near the hospital. It takes us twenty minutes to walk there, and we are both aware of the mountain behind us, a looming presence. There is menace as well as promise in Goma.

'What will we say?' I ask Manny.

'All we can do is ask if they know her name and where we can find her.'

'In French?' I ask.

'I suppose so.' he replies. 'I'd better have a few phrases ready.' We stop under a palm tree while he searches his phone for a relevant phrase.

'*Vous connaissez Madame Deng, s'il vous plaît? Elle travaille ici*?' Manny mutters to himself.

The hospital is an array of low buildings separated by concrete paths with areas of grass and shrubs in between. A sign points to reception, Manny goes up to the desk and asks his questions. The receptionist seems bemused.

'*Madame Deng*.' repeats Manny. '*Ici*?'

'*Non, peut-être dans un autre immeuble*.' She waves a hand towards the neighbouring buildings. We take this as an invitation to enter the compound. We ask the same question at each of the single-story concrete buildings. Sometimes we are met by blank stares, sometimes by a firm. '*Non*.' In one block we find a doctor who speaks English. Manny explains our quest.

'Give me a moment, I have to check on a catheter, then I'll have a look on our system.' He dashes off and we wait on the open porch. The sun has boiled away the cloud from the mountain and it stands over the town like a green cloak.

'Right,' says the doctor. 'Let's have a look.' He moves the mouse confidently. 'I have our staff list up. What was the name again? Deng? There are several – James, Guor, Deng Mobutu. No women. Have you tried at reception?'

'The receptionist only spoke French so we could not explain fully.' I reply.

'Try again later.' he advises. 'There'll be a change of shift at five.' We thank him and try the rest of the blocks without finding out anything more. Manny is despondent.

'I don't think she's here. The uncle must be mistaken. Or she's left.' he says. In both our minds is the thought that we have travelled all this way and are too late. Something has happened. She has moved again, become ill, or worse, a fear we dare not name.

'It's four o'clock. Why don't we find a cup of tea and come back at five?' Two mugs of tea and a pack of biscuits in front of us, we sit at a table in silence. I pray that we can find one woman in this city of many hundreds of thousands.

'We never mentioned that she was a counsellor.' I say. 'Those buildings were all surgical wards, apart from the maternity block. Perhaps there is a different place for counsellors.' Manny takes out his phone.

'French for councillor is *conseillère*. We could try!' We head back to the hospital and wait at the reception desk, which has a queue of people. Eventually it is our turn.

'*Madame Deng. Conseillère. Travaille ici?*'

'*Non, pas des conseillères ici...*' replies the man behind the desk. There follows a long explanation that Manny clearly does not understand. We stand dumbly staring at him, desperate to communicate but unable to say more.

'Lord, help us.' I pray silently.

'Amereecan?' he asks.

'Yes.'

'*Attendez un moment, s'il vous plaît.*' Manny turns to me.

'I think he's asking us to wait.' We stand together, a man coughs behind us and we turn to see a line of weary people whose eyes show their anxiety at the delay. The man returns with a woman with Asian features and straight black hair caught up in an Alice band.

'You are asking for a counsellor?' she says. Manny explains our mission.

'The counsellors are part of our *Aide pour le Lac* project. They work in the communities and villages around Goma. You'll need to go to the project office. It is off Avenue de la Paix, behind the Yole Africa building. They will be closed now until eight in the morning. You can take a bus from here.' We thank her and make our way back to Maison Matu for supper and an early bed. We are weary and unsure whether to be encouraged or not.

'At least we know there are counsellors associated with the hospital.' I comment.

'We only have two more days here.'

'All we can do is pray, Manny, and get some sleep.'

At first light the following morning we ask the proprietor to order a boda-boda for us and take a rapid trip through the city on the back of the motorcycle. I can feel Manny's weight pressing into me as his arms hold me tight, but I am terrified that he will fall off the back, or that we will all tip over as we weave through the cars, vans and bicycle drawn trailers that cram the streets. The air smells of diesel fumes and goat manure, with an overlay of fish. As we cross the city the smell of fish becomes stronger. The noise of the boda-boda is irregular and the rush of air past my head makes me dizzy. We whizz between tall buildings and along a broad dirt road past large houses. Manny leans towards me and shouts in my ear. 'Lake Kivu on the left.' and I catch a glimpse of grey-green water glittering in the early morning sunlight. The boda boda makes a sudden turn, that nearly unseats me, dives between two buildings, and pulls up outside a two-storey block with the Guérir les Gens logo on the door.

'*Vous retournez dans une heure, s'il vous plaît*' says Manny as he hands over the payment.

'*Bien sur.*' replies the driver as he wheels round and shoots off again.

'I've asked him to come back in an hour.' says Manny. 'Let's try our luck.' he adds.

I'm not sure luck is going to help us. I am praying hard that we find someone who can connect us to Elizabeth Deng.

'*Bonjour.*' says Manny to the woman in nurse's uniform behind the reception desk. '*Nous cherchons une femme qui s'appelle Elizabeth Deng, une conseillère.*' The response is too rapid to understand. She sees his puzzled expression.

'American?' she asks.

'Yes.' we reply.

'You are searching for Counsellor Elizabeth Deng? For what reason?'

'She is my mother.' Manny replies. 'We lost touch in the conflict.'

'Sorry.' she responds. 'Do you have your passport? I need to see it before I share information.' We pass over our documents, and she checks them carefully and hands them back.

'I know Mama Elizabeth Deng.' is her astonishing response. 'She works in our community project in Bukavu.'

'Bukavu!' I repeat.

'Where is that?' Manny asks simultaneously.

'It's at the other end of the lake. You can reach it by boat. Do you have her phone number?'

'An uncle gave us this number, but it does not ring through.' She picks a phone up from her desk and scans it.

'That's an old number. Here's the new one.' She reads it out and Manny enters it on his phone.

'Thank you.' we say together.

'Do you think we've found her?' Manny exclaims when we are outside.

'Oh, Manny. I'm so glad.' We embrace and cling to each other. It has been a long search. 'Shall we call?' I encourage him.

'Not yet.' he says. 'Let's go to the lakeside and see if we can get a drink.'

We sit with a can of beer each, watching the waves lap against the grass.

'I'm going to find out about the ferry before I call.' he says.

I watch the birds at the edge of the lake. Hamerkops with their sharp beaks and backward sloping feathered crests peck about in the grass. White egrets wade in the shallows. The sun is high in the sky and the lake is a deep blue. A few local fishing boats bob in the water to my left, making their way slowly towards a line of homes on the Rwandan side of the lake. Far out waves ruffle the water. Manny breaks into my thoughts:

'We can get a ferry at seven thirty in the morning, and it takes three hours.' he says, 'There is a return boat at two in the afternoon. We would have about three hours there. I'm going to call her number.' I watch the waves ripple and pray as I have never prayed before that this conversation will go well.

'Hallo, am I speaking to Elizabeth Deng?'

I can hear a woman's voice answering.

'This is Emmanuel Deng.'

The voice on the other end sounds suspicious.

'I am the one they called "Kor." Yes, my goat had a brown cross on his back and white tips to his ears.'

Excitement and delight. I cannot hear the words, but the intonation is full of emotion.

'Yes, after all the years.'

A question.

'I live in Juba, with my wife, Maria, and daughter, Rose. My sister, Esther, Nyadena as she now is, is in Juba also.'

There are loud exclamations on the other end.

'She had two boys after Eliza. They are Luko and Barni.'

Concern.

'Yes, they are doing well. I'm in Goma with Maria. Can we meet with you?'

Long explanation.

'Yes, we'd like that. Where shall we find you?'

Instructions.

'Okay, we will be there.'

Delight.

'God bless you too, Mama.' he rings off.

'I knew her voice.' smiles my husband. 'I knew straight away. She's coming to Goma tomorrow. She comes every month to meet my sister, Hannah, and son, he's my nephew, I guess.'

'Oh Manny, that's wonderful.

'My mother says Esther wrote about us, but she didn't know what to believe.'

We order another beer and enjoy the sense of relief. We risked so much on this journey, and I am thankful that it has been successful but when I heard him say 'my mother' for the first time I realised I will shortly meet my mother-in-law for the first time. I hope we go well together.

12 ELIZABETH

I lean against a rusted rail and watch the water slap against the quay, oily and clogged with decayed vegetation. Manny takes a stick and pokes a coke bottle bobbing in the detritus, now bumping up against the posts, then drifting away again. Rain clouds shroud the lake but the torrential downpour that soaked us when booked our Covid tests this morning has ceased.

The drumming of rain on the roof of the hostel enforced a rest and we lay on the bed, content to let our bodies relax and our minds sift the events of recent days. A text from Peter reassures us that Rose is being a good girl for her cousins. How I miss her cheerful babble and her body pressing into mine.

There is a rumble of thunder from the direction of Mount Nyiragongo. The air is moist and heavy. There is an acrid taste on the back of my throat and faint whiff of rotten eggs, which Manny thinks is due to the mountain. I peer into the mist for a boat approaching and wonder what my mother-in-law will be like. I fear she will find it difficult to share her son with a wife she did not know about till yesterday. Will we get on? Manny, standing next to me, hums to himself.

The mist is disorientating but I can hear a dull throbbing. The coke tin bobs more quickly in time to a hidden rhythm, and there is the boat. A white prow, scraped in places and stained with rust, carves through the mist, the hull, end on, narrow in the water, and top heavy. Engines throb and the sound reverberates against the low ceiling of cloud. Manny's humming ceases but he is alert, body still but muscles tensed, a cat wakened from slumber and ready to pounce.

Ropes flung from the bows are caught and looped round concrete bollards on the quayside. The ferry edges cautiously in, turning sideways and sliding into the quayside. Brown faces appear behind the misted windows and a queue to disembark forms on the upper deck. Half a dozen men in light weight business suits come down the gangway. A woman in a tailored kitenge dress in petrol blue and gold with a matching headscarf is next, her high heels clattering as she walks down the metal gangplank. She nods her thanks to the men holding the ropes. Another gate is opened on board and a crowd of young men, some with colourful bags, others carrying sacks, pour down the gangway and scatter across the quayside, heading in different directions at the main road. Finally, a small group of older women, some with holdalls or plastic bags walk slowly down the ramp. They are met by friends and family and escorted towards the bus stop. The stream of passengers disperses. The quayside is empty except for the crew.

'We must have missed her.' says Manny. 'I'll check she was on the boat.' He walks across to the gangplank, talks to the nearest crew member, and disappears inside.

'Have we been deceived,' I wonder, 'or just foolish? We should have arranged a sign. I recognised Manny when he first arrived off the train in Bristol. He recognised Nyadena when she came off the Nile ferry. I thought there would be instant recognition of his mother.

'Madame Deng?' The smartly dressed woman who came off the boat first is standing in front of me, a younger woman just behind her.

'Yes.'

'I am your mother-in-law, Elizabeth Deng. This is Hannah, my daughter. Where is my son?'

'We thought we'd missed you!' I gasp. 'He's gone on board to check.' There is an awkward pause.

'He never could stand still.' she laughs. I see the high cheek bones and slanting eyes of Nyadena mirrored in her face. Her skin has a bronze glowing tone and there is a faint line of kohl around her eyes. I feel under dressed in holiday jeans and a green shirt splashed with sprigs of orange flowers. There is a familiarity about her movements. A lost memory flashes back of a Palm Sunday parade in Nimule in childhood, Manny joining the men drumming at the head of the procession and his mother reminding him sharply to stay with his brother and tuck his shirt in.

Manny's head appears above the metal sides of the gangplank, and I wave furiously. He strides over to us, eyebrows raised in query.

'Manny, Madame Deng was one of the first off the boat, and this is your sister, Hannah.'

'Mama?' He sounds incredulous and Madame Deng laughs again.

'You are Emmanuel. You are bigger than the boy I remember but I would know you anywhere.' She stretches her arms wide, and Manny walks into them. He is taller than she is, but as her arms reach up, his enfold her and they embrace for a long time. Hannah and I stand mesmerised by the love. Manny breaks off and turns to Hannah.

'My big sister.' He laughs and envelopes her in a hug. She is taller than her mother but willowy and frail in appearance. I can see Manny moderating his hug to a gentle embrace. Her eyes are wet with tears as they step back from each other. I am astonished at Manny's ease. Something has changed. The hesitancy and suspicion that he had with Nyadena and Reuben has vanished.

'You will join us for lunch,' states Madame Deng, 'Hannah and I usually eat at Chez Luis.'

Her manner is decisive. This is an instruction not a request, but I am relieved she is taking charge. The similarity in manner between Manny and his mother is striking. They are not physically alike. Manny has the strong jawline and flared nose of his father but something about their manner of speech and gesture is similar. As they walk together towards Chez Luis I turn to Hannah.

'Your mother mentioned that you have a son. How old is he?' Her dark face colours slightly but she replies calmly.

'He is fifteen, nearly sixteen. He is playing football with his friends.'

'And you are a seamstress?'

'Yes. I make clothes for the ladies and children.' Her English is halting with a French accent.

'You know Esther?' she asks.

'No. Er, yes. She is called Nyadena now.'

'She ees well?'

'Yes.' I assure her. 'Emmanuel met her in Pagak, near the Ethiopian border but her husband has been posted to Juba. She came on a ferry up the Nile with the children. They came to lunch, and I have visited at her house several times.' I sense that Hannah is hanging on every word I say but is too shy to ask questions, so I continue. 'She is working as a seamstress.'

'She do not like sewing!' Hannah speaks quietly but there is astonishment in her tone.

'Nyadena has to take work in to pay for the children's schooling.' I explain.

We have reached the restaurant and Manny's mother leads the way inside.

'*Quatre personnes, s'il vous plaît.*' she says to the door attendant. He nods and leads us to a table on the far side, facing out onto a small courtyard, where a pleasant breeze blows through the unglazed window. We order drinks and food and talk inconsequentially about our journey here, her boat trip, our search for her at the hospital and the good fortune of finding someone who knows her.

'I trained the staff in Goma before I moved to Bukavu.' Mama Elizabeth explains. My eyes meet Manny's. Whatever we expected at the end of our search, it was not this dynamic, assertive, fashionable woman. She intercepts our glance and the corners of her mouth curve in a smile, but she makes no comment, other than to ask if we wish to order a dessert.

'Mama, this is on us.' Manny says firmly.

'Emmanuel,' is the reply. 'I have spent twenty-five

years wondering if you were alive and whether you had enough to eat. Let me feed you today.' To my surprise Manny looks abashed and fidgets with the tail of his shirt, which as usual has escaped. We order flambéed lady finger bananas with cardamom and ground nut sauce, and a pot of tea.

'Now, no more formality. Maria, you may call me *tante* Elizabeth, or Aunt Elizabeth if you prefer. Emmanuel, you have changed your name.'

'I haven't changed it, Mama. I was in the US, in Baltimore. That's how the Americans abbreviate 'Emmanuel'.'

'America. I see.' Manny tells them the story of his long walk with the other Lost Boys across South Sudan to Ethiopia, their arduous journey into Kenya, and his good fortune in being chosen to go to the US.

'I was blessed to have a good sponsor who treated me like a son.' he finishes. 'He helped me qualify as a family lawyer and to find work in Baltimore.

'And now you live in Juba?' she prompts.

'We decided to return to South Sudan to be near Maria's family in Nimule. We want to help rebuild our country.'

'My granddaughter, Rose, is not with you?' Aunt Elizabeth's face softens and a look of longing creeps into her eyes. The similarity to Nyadena is more marked.

'We left her in Nimule, with Maria's family, but you will see her soon, we will arrange it.' He assures his mother, and I nod in affirmation. She is Rose's only grandmother now. 'Tell us what happened to you and Hannah, Mama.' Manny prompts in turn.

'We fled to Uganda and stayed in a refugee camp for several years. Your father went back to avenge the massacre of our town. When the Lord's Resistance Army swept into north Uganda there was little food, so we came to Bunia, where my relatives lived. They loaned me money for a sewing machine, and I started to make clothes and bed linen. I was able to pay school fees for both girls for a few years until Hannah was old enough to help me with the sewing business. They learned to speak French at school. We spoke Dinka at home. My business grew because many people lost their clothes and bed linen when Mount Nyiragongo erupted a few years earlier. People trusted us to make good plain clothes. I was able to pay my uncles back. Hannah became a gifted seamstress. Esther was doing well at school in languages and bookkeeping. I planned to expand the business.' She pauses for a moment then continues, 'There were brigands around from both sides of the Rwandan war who had fled into the forests, and rebel groups fighting against the government of Congo. Hannah is the one to tell you what happened.' She turns to her daughter who has said little throughout the meal. Hannah's eyes fill with tears. She looks at us with fear and defiance in equal measure. Her voice is still quiet but there is a fierce anger underneath.

'I deliver some sheets to one of our neighbours.' she says in her heavily accented English. 'The men attack me. I cry out and ask them not to, but soldiers think it is their right to take from a woman. I fall pregnant. My uncles say is my fault, I must stop the baby. It is a bad thing to take a child's life. Our neighbours do not come for sewing any more. We come to Goma.'

'It was best to start again.' says Aunt Elizabeth. 'We made up a story to explain Adam's lack of a father.'

'Adam is my son.' adds Hannah, 'We say his baba is a soldier and is dead now. Maybe it is true.'

The story she tells is a harsh one. How can people be so unfair to a woman who has been abused in this way. I know from Manny's work that similar things happen in the conflicts in South Sudan. It is a brutal method of war, to make local women bear children. I want to hug her and tell her 'It is alright,' we understand but I am not sure how to reach her.

'When Adam was two, I was able to get work at the local clinic.' continues Elizabeth. 'The new hospital opened; they were looking for staff. I was taken on and trained and Hannah took over the sewing business.'

'I pay for Adam to go to school.' Hannah adds proudly.

'It was hard for Esther. She missed her school friends. She was fifteen then and loved the baby at first, wanting to cuddle him and play with him but as he started to walk and chatter, she became impatient. She stayed at school long enough to get her qualifications and enter the police force. I realise now she needed her own life.'

Elizabeth pauses. Her beautiful slanting eyes are filled with regret and disappointment. She has been hurt, I can see, but she is proud, and independent. There is fire in her. Manny and Nyadena have inherited that strength. Aunt Elizabeth turns to me.

'You have visited Esther?'

'Yes. She lives in Juba now. Her husband is a chaplain in the army.'

''You have seen the children?' she asks.

'Yes, Eliza, Luko, and little Barni. Now they have Isaac too.'

'Another baby! Manny did not tell me.' She is thrilled but I hasten to explain:

'No, he is older than Eliza, he attached himself to them on the boat to Juba. He has many problems.'

'I see.' She does not press it further. The restaurant has emptied, and Aunt Elizabeth asks for the bill.'

'Do you miss your sister?' I ask Hannah. She nods but adds.

'It is better now. Adam is a man, and the cloth-es do well.' She pronounces it as if it were two words.

'Will Adam join the business?' Manny asks.

'No, he want to be doctor, but it is much money.'

Aunt Elizabeth suggests that we walk to the end of the harbour where there is an unobstructed view of the lake and a cafe where we can take some tea later. Hannah excuses herself, she must deliver orders and make Adam's tea.

'She is a good girl.' says her mother. 'She has worked hard and is financially independent, but she has never married. Adam is her only child. Now, Maria,' she adds as we walk towards the lake, 'you must tell me how you and Manny met.' I explain to her how I came to the UK and worked at the Olaudah Trust Hostel in Bristol until Manny came to Bristol to find me.

'We decided to come back to South Sudan.' I add. 'Manny was offered a government job and I was able to continue working for the Olaudah Trust one day a week. I also have a hairdressing business.' Elizabeth appears surprised, which makes me determined to show her that I too am a strong woman. 'I will send you a copy of my story.' I tell her. 'My colleague Jane is married to a journalist, and he wrote a book about me.' She nods in reply and her eyes stare straight into mine. We turn along the shore of the lake. There are clouds overhead but a strong breeze from the lake cools us.

'How long have you been in Bukavu, Mama?' Manny asks.

'Six months' she replies. 'I was moved to the mental health unit, as an administrator. I learned how to type, and then to use a computer. I started to help women who came to the hospital as victims of rape. Many of them needed extensive surgery, but they also needed counselling for the trauma. I had the opportunity to train as a counsellor myself. I wish my job was not needed,' she adds, 'but while there is still fighting and rape there are many who need help.

'Is it rebels who do these things?' I ask.

'There are militant groups of Hutus and Tutsis who fled after the genocide and continue their conflict here, and rebels fighting the Kinshasa government. They live in the forests and mountains, but they must come into the towns for food and weapons. It is a tough situation; many women have been traumatised.'

'You provide counselling?' I ask.

'Yes, I train people to be counsellors.' I glance across the table at Manny to see how he is reacting. He looks shocked and unsure of himself.

We thought his mother was dead. When we contacted Nyadena he worried that she was ill or suffering in some way. We had not expected this sharp eyed professional, training others in specialised work.

We reach the end of a headland jutting out into the lake, where we order a pot of tea from a small hut. Clouds are gathering to the south and rain will surely fall again but the lake sparkles in a brief patch of sun.

'The lake is our road.' says Elizabeth. 'It takes more than a day to travel by bus to Bukavu, and when there is fighting the road is closed but the boat takes six hours.'

'It's beautiful place.' responds Manny. 'We are staying in the north of the city. Esther referred to a mountain that smoked but we didn't understand until we saw Nyiragongo.

'It's a dangerous mountain.' Elizabeth replies. 'A few years before we arrived the crater exploded, and gas and rock flowed down into the city. Many houses were destroyed. You can still see the black areas where the fire hardened into rock and no houses can be built. The sailors say the lake boiled and the water rose like a fountain.' We watch the shadows on the lake shift and change.

'What are your plans for tomorrow?' Elizabeth asks. I raise my eyebrows at Manny, silently questioning whether we will stick to our plan to leave in the morning.

'We have an appointment for a Covid test at four tomorrow.' he says. 'If that's clear then we drive back through Uganda and meet a friend and his fiancée in Entebbe.'

'Aie, aie' she responds, lapsing into the sounds of our childhood. 'So soon!'

'We've been here several days, Mama, it took time to find you.'

'You haven't met Adam. Will you come to Hannah's house? It will be an African style meal.'

'We are Africans!' Manny responds. We laugh together and it is a good moment. Elizabeth has a powerful personality and a drive which I see in Manny, but which has been suppressed in recent months.

She waves farewell and leaves for Hannah's house.

'*A bientôt.*' are her final words.

'What does that mean?' I ask Manny.

'See you soon.' he replies.

We retrace our footsteps to the hostel, clutching a piece of paper on which she has written directions.

'It's okay, isn't it?' I say.

'It's okay, Princess. Something clicked into place as soon as I heard her voice on the phone.' He is silent for a moment. We walk along the street hand in hand. I am thanking God for helping us find his mother.

'She called me Emmanuel.' he says. 'No-one has said my name like that since I was a child. In America they swallow the syllables.' We are walking up an avenue shaded by palm trees.

'I love you, Em-man-u-el.' I reply, and we turn into each other's arms, and kiss. The long leaves rustle above us and the dappled light falling through the fronds wraps us in its filtered peace.

Hannah's home is a single storey two roomed concrete house, painted pastel orange with a turquoise stripe at shoulder height, a blue galvanised roof, and a latrine and wash house round the back. There is a small yard filled with vegetables, and a cooking area. She is bent over a charcoal stove when we arrive.

'*Bonsoir. Bienvenue.*' she murmurs and signals for us to sit on a bench beside the front door. Manny places the rucksack he has been carrying under the bench and we settle ourselves against the wall of the house. She goes into the house and returns with freshly made lemon juice and a tray of tiny tomatoes and green chillies. Manny loves chillies and is immediately at ease. I feel more tentative. It is a new experience for me to be with Manny's family. I met his father and brother briefly before we married, and they came to our wedding, but I have never visited with Manny's family.

The lemon juice is cool and refreshing and I savour it. Similar houses surround us on either side. Beyond the tarmacked road in front of us, I can see the slopes of the mountain, the peak still cloud covered. The sun is setting, and long shadows highlight the homes and fields on the lower slopes. The view fades to flickers of light provided by small generators. Hannah brings a lantern. A young man comes round the side of the house, half hidden behind a wooden table, which he sets down in front of us, and then awkwardly lays a cloth over it. Elizabeth appears with a large bowl of steaming stew and sets it down in front of us.

'Good evening.' she greets us, and with a flourish of one arm adds, 'This is your nephew, Adam.'

He is as tall and dark as Manny, but fine featured like his mother and grandmother. He mumbles 'Hallo' and then retreats into the house.

'He's shy.' apologises his grandmother.

Hannah comes out of the house, inspects the saucepan simmering on the brazier, gives it a stir and brings it to the table. Adam lays knives and forks and then fetches three wooden chairs from inside. The meal is simple but delicious. Tender chicken with onions, maize, tomatoes beans, and chillies in a spicy sauce.

'Now,' says Elizabeth, as we mop up the last of the delicious sauce with extra spoonsful of rice, 'we must make plans.' Manny looks startled and Hannah seems nervous. Adam concentrates on his food. 'My work in Bukavu ends in December. By then all the councillors will be trained. There may be some final administration to be done but I expect to finish in early 2021. Adam will complete his exams. We have applied for him to attend the Juba Model Secondary School from the start of the year. Hannah can move her business to Juba. Guérir Les Gens are opening a counselling service in South Sudan. I have applied for a job as a trainer in the new service. If I'm appointed, I'll start in February 2021. We are coming home!'

'Wow.' Manny reacts quickly. 'Time to celebrate.' He bends down to retrieve the rucksack. I am taken aback. Not only do I suddenly have a mother-in-law, but she will be in the same city.

'We have been waiting for the right moment!' Manny brandishes a bottle of sparkling wine. 'Do you have more glasses?' he asks Hannah.

'Yes. What ees it?' she asks.

'In the US and Europe, we celebrate good

news with wine.' he says. 'It's like beer but made with grapes. Adam raises his eyes off his plate for the first time and seems impressed.

'Bravo!' cries Elizabeth. Hannah is already on her feet and returns with five glass tumblers. Manny pours a small amount into each glass and raises his.

'To South Sudan!' he shouts and slaps his thigh.

'To South Sudan!' we all cry and clink our glasses, a new experience, it seems for Hannah and Adam.

A warmth permeates our gathering. Elizabeth tells us why she is keen to return to her own country. We warn them that it is not easy, the shortages, the erratic electricity and phone signal, the corruption and political instability, above all the lack of unity in the army and the unpredictable outbreaks of violence.

'*Ici aussi,*' responds Adam. '*et nous avons un volcan!*'

'He's talking about the volcano erupting.' Manny interprets. I am alarmed but his mother chides him.

'*Non, Adam, ne dit pas cela!* Another eruption is expected.' She explains. 'We have every reason to return with you and Esther.'

We stay late talking about many things, they are concerned about Nyadena, Esther as they call her, particularly when we explain about Isaac and the difficulties of his behaviour. They share our Christian beliefs and attend the local Catholic church. They complain about the government in Kinshasa, the letting of contracts for mineral exploitation in return for developments, which are slow to appear. They tell us stories of the common experience of rape among young women and the damage it causes. Manny talks about his work as a family lawyer in Baltimore and his dream of developing family courts in South Sudan. We exchange phone numbers and addresses and make plans to meet next year in Juba. Hannah and Adam walk us down the road to where we have parked the car.

'I will help you find a place for your business.' I offer Hannah.

'Perhaps.' she replies. '*Maman a toujours des projets.*' I do not understand but I see Manny's surprise and wonder what she has said. We drive off waving furiously and I watch as mother and son make their way back up the hill together.

'What was the last thing Hannah said?' I ask as we drive back to the hostel.

'Mama always has projects.' he replies.

'She said 'perhaps' when we offered to help with the business. What is that about?' I wonder.

'Mama was always the planner when I was a child. Hannah is more cautious.'

In the morning as we wait anxiously for our test results, I ponder how it will be having Elizabeth in Juba. Jessica and other friends complain about their husbands' mothers, and I am beginning to see that it could be difficult.

'You are quiet, Princess. Are you worried about our tests?'

'There is nothing we can do about that. I'm thinking about last night.'

'You were right all along, Princess. It's a relief to know what happened. Hannah and Mama will help with Esther and the children.'

'We'll see how things work out.' I say, as calmly as I can, but I feel a sense of panic. After years of having no contact with my family at all it has been wonderful to visit Nimule and spend as long as I want with them. I have never thought of how Manny feels about it. He was always kind to my mother, and respectful to Uncle Amos and my siblings, but now there is another family to consider, and we must share our time with them.

We endure another long day of driving and arrive at the hotel in Entebbe around midnight. I am dazedly aware that we are being shown to a spacious room with a large bathroom. A quick shower, cup of tea and straight to bed is all we are capable of.

I wake at five, thirsty, from a dream of Elizabeth's heels tap tapping across our apartment. Further sleep is impossible. I watch the soft light of dawn seep through the haze of the mosquito net. Our double bed occupies one half of the room with the door on my left, a large window on the right, and the bathroom opposite. The room turns a corner around the bathroom and a single bed occupies the space beyond, with another large window facing the same way as the one behind us. I pad across to the bathroom to get a drink of water and then cross to the second window. Behind the mosquito screen is a glazed door onto a small balcony. I sit at a table looking at the view across Lake Victoria. The garden of the hotel slopes down to the water, waves lapping gently onto the course grass. As the sun rises it picks out the white feathers of two egrets strutting along the water's edge. Hamerkops join them, their beaks picked out in golden light, their brown feathers glowing. It is entrancing. Garang is paying for our stay here as a thank you for getting him out of Juba. It is the perfect place to relax.

We have breakfast in the garden where the contented twittering of the birds as they sift through the mud for food is a gentle symphony. I spend the morning dozing as much as reading until it is too hot to stay in the sun. I return to our room. Manny has unpacked and is lying on the single bed, snoring. I fetch a glass of water and resume my reading on the balcony. A local fisherman in a dugout canoe drifts across the lake and ibis fly overhead. A palm fringed bay stretches beyond the hotel on one side and on the other there is a field, occupied by a single cow, with a wooded area beyond. Manny rouses me an hour later.

'Wake up, Princess, we are still on Congo time, but it's nearly one o'clock. If we don't hurry, we'll miss lunch.' We must have slept again after lunch because it is four o' clock when we hear car doors slam and voices below.

'Manny, wake up. They're here.'

We wait in the reception area as they finish checking in and then announce ourselves.

'Manny, Maria, you made it!' Garang looks well. He is nearly as tall as Manny, but with a slight, lean figure. He is thinner than when I last saw him, and his face is lined but there is a bounce in his step and his deep brown eyes are as piercing as ever. We hug. He clings to each of us in turn. 'Thank you, for all you did.' There are tears in our eyes. This is a precious friendship we thought was lost for ever. Garang turns towards his partner.

'Zilpah, my fiancée.' he says. She is shorter than the three of us, round faced, with a soft curving figure. There a poise and calmness about her that contrasts with Garang's intensity and restless energy.

'Hallo.' The smile is in her eyes, not just on

her lips. I get the impression of gentleness and inner strength.

'Hey,' says Garang. 'We need to freshen up and settle in. There's a great bar by the lake, I thought we could have a drink and a dish there. Shall we see you down here in an hour?'

The bar is no more than a row of wooden tables under the palm trees at the edge of the lake. Food and drinks are dispensed from behind a bamboo screen between the tables and the road, which has little traffic. We order beers and curry. The evening breeze soughs in the palm fronds. The fisherman is back, paddling his way home in the evening light. The lake is iridescent with small waves, lit by the setting sun. They make soft slapping noises where the roots of the trees protrude into the water. The scent of spices mingles with a faint aroma of palm oil from fruits squashed underfoot. At tables around us people chat quietly, winding down from the working day.

'How has your trip gone?' Garang asks. 'Has your quest been successful?'

'We finally tracked down Manny's family yesterday.' I reply.

'You did it! That's great! Zilpah knows this was a big deal for you. Did your mom recognise you, Man?'

'Straight away and started telling me off almost immediately!'

'They are well?' asks Zilpah.

'They've had some tough times, but they're doing okay now.' replies Manny. 'They're planning to return to South Sudan next year. My nephew has applied for Juba Model Secondary School.' My husband sounds excited and happy.

'How about you?' asks Manny.

'Thanks to the prompt action of you and the other Boys, I'm fully recovered. There are some scars of course but I'm back at work, covering western Kenya and Uganda.' He raises clasped hands above his head in a gesture of triumph, then drops his voice to a murmur. 'I'll never be able to have children. Those brutes destroyed the nerves in my equipment.'

'Oh, Garang! Is there nothing they can do?'

'We are planning to adopt as soon as we're married.' says Zilpah. 'Many children are born without love or have lost their parents.' I look at her to see whether she really means this or if it is just to cover her embarrassment. There is intense concern in her eyes and a hint of challenge. She means what she says.

'I was separated from my parents at the age of twelve.' I tell her. 'Manny's sister, Nyadena, has taken in a boy of about that age, who was being abused.' Zilpah glances across at Garang but he is deep in conversation with Manny.

'I work in a village for orphaned children in Nairobi. They do well with our help, but it's better if children grow up in families.' Zilpah explains.

'You will adopt one of the children in the village?' I suggest.

'It would be difficult to choose one child.' she replies. We'll find another way.' I like her. Garang is fortunate to have found such a warm and sensible woman.

The stars are coming out. We sit and talk till late, hearing news of Garang's work. Nairobi has given him new opportunities to investigate South Sudanese issues, though he does not write about these in his own name.

'Do you realise,' he tells us, 'Salvador Kiir, our President, and Riek Machar, our Vice president both have luxury villas in the same residential suburb of Nairobi, heavily guarded, of course? Their families live a life of luxury, swimming pools, beautiful gardens. We launch into a lengthy debate about what can be done to help our country. Sadly, there is no answer to this. Until the armed forces agree to become a single national force and to stop the 'cattle raiding' attacks on each other, and our corrupt rulers refrain from taking government money to protect their wealthy lifestyle, things will not improve. We agree that we must continue to do what we can, though for Garang, this will be from Nairobi for the foreseeable future.

The last two days of our holiday are truly a rest and a chance to process all that has happened since we left Nimule. The park I spotted next to the hotel is the Botanical Gardens, and we spend a peaceful afternoon walking there, wondering at the range of beautiful plants that grow in Uganda. We visit the site of the Tombs of the Bugandan Kings at Kasubi in Kampala, a reminder of the splendour of our ancient kingdoms and the reverence that our tribal chiefs once commanded. We relax in the garden at the hotel and watch the birds feeding at the water's edge. It has been a time of reflection, which has passed too quickly.

We wish Garang and Zilpah well for their wedding next month and collect their good wishes for friends in Juba. Our holiday is over. It has changed our lives.

13 REUNION

Rain cascades over the corrugated rooves of Lologo village. Water drips off the eaves and forms small trenches around each hut, such is the vehemence of the downpour. The rainy season should have ended, the humidity of the last few months would usually be replaced by drier air from the Sahara but this morning the downpour lashes the township, reluctant to release its hold.

Nyadena rounds the corner onto her street, a bundle of washing balanced on her head and an umbrella held over it. She slithers on the sloped edge of the street as she tries to avoid the torrent of mud cascading down the centre of the track. She reaches the door and undoes the padlock, pitching the bundle forward onto the double bed.

There is little furniture, a small cupboard next to the bed, a clothes chest, a plastic chair, two sacks of grain leaning against the back wall, and a small charcoal brazier. The earth floor is slightly sticky where rain has seeped in under the door. She opens the shutter to let more light in, but hastily closes it as the rain blows in. She peers anxiously out of the door, hoping that the rain will ease so that she can boil water to wash the clothes she has just collected. Her naturally optimistic nature is straining to stay positive and the difficulties of providing food and caring for the children during the week, when Reuben is at the barracks threaten to overwhelm her.

'Nyadena?' A loud voice hails her, and a tall figure appears in the doorway, hunched forward with the weight of a rucksack.

'It's Maria, can I come in?' Nyadena pulls her inside, grateful for company to lift her spirits. She shakes out the umbrella Maria is carrying and offers her the chair while she sits on the bed, their dim figures outlined in the light of the doorway.

'Adut sent some vegetables from her garden.' Maria explains. 'There are onions, sweet potatoes, tomatoes, and greens.' She opens the top of the rucksack.

'Thank you. Who is Adut?'

'She is my niece, my sister Rachel's daughter. She learned to grow vegetables in Kakuma refugee camp and now she has a small garden near my family's compound in Nimule. She wanted to send you a gift.' Nyadena, caught off guard by the generosity of this present, stutters:

'We, ...we have no vegetables. The children need them. Isaac, he is hungry, always. More old than he looks. His voice change. He is a youth now.'

'Where will he go? You cannot keep him for ever. What about his parents?'

'The friend from Pagak, Miriam, she has checked with police post in Pibor, to find if they can know his parents. People come, but for small children. No one for a youth.'

'Is Isaac his birth name?' Maria asks. Nyadena shakes her head and laughs.

'No, we give him that name. The master call him *Boy*.'

'Does he have any papers?

'No, it is many shillings to get papers. When the child is born it is small amount but if the papers are lost there are many charges.' My understanding from Manny is that the cost of registration papers is set at a low enough rate for even poor families to afford, so there is clearly some corruption involved here.

'Please tell me the list of charges you have been asked to pay. I will check with Manny.' I say.

'Thank you.' Nyadena replies. She scribbles for a few moments on a piece of lined paper and hands it to me.

'What will you do about Isaac?' I ask her.

'Miriam look for a place.' I make no reply. Orphanages in South Sudan have more children than they can care for, and there is no system for fostering or legal adoption.

'You will have to find something soon.' I add. 'It is affecting your own children.'

'Eliza love him. Luko see Isaac do bad things. It is difficult. When he is bad at school, they send him away. I cannot work when he is here. Pastor says we must pray and have faith.'

'Yes of course, but I will also see if there is anything more we can do. What would be best for Isaac, do you think?'

'He is friendly when he is calm. He like to play games and go to school. Then a thing happen that he do not understand. He need a wise person to help him. I talk with him, but my own children need me. Isaac need his own Mama and Baba.'

'Would Isaac cope with moving to a new place?'

'He is brave. He is clever. He like to be in a new place. He need love.' Nyadena hugs herself in an expressive gesture.

'We will talk with our friends. Nyadena there is something else.' Manny is here too; he is waiting under the trees. May I bring him in.'

'Of course. Why he not come with you?'

'He wanted to make sure it is a good time.' Maria says, and leaving Nyadena puzzled and concerned goes to the door and waves her arm urgently towards the palm trees. A dark dripping shape emerges. Manny holds a large black umbrella over his head, but his suit is wet and his leather shoes are splashed with mud. He stumbles across the sodden path to Nyadena's front door and enters shaking himself like a wet dog.

'Mr Deng, you are wet. Please, here is a towel.' Nyadena hands him a threadbare towel and watches anxiously as Manny dries his shoes and trouser legs.

'I make you some tea?' Nyadena asks.

'No, I am fine.' He says and draws a deep breath. 'We went to Goma, Maria, and me. We met with Mama Elizabeth. She recognised me straight away and as soon as I heard her voice, I knew Mama. You are Esther. We are brother and sister. I am sorry I could not believe this straight away.'

'You are Kor?'

'I am Kor, and you are my little sister, who I have not seen since you were a baby. I am sorry it has been so long.' Esther stares at her brother for a long time, examining his face, and figure. Maria has sat down again and watches in silence, a smile curving her wide mouth until her teeth gleam in the darkness.

'You were a youth, very thin. Now you are big man in the government. It is not possible.'

'I am a foolish man in a damp suit, but I would like to greet my little sister.' Nyadena moves towards him and he envelopes her thin, strong, body in a bear hug.

'You are Kor.' She murmurs. 'Not dead. Come from far.'

'I have come a long way from the Bor to Ethiopia and Kenya, the US and Goma but now I am here, with my family.' They break apart and Manny suggests:

'Mama Maria, you are sisters.' Maria stands and gives her sister-in-law a hug.

'I could not wish for a better sister.' She says. The two women clasp each other with tears and laughter while Manny smiles indulgently.

'Our mother.' he pauses as they break off, wiping tears away.

'Yes..?'

'She is well. She is a councillor for the Guerir les Gens Hospital. She works in Bukavu but she comes back to Goma every couple of weeks. Hannah is running the sewing business and Adam is studying for his school certificate. We had lunch with them, and then Hannah invited us to their home that evening and gave us a beautiful meal. They send all their love.'

'They are sad with me.'

'Only because they have lost touch, but that will change. They are planning to come to Juba for Adam to study and work in this country. Mama is waiting to hear about a job in Juba and Hannah will move her business here. They are coming home!'

'We will all be in Juba. God is good!' Nyadena marvels at this sudden change in her circumstances. Then she remembers Manny's reference to his father the day she and her family lunched with Manny and Maria.

'Baba?' she asks shyly. Manny's face sets hard for a second then he explains gently.

'Father has remarried. He has three children by his new wife.'

'Oh, he did not come for us.'

'No. Our older brothers, by his first wife, were killed. He is bitter. He wants to forget and start again.'

'Perhaps he will relent, in time.' Maria interjects and Nyadena is grateful as she tries to reconcile her childhood memory of an indulgent father, with a bitter old man and his new wife. One step, one time as Mama used to say.

'Mama and Hannah come soon?' she asks. 'And Adam?'

'We don't know yet.' Manny replies. Maria chips in:

'We would like you all to come for lunch again. Or we could go to one of the cafés near the river?'

'The children like the river.' Nyadena smiles gratefully. It is easier to control Isaac's moods and Luko's irritation when he gets in a fight if they are in a more open space, and Eliza and Barni will love any new experience.

'I will book a table and send Reuben the details and time.'

'I tell Reuben.' agrees Nyadena.

'And I will see what we can do about Isaac's

papers.' adds Maria.

'Yes, praise God, Isaac need that paper.' Nyadena's heart is full as she hands them the damp umbrellas and waves them off. The feeling of relief is overwhelming. She is not alone. She has a family, a brother in a big job, her mother and sister coming soon. Eliza, Luko, and Barni will have a big cousin to look up to and admire. Perhaps something can be done for Isaac. God is very good.

A week later Nyadena leans back against the plastic back of the car gazing at the tall buildings near the airport. Barni is sandwiched between her and Reuben. Eliza, Luko, and Isaac are in the back seat. She can feel Isaac twisting as he follows a particular car as it streaks past them and muttering. 'Mercedes, Subaru' Luko is more interested in the small blue tankers that carry drinking water to the apartments and offices. The smell and noise that clearly excites the children is making Nyadena feel nauseous, perhaps with trepidation at the thought of seeing her mother again after all these years and her desertion of the only family she knew. Memories flood back. Mama, her strength, her wisdom, but also her sharp tongue and her strong opinions. How will it go with Reuben, and what about the children.

Maria is in the front passenger seat, an elegant bow in her hair and her shoulders upright in her dress, brightly patterned in green and pink. Nyadena feels her own hair cautiously. Maria took her to the salon, washed and straightened her hair and then delivered her next door for a manicure. She has a new dress of deep blue, decked with white flowers and green leaves that perfectly complements her bronze tinted skin. For the first time since Eliza was born, she feels fresh, smart, and fashionable.

The car slides through metal railings and parks in front of the airport hotel. Marie and Manny greet the woman on reception warmly. The Thon family follow them through a cafe style restaurant and into a large lounge with couches and armchairs round the walls and a large circular table in the middle.

'I've ordered tea for half an hour's time.' Manny tells them. Maria and I will greet Mama as she arrives and bring her here.' The Thon's wait nervously. The children are in their best clothes. Reuben is silent and thoughtful. Nyadena watches the children wondering how she will keep them entertained but they are so overawed by the size of the room, the pictures on the walls and the fascination of meeting a grandmother who arrives by plane that they sit quietly, occasionally pointing something out to each other. When tea arrives, they are stunned into silence by the magnificence of the cups and saucers, the shiny chrome teapot, and the bowl full of sachets of sugar. Nyadena rashly allows them to have one each.

There is a sound of voices outside and a noisy clatter of heels on the tiled floor. The door opens and Nyadena and Reuben rise, telling the children to sit and wait their turn. Mama Elizabeth enters wearing a loose-fitting kaftan in a kitenge material of deep red and blue. Her blue patent sling back shoes clack as she crosses the floor, a string of large blue and gold glass beads jangle at her neck, and similar earrings dangle, her hair is piled high on her head and dressed with a matching red and blue scarf.

'Mama?' Nyadena's voice quivers at this smart figure. Last time she saw her mother she was thin and worn, worried by Hannah's health, and the care of baby Adam. How did she become this well dressed, well covered matron with her polished nails, her elegant hair, and her air of authority.

'Esther. Dear girl. We have missed you!' She is enveloped in a warm embrace. 'Dear child, how I have longed to see you.' Elizabeth stands back and holds Nyadena at arm's length, a hand on each shoulder. 'You look well.' She states, and Nyadena feels well. Gratitude to Maria for helping her to look smart floods through her. It would have been alarming to meet this changed Mama in her usual faded dress and dusty hair.

'The children.' Mama Elizabeth turns to them. 'Eliza, Luko, I recognise.' Eliza has remembered her grandmother's voice and runs towards her to be hugged in her turn. Luko is more cautious but follows his sister's lead and submits to the hug. Barni eyes his strange Grandmama with some uncertainty, but she claps her hands and makes her earrings dance and he laughs and runs towards her for his hug.

'And this young man must be Isaac.' Mama Elizabeth walks over to the armchair in which Isaac is slumped. 'Will you shake hands?' she asks. Shyly he extends a hand. Elizabeth looks deep into his eyes, noting the trauma and the fear, with a councillor's eye. Isaac jumps like a nervous cat, but she holds him with her eyes and he returns her smile.

'Reuben.' Elizabeth turns towards him. 'It is good to see you again. You have a fine family. Congratulations on your posting as a chaplain.'

Maria pours the tea, and they pull the armchairs

closer and sit around the table. Elizabeth is the centre of attention. She tells them of her role at the hospital, heading up a training programme for counsellors, and working with the Ministry of Health on a programme for the rural towns.

'I will make many journeys.' she tells them, 'But first I must find somewhere to live in Juba with three rooms so that Hannah and Adam can join me. but first I must make a home in Juba. Manny and Maria, you can show me how to find a good apartment with three rooms for when Hannah and Adam join me.

'Yes, of course, Mama.' Manny murmurs.

'I meet with my new team tomorrow and Friday, then Saturday, we will find the right place. Now, these children need to be outside' Elizabeth continues.

'Come, boys, Eliza, let's go for a walk.' Reuben responds immediately.

'Rose and I will come too.' offers Maria. 'Where can we go, Manny?'

'Ummm. How about Lily's Supermarket for an ice cream.' he replies.

'Perfect.' says Elizabeth. 'You can show them where to go.' The children shuffle out obediently with the three adults leaving Elizabeth and Nyadena alone. Elizabeth moves to the armchair next to Nyadena and turns to her:

'Now we can talk. Esther, my precious girl, tell me everything since you left Ezo.' She reaches for Nyadena's hand and clasps it. Nyadena clings to her mother and feels the moisture of her tears trickle down her cheeks.

'Oh, Maman. Sorry I did not call you from

Pagak. There was no signal for South Sudan and Reuben's phone was expensive. I should have sent a letter sooner.' They speak in French and Nyadena finds the language she learned as a teenager feels familiar to her tongue, the precise vowels, and the consonants at the front of the mouth forming more easily than English, which she has never been taught. She tells of the time in Pagak, the hardship but also the beauty and the closeness between the women. She recounts the journey to Juba, the addition of Isaac to their family and the daily grind of finding food for the children during the curfew.

'And now,' asks her mother.

'It is easier. Reuben has completed his chaplain training and is paid more. Maria's family are generous with vegetables. Whenever Maria and Manny visit Nimule, they bring back a bag full. The children do well at school. Barni will start next year. Only Isaac does not find school easy.'

'He is a troubled boy.' She replies. 'You can see in his eyes.'

'And you, Maman. How is it for you and Hannah. Adam, he is a man now?'

'He is taller than Hannah and me, and a fine boy. He studies hard. We are proud of him. He wants to continue his education here. He is studying English, but he needs practice.'

'The sewing business is going well?'

'Yes, Hannah has a gift for it. She has many customers. She will start again in Juba.'

'We can help her. For sure Maria will tell the clients who come to the salon.'

'She is a good woman. Manny has made a wise choice. Oh Esther, I have been afraid for you all these years and I find you are well settled with a fine family.'

'Oh, Maman, we are not well off, like Manny and Maria, but we are happy.'

'My darling girl, give me another hug.' They do not hear Manny enter. Nyadena opens her eyes and sees him standing in the doorway.

'Thank you, my brother,' she says in English. 'to bring Maman back.'

'Not me.' he says. 'I believed that you had died in the massacre. It was Maria who insisted that you might still be alive.'

'You have spoken with your father?' Elizabeth asks.

'Yes, Mama. I am sorry but he has another woman now and three young children.'

'I thought that is how it must be.' she says calmly. 'Does he know we are all together.'

'Not yet, Mama. He knows that Esther and I have been in touch.'

'Do not be troubled over this matter. If you have a number, I will call him. He must be told that Hannah is alive and that he has a grown-up grandson.'

Later, Nyadena tries explaining to Reuben how different she feels. Being with her mother rekindled a part of her that was buried. Somehow speaking French reconnected her with her girlhood and brought good memories to the surface, the closeness with her sister, the intense joy of Adam's birth. The struggles and achievements of her time in secondary school. There is sorrow that her family were not there to see her married to Reuben, but joy at her mother's delight in the children.

'I should have been more grateful.' Nyadena says to Reuben, but somehow there was never time to think.'

She hears from Maria, who visits regularly, that the search for a three bedroomed apartment has not been successful. Instead, Elizabeth has taken three separate rooms in a boarding house, with a shared bathroom and use of a kitchen. For all of them this will be a time of rebuilding. They have done it before, in Uganda, In Goma, they can do it again.

Ten weeks later

Nyadena and Maria stand outside the airport building, trying to ignore the noise and confusion as cars pull up on the dusty road to discharge passengers. In front of her a long queue snakes from the entrance of the terminal building, under a covered canopy and out onto the same stretch of road where the cars are pulling in. People carrying cases, small children, sacks of vegetables and large plastic carrier bags of shopping stand waiting in the heat of the day. There has been no perceptible movement of the queue.

It has been over an hour since her mother texted to say that the plane had landed, and that she, Hannah, and Adam were waiting for their luggage. Manny has jumped the queue by showing his government pass and has disappeared inside to find them.

'It is always chaos here.' Maria comments. 'A small provincial airport has become an international hub. Nyadena nods in agreement as she observes the chaos. People try to join the end of the queue but there is no space for their bags. Taxi drivers compete for the few passengers who do emerge. Unemployed youths jostle to catch the attention of those who might give a generous tip for having their bags carried to the car.

At last Manny emerges with his mother, dragging a huge, wheeled suitcase, with a large box strapped on top.

'Whew,' he says. 'A Mama dropped a bag of nuts onto the baggage carousel. The bag burst and the nuts tumbled out and went into the machinery. The carousel was stopped until the mess was cleared up and all the nuts collected. '

'Esther, Maria.' Elizabeth greets them with a warm embrace.' We are here at last. Hannah and Adam are behind somewhere.'

'Over here. Ici!' Manny yells and a slim bronzed figure in a shiny blue dress and matching turban steps forward from the exit, followed by a stocky, youth, brown skin shining with the exertion of hauling two more suitcases behind him. Hannah! Her companion through a troubled childhood of flight, refugee camps and the struggle to get established in Goma. Hannah who had needed her so much when ill and giving birth to a baby son. Hannah, who she deserted in order to follow her selfish ambitions.

'Hannah.' Nyadena whispers.

'My sister.' She feels herself gathered into a soft embrace, and something deep in Nyadena's heart softens. She returns her sister's embrace.

'I'm sorry, very sorry. Always I think of you.'

'I miss you, my sister, but we are here, together again. Praise God. Ah, here is Adam.' Nyadena turns to greet him.

'Adam? Can this be so?' He was a baby last time she saw him, dependent on her and his grandmother because his mother was too sick and shocked to look after him. 'You are grown.' Is all Nyadena can say. Hannah and Elizabeth laugh as she shakes hands with the strong young man standing in front of her. He is too tongue tied to say anything, in this strange land, that he has never entered before, amongst relatives he had never heard of until the last few months.

'*Bonjour, tante Esther.*' he stutters.

'*Bonjour, Adam.*' she replies placing a hand on each shoulder and looking up to the tall young man in front of her.

'Let's go.' Manny is impatient to whisk them away, past the hospital and along Havana Street to Elizabeth's new home. It has not been possible to find an apartment. Instead, a row of three bedrooms in a single-story boarding house must suffice. Manny pulls up in front of the colonnaded building. He and Adam unload the bags and carry them one to each room. The box containing Hannah's best sewing machine, which she has retained to start her new business in Juba, is unloaded into her room. The bathroom, with its shower and flushing toilet, shared between the eight rooms in the block, is admired.

'We'll leave you to wash.' Manny says.

'See you about six o'clock for supper.' adds Maria. 'It takes about half an hour to walk. We'll run Nyadena home after that.' Nyadena enjoys the evening more than she could have imagined. The prospect of her mother and sister living nearby is changing her. At the right moment she will suggest to Reuben that she revert to the name Esther. Once Barni is at school, she can apply to join the Police Force again, resuming the name shown on her papers, Esther Thon. Nyadena feels hopeful at the thought of the two halves of her life coming together again. There is an end to this hardship in sight. *'Jesu Christo Rhudoa,'* she prays in the Dinka tongue. 'May you find Isaac a future and bring Reuben and I to a new home where we can bring up our children to build a better country. A place where families are not split apart by fighting, and children can grow up in peace.'

14. NAIROBI, KENYA

There was a sudden thunderstorm last night and the uneven pavement is dotted with muddy puddles. Rose, toddling along beside me, is delighted, splashing through them in her tiny rubber boots. I am more concerned with keeping my dress out of the way so that it is clean enough to visit my mother-in-law.

In many ways Elizabeth's arrival in Juba has helped us. She is a willing baby-sitter in the evening so Manny and I can go out for a meal. She is an enthusiastic and generous grandmother, who delights to bring her grandchildren presents of toys and clothes. This has been life changing for Nyadena's family but resulted in Rose being rather spoiled as Manny and I try to find places to store all her toys in our tiny apartment. Manny is proud to have family of his own nearby. We are both warmed by the closeness of Hannah and Esther, as she now is and proud of her acceptance into the police force in a part-time post.

Elizabeth is a disturbing presence. Her energy and her demands can be unnerving. She has been relentless in her search for a suitable apartment, driving Manny and Hannah mad with her demands to visit yet another site, which she then dismisses as too small, not clean enough or lacking amenities. We have at last located something suitable and Rose and I are on our way to visit.

'See Ganmaman's new house.' I tell Rose.

'Rose sleep at Ganmaman's?' she asks hopefully.

'No, not today, there is too much to do.'

As we reach the second floor and approach the door of the apartment, we can hear Elizabeth's strident tones.

'Yes, over there. No, no, a little to the right, and pushed back into the window. Yes.'

We ring the bell, and the door opens to reveal Manny and Hannah, dusty and weary, pushing a large sofa into the window bay.

'Maria, and my little Rosebud!' She sweeps Rose into her arms. 'Look who I have here. Time for a coffee.' Hannah moves quietly into the kitchen while Manny collapses on the sofa, wiping his brow. His eyes meet mine. Nothing is said but I am aware that it has been a difficult afternoon for him.

'You have made it look very comfortable,' I tell them, looking round the room at two armchairs positioned against the opposite wall with a locally carved coffee table in front of them.

'Come and see.' invites Elizabeth, and bearing Rose with her, she shows me the small shower room, two double bedrooms and a narrow room, which just takes a mattress for Adam, who will return from school later. The bedrooms are connected to the lounge by a dark corridor where Elizabeth has hung brightly coloured pictures, brought with her from Goma.

'*Le café est prêt.*' calls Hannah.

'I go to join Manny on the sofa but Elizabeth

insists on taking the seat next to Manny, with Rose between them, so that I can admire the view of the river and the hills beyond.

'Very nice.' I agree, but will it be hot in the middle of the day?'

'We shall not be here.' states Elizabeth. 'I shall be at the office or travelling and Hannah has hired a small shed at the end of the road where she has set up her sewing machine. She already has some orders for pillowcases and dresses.'

'Congratulations, Hannah.' I tell her. 'Please give me something fashionable that I can hang in the salon so we can get some orders from my customers for you.'

'Thank you.' she replies. Hannah is as gentle as her mother is strident but there is a tough quality beneath her quietness. She remains calm and pursues her own interests, respecting her mother's wishes but not allowing herself to be dominated. She is a difficult person to get to know, but I feel a great admiration for her.

'We are settled now.' states Elizabeth with satisfaction sipping her coffee. 'We must do something for Esther. She cannot continue looking after that difficult boy, it is too much. Where are his parents?'

'They can't be found. Nyadena's, I mean Esther's, friend, Miriam has been in touch with Pibor, where they first saw him, and no one has come forward. We have tried the Red Cross and other agencies. He has been registered as having no parents., with Reuben and Esther as his foster parents.'

'It is wearing Esther down.' Elizabeth continues. 'We should find another place for him.'

'Mama, you do not understand.' says Manny defensively. 'We have the laws to protect children, but there is no system, and all the orphanages are full. If no one takes them in, children with no parents roam the streets.'

'Well, that is not good.' agrees Elizabeth. 'But we cannot allow Esther to be worn down with worry, like this. It is not good for my grandchildren.'

That evening Jacob joins Manny and me for supper. He has been in Nairobi on business for the bishop and has been able to visit Garang and Zilpah.

'How are they?' we ask.

'They are well.' he reports. 'They have a nice apartment. Garang has plenty of new commissions. His time in detention has increased his opportunities as a journalist. He has become a spokesperson on political detention and is in demand with global news services. Zilpah loves her work with children. Their only sadness is that they cannot have a family. They are looking to adopt but Garang wants to give a home to a South Sudanese. I think Zilpah would be happy with any child. She is a beautiful wife for him.'

'Yes, it is good that he has someone to support him.' agrees Manny.

'How are your family getting on, Manny?' Jacob asks.

'I had forgotten how exhausting my mother can be.' he laughs in reply. 'They are settled into an apartment; we moved her new sofa in this afternoon. Hannah has a lock up shed for her business and already has some orders. The only worry is Esther, Nyadena, my younger sister. She still has that difficult boy as well as her own three children.' They continue to chat as I clear the table and bring some beers. A thought I hardly dare capture has fluttered into my head. I listen as they talk about their work and the continued conflict between our leaders.

Isaac? There are problems but with undivided attention he might be able to settle down. I wait until there is a pause in their discussion.

'What about Isaac?' I interject. Jacob eyes crinkle as he tries to puzzle out who I am talking about.

'Manny's younger sister, the one in Juba, has rescued a slave boy who ran away.' I explain. 'He is living with them, but she already has three younger children. They know nothing of his background, but we think he is around twelve. His parents cannot be found.'

'That is a challenge.' Jacob says.

'Yes, he is desperate to please and constantly hungry. He tries to be good but has sudden outbreaks of anger and frustration that get him into trouble at school and with older boys. He's often sent home and Esther has to deal with it.'

'Garang would never take it on, not after all he has been through.' says Manny.

'I'm not sure.' replies Jacob. 'It might be just what he needs. Should I try to sound him out?'

Manny and I never tire of the view from Gordon's Hill, the high escarpment north of Nimule, which overlooks the winding ribbon of the Nile, as it turns through a ninety-degree bend on its way from Uganda into South Sudan. The river is fed from Lake Victoria, through Lake Kyoga, tumbling over the edge of the Rift Valley at Murchison Falls, and flowing out of the northern end of Lake Albert. By the time it reaches Nimule it has gathered momentum for its journey north to Juba. It is eight in the morning and the sun's heat is not yet overpowering. It dances off the ripples far below us making the narrow ribbon of the Nile shimmer.

We are here for a special purpose. Reuben, Esther and Isaac stand with us, waiting anxiously for my uncle Amos's car to pull up and Garang and Zilpah to join us. It is too dangerous for Garang to enter South Sudan officially. He and Zilpah left their car at the border and crossed on foot, disguised as one of the many thousands who commute each day from the Uganda refugee camps to their work or families in Nimule. Amos has kindly loaned them his car for this journey to an isolated spot where they can meet Isaac. We are all nervous, Manny for the safety of his friend, Esther and Reuben for the future of their foster child. What if my suggestion that Garang and Zilpah adopt Isaac does not work out? I fear that they will not like each other, that the papers will be too difficult, that the artificiality of the meeting today will constrain us all. Only Isaac seems unflustered, excited by another car journey, eager for a new future. I envy him his energy. He must have an adventurous spirit or he would not have run away thrust himself upon Esther and her children. A car pulls up and two familiar figures climb out.

'Shall we walk back down to meet them.' I suggest. Isaac is eager, leaping between thorn bushes and jumping clumps of grass and piles of stones. Reuben, Esther and I follow more cautiously.

'Are you OK?' I ask.

'Yes. Isaac will have a good life.' she says.

'Will you miss him?'

'Yes, of course, he is our family.'

Garang and Zilpah have intercepted Isaac and Reuben. There are handshakes all round and hugs between Manny and Garang. From a distance it looks like just another family reunion, which perhaps it is, if all goes well.

'Maria., good to see you.' Garang greets me with a hand on each shoulder. He looks well, but older, the harshness of his torture in the Blue House will always be etched on his face.

'Garang, meet Esther, Isaacs foster mother.'

'God bless you, mama,' is his unexpected response, but Esther smiles and shakes his outstretched hand. I turn and embrace Zilpah. We do not know each other well but she is a woman I feel immediately comfortable with. Her gentle smile is ready, but her eyes watch Isaac, noting his reaction to all that is going on.

'Isaac.' She says. 'You know the way, take us to this lovely view we've heard about.' He eagerly jumps ahead and laughing Zilpah follows him.

'She knows how to talk to children.' exclaims Manny.

'All children love her.' Garang replies. He turns to Reuben. 'Tell me the issues.' he says. Reuben explains Isaac's background and his efforts to settle down, marred by the unpredictable losses of control.

'How do you handle it when that happens?' Garang enquires.

'We talk to him, reassure him, try to find out what has triggered the behaviour, usually it is some reminder of past brutality. We tell him what we expect but we also make allowances. It's been difficult for our own children to accept that, even Eliza, who brought him into the family. We will miss him,' adds Reuben, 'but we cannot give him the attention he needs.'

By the time we catch up with Isaac and Zilpah he is eagerly telling her about the cars he has seen on the way. We walk along the ridge of the escarpment. Garang taking Zilpah's place to chat with Isaac while the rest of us watch anxiously as we follow them.

'It is okay.' Esther whispers to me.

'It looks like it.' I agree. As the sun climbs higher, we adjourn to a tree and share the tea and soft white rolls that my sister, Deborah, has prepared for us. There is a sense of peace over our group. Reuben and Esther seem content. Isaac is relaxed. Garang and Zilpah seem pleased. Manny seems thoughtful. I am relieved that this risky meeting seems to have gone well.

Later that evening Manny and I enjoy a cool beer in a bar by the river. Esther, Reuben and Isaac have returned home, to join Elizabeth who has been looking after the children. Rose has had a busy day with Aunt Roselyn and is asleep.

'That went well.' I say with relief.

'Yes, well done. I think your idea will work.'

'You went very thoughtful when we were having tea.'

'I was thinking about Isaac. He will have little memory of his childhood. If this works out, Garang and Reuben will be his parents. I havn't thought of Kenny and Mary for months with all this family business going on, but they will always be the people who seem most like parents to me. They guided and helped me at a low point in my life.

'Tell me.'

'Kenny and Mary? I hated them at first, Mary particularly. She'd come round to the flat we'd been allocated, butting her head into whatever we were doing. Jacob was fine with that, but she used to annoy me, always there, always telling us what we were doing wrong. She'd insist on going to the shops with us and telling us what to buy, making us add up what it was costing as we went round. Then she'd stand over us while we cooked and tell us what we were doing wrong. I could never get the hang of it, but Garang was good at following her recipes and making something decent. Then she was on at us to go to English and Math classes and to start training for a job. We wanted to do something that would be useful in the refugee camp, like carpentry or metalwork. Mary kept on at us. "You're bright boys!" she'd say. "You need to get a qualification that will help to rebuild your country." Garang decided he'd do a course in journalism, then Jacob started doing business administration. I kinda switched off from Mary and just let her nag the other two but I felt bad about. She'd helped us more than we had realised. We had phones by then and were texting the other Lost Boys. They were in cities all over the US, Dallas, Chicago. They had mentors but not like Kenny and Mary. They'd got into difficulties with money and not been able to get into education.'

'She must be a kind person to give you so much of her time.'

'She is, fierce, but kind. She's tiny, very smart, hair

very stiff, wears heels so high you'd think she'd fall over but she's like one of those dogs that won't let go.'

'A terrier?'

'Yeah. She didn't yap like they do but she never forgot anything, and she'd check up on us constantly. We kicked against it, but it helped. We kept going, got ourselves organised. She brought Kenny along when we'd been in the apartment about a year. He seemed very aloof. He told me he was a lawyer, and I didn't know what that was but when he explained I realised that's what I wanted to do. His mind works the same way mine does. I continued with English and Math. Then I added sociology. I thought it might help me understand how people behave. It was a good choice because it helped me into family law.'

'What's Kenny like?'

'He's not scary like Mary is but kinda reserved. He seems easy going but you never know what he's thinking. He's one of the senior attorneys in Maryland. He helped me know where to study and paid for some of it. I wondered if it would be worth all the years of training. He encouraged me. He was quite proud when I got the job in Baltimore. When you get to know him, he's a fun guy. He plays songs from the old musicals on the piano and Mary sings along. I used to do a bit of drumming for them when they had a big party or something.'

'They sound great!'

'Yeah, they got me sorted out. I'd never had much encouragement before.'

'You miss it, don't you?' I ask him. It worries

me that he had such a good life in Baltimore. By the time he had qualified and worked for a couple of years he was earning a high salary. He takes my hand.

'One day, I'll take you there, Princess. We could leave Rose with your aunt for a few days. Kenny would put us up.'

'Manny, that would be ridiculously expensive.'

'We'll see how things work out with Esther. Reuben thinks they may be able to afford a proper house with Esther working in the Police Force again. We must wait and see how things go with Isaac. I want it to be right for Garang and Zilpah before we decide anything.'

Our hotel room overlooks the corner if Kenyatta Avenue in Central Nairobi, but no sound of the busy streets below penetrates the thickly glazed windows. Manny is sprawled on a double bed covered in rich red brocade. Reuben and Isaac are in the adjacent room. I am seated in an armchair by the window enjoying the hustle and bustle of people going home from work or setting off for their evening out. It is dusk, and there is a sense of urgency, tasks to be done, preparations to be made before the sun sets and the cooler evening air brings a new burst of activity. A white Subaru taxi sweeps under the porch of the hotel and disappears from view, a few minutes later it appears from the opposite side and re-joins the line of traffic down Kenyatta Avenue. I imagine the relief of the group of travellers as they enter through the double doors and seek the sanctuary of their rooms.

Our flight from Juba was swift and trouble free but the queue at the airport was arduous, with a restless teenage boy. Manny, Reuben, and I took it in turns to keep Isaac quiet. Reuben is more an uncle or a big brother to him and seems able to calm him with just a hand on the shoulder. Garang and Zilpah have paid for our journey here and hotel rooms.

Manny and Garang have been months filing the necessary paperwork with the South Sudanese and Kenyan authorities for Isaac's adoption. They have been frustrated by an apparently simple task of taking one boy to a new family requiring so much documentation, whilst thousands of children pass from desperate families to the childless, or an abuser, without any judicial control. At each stage of the process, officials requested unauthorised 'special payments' which Manny refused to pay, resulting in delays, and sometimes necessitating intervention from senior officials.

There is a loud crash and a knock on the door. I am reluctant to open it in case Manny wakes.

'Aunt Maria, can I come in and look out of your window, I can only see the shops from ours?'

'You must be quiet and not wake Manny.' I whisper, glaring at Isaac fiercely, and he cowers, then rallies.

'Okay.' he whispers and sidles past. He is small but well-muscled. His frame has filled out since I first met him. His eyes are huge with dark circles around them, his hair thin due to childhood malnutrition but with a tendency to spring sideways above the ears. He has the alertness of a wild cat. I let him stand in the window and watch the cars. He is totally engrossed, head turning one way, then the other, following one car, then the next. I have a sudden fear for him. I too remember a profound change in the teenage years. I was fortunate that I had two good people, fellow servants who guided me, but I missed my family. Isaac has no memory of his parents. A child alone, who must make his way in the world, with Garang and Zilpah's help. We were unable to attend their wedding in November because of an increase in Covid infections in Kenya. Five months later they are taking on a teenage child. Zilpah is experience with troubled children and Garang is eager to help another 'lost boy,' but it is bound to be a challenge for all three of them.

At seven we go down to the bar to await their arrival. Isaac seems calm, excited even.

'What do you think of your new city so far?' I ask him. He sips a cola cautiously, the first time he has had one, and the bubbles cause some excitement, but I can see he is trying to be grown up, perched on the edge of his chair in his new jeans and T shirt.

'It's fun! I want a car like the one that brought us from the airport.'

'Whoa!' exclaims Manny. 'You'll have to earn big money for that.' I glare at him. The boy is only dreaming and contradicting him could get him worked up. His small body is swamped by the capacious padded armchair. His passport states that he is thirteen. Nyadena had estimated him to be eleven or twelve when he first came to them, but we think his small size and bouts of immature behaviour are misleading. His small frame is filling out, whether that is the onset of puberty, or the result of regular meals is difficult to know.

'Cheers.' says Manny raising his glass.

'Thanks, Manny. Cheers.' Reuben responds

quietly. Isaac is looking around the bar, his sharp eyes darting from one object to the next.

'I like this place.' he announces. 'I like those things in the ceiling and the.' We follow his gaze. The ceiling fans are polished brass, their five blades whirr gently creating a cool downdraft. The bar is a rich, dark, mahogany. Rows of bottles filled with liquids of assorted colours are arranged along it, blue, golden, yellow, green, red. People in business clothes are seated near the bar. Families have grouped their armchairs together and lean in to laugh at each other's jokes. Two women chatting over cocktails at the small circular table next to ours, glance at the small lad in the huge chair. I hope they do not make Isaac self-conscious; he can get agitated if he feels he is being observed. Thankfully, they resume their conversation and take no further notice of us. The space is vast, and clusters of armchairs stretch away from us in each direction.

Reuben and Manny get on well now and are deep in conversation. Isaac sips his drink and cautiously and watches the fans rotate. He seems fascinated by anything mechanical, and I ask him how he thinks they work. He studies the shaft of the fan above us and identifies the thickened area where the motor sits. He chatters happily about rotors, and I let him prattle on, wondering how he has managed to pick up so much in his stunted childhood. I like this place too. There are thick swagged curtains in the window with nets in between, concealing the bustling street. It has similar proportions to Avon View House, lofty ceilings, generous windows, wooden pillars. It feels comfortably luxurious.

Manny breaks off his discussion with Reuben and gets to his feet.

'Garang, Zilpah, great to see you.' Manny greets them. Reuben jumps to his feet, bumps elbows politely and turns to beckon to Isaac.

Isaac looks mutinous and only Reuben's hand is restraining him from bolting.

'Hallo, Isaac,' says Zilpah slowly. 'What do you like best about Nairobi?'

'The cars.' he responds eagerly.

'Which make is the best?' Zilpah prompts him.

'The Subaru saloons are strong. They last a long time, but the Volkswagen we came in from the airport as a better engine.'

'Great.' responds Zilpah. 'Let's go to the window and you can show me.' She sets off for the widest expanse of net curtain with Isaac in tow and we watch in amazement as they push aside the nets and stand together enclosed in their own space watching the traffic.

The waiter arrives with the drinks Garang has ordered. Isaac and Zilpah return and for a moment there is confusion as Isaac demands another cola and is reprimanded by Reuben. Garang looks at Zilpah for direction and she shakes her head.

'You can go to the bar and choose some sparkling water.' she says, raising an eyebrow at Garang. Isaac and Garang walk to the bar together and I watch Isaac excitedly run his hands along the smooth wood and talk with the bar tender about the choices available. He returns with a glass of fizzy water topped by a slice of cucumber and sprig of mint, chatting animatedly. By the end of our meal together Isaac seems settled with both Garang and Zilpah. Reuben will stay on for a few more days and then, if all goes to plan, Isaac will have the security of two loving parents, and our friends will have a ready-made family.

As we settle in our seats for the flight home I turn to Manny:

'That went okay, didn't it?'

'Yeah, Isaac's a lucky boy. He'll have opportunities Juba can't offer yet.'

'Do you think it will cause jealousy with Reuben and Esther's children?'

'Reuben is a good man. He'll do his best and my sister is innovative. They'll provide for their three somehow.'

I watch the clouds slip past below me, set thoughts of Isaac to one side, and turn to the week ahead. Rose will be tired after a stimulating twenty-four hours with my aunt. Hopefully, she will go to sleep early, which should give me time to catch up. Another plane is visible beneath us. It appears smaller as it drops away and loses height to land. More planes, more people coming to Juba. Now these family problems are resolved, maybe we can save up for a house again, and the visit to Kenny and Mary in the USA that we planned so many months ago.

15 WASHINGTON

'*The strength of the human spirit to overcome challenges comes from maintaining strong family connections and pride in one's heritage.*' I read the words on the bronze plaque slowly aloud. These raised letters stir something deep within me. Manny and I have made decisions that have allowed us to reunite with our families and reconnect with our heritage. We have returned to our roots in South Sudan, but it has been costly. I can see that now that we are far away from the places I know.

We are visiting Annapolis forty kilometres from the city of Baltimore, Maryland, where Manny lived for ten years while he studied and then worked for a family law firm. I have been speaking at a conference on human rights at the United Nations in Washington, paid for by the Olaudah Trust, who agreed to delay my return flight by a few days so that Manny and I could visit Kenny and Mary. Manny spent yesterday with some of the Lost Boys who have stayed in the US. We met at Baltimore Airport this morning and hired a car so that Manny can show me his favourite places before we stay for a couple of nights at Kenny and Mary's home in Washington.

'I used to come here by the light rail link at the weekend,' he says, 'and wander round the old town and the harbour. I felt I had a connection with the millions of people from Africa who were forced to come here. I chose to come here, it was an opportunity, but it was still hard to be cut off from my country.'

The bronze figure of Alex Haley is seated on the harbour wall. The children lying on the ground around him are relaxed, casual, their tilted bronze heads contrasting with the red brick paving. Are they listening to the story?

'Have you read the book? I ask Manny.

'Parts.' he replies. 'It was on the curriculum for the English Language examination I had to take when I first arrived here at eighteen. I found it very strange. It's about his ancestor, Kinte Kunta, who came from Gambia. He was a well-respected man in his community, who was tricked and taken, along with millions of others. They were not well treated.'

We gaze out across the water, lined with renovated warehouses and parkland, reclaimed from former dock areas. The creek is as wide as the river Thames, we can just see where it opens into Chesapeake Bay. From there ships pass into the Atlantic and thousands of miles away to the continent we have flown from in a matter of hours. Once fellow Africans endured weeks of appalling hardship, this serene scene was a bustling hell of human lives for sale. I was fortunate that kind people released me and helped me.

'Seen enough?' Manny asks. 'Shall we grab some lunch?' I nod and he leads the way across the square beyond the memorial to a tavern with tables outside under a red and white striped awning.

'Here, okay?' I follow him to the corner closest to the harbour.

'Perfect.' I say.

'So, the conference went well?' he asks when we have ordered.

'Yes, both Jane and I spoke. Then she went to the discussion on how to help victims of trafficking, while I went to the one on prevention.'

'Did they come up with any good ideas?'

'Loads of them but nothing practical. I tried to explain what it is like having children with no means to support them, and that for some selling a child into slavery is the only way to keep other family members alive.'

'Like Isaac.'

'I used Isaac as an example, no names of course. Some of the agencies won't release funds to South Sudan because they fear they will be misdirected.'

'Yeah, they're right.' He drums one hand on the table, then asks 'All well at Avon View House?'

'They're busier than ever. Jane is worried the council support grants will not be enough to cover the increased costs of food because of the effects of the pandemic on the European economy.' He frowns.

'Did you have a good time with the Boys?' I ask.

'Yeah, they're mostly fine. One or two are still out of work but mostly they have established a good life here. They watch what is happening and keep in touch with each other and news networks. There are plans.' he says. 'I cannot say more, but some of them would like to return when it's a bit safer.'

He reaches across the table for my hand. 'Enough of problems and plans,' he continues, 'let's enjoy our holiday. I told Kenny we'd turn up around four, so we can take our time.' We raise the beers we ordered and clink.

'Cheers, here's to us!' We have not had a break since that long drive to Goma. Rose now goes to a nursery which started up when our schools reopened in May. I have more time for the Olaudah Trust work and with Manny's salary coming through regularly we have built up our savings towards buying the materials for a house. In other ways it has been a difficult year. As I feared, Elizabeth's strong personality has caused difficulties. Manny spent days helping her to find an acceptable apartment. She was appalled by Nyadena's situation and offended Reuben by saying so. Relationships were strained for a while, but Reuben and Nyadena have rented some land in a better area and are hoping to build a house. Elizabeth causes offence without meaning to. She runs her finger along our table and inspects it for dust or detritus from Rose's meals. She irritates Manny by telling him he should put his shoes away when he comes home from work. Fortunately, Adam's arrival has diverted some of her energy to him. Adam adores his grandmother, and she seems more mellow with him than with the rest of us.

'Why the smile?' Manny asks.

'I was thinking about your mother. She seems pleased to have Adam around.'

'Mama needs people.' he says drily. 'She'll be calmer now her work is picking up and she has Adam as a project.'

'Was she like that when you were a child?'

'I suppose so. She had my older brothers to

deal with, and my father to drive forward. She was always the one with the energy.'

'I shall enlist her help to find new customers for the salon.' I suggest.

'Good idea, she can bring all the new people at the hospital.'

We linger over our meal. Troubles and responsibilities dissipate in the breeze and dance away across the water. Hand in hand we walk back to the car past the beautiful Maryland State House, red bricks glowing, the cupola above glistening white in the afternoon sun.

'Happy, Princess?'

'Yes, and puzzled, why did you leave, give up all this to come to Juba?'

'Same as why you left Bristol. It never felt comfortable.' We link arms and saunter back to the car park and drive on to Silver Spring, the suburb of Washington where Kenny and Mary have lived since Manny first knew them at the age of eighteen.

A dense thicket of dogwood and hickory hides the house, arching over the drive to form a green tunnel. Manny swings the car round a sharp turn and stops in front of an imposing house with a double height colonnade.

'Mary said if they are out to leave our stuff on the porch and go round the back.' says Manny. He unloads our modest bags and pulls a cord at the side of the wide front door. A bell clangs somewhere deep within the house. We wait and then put our bags down. As I straighten up there is a faint footfall behind the door.

'Manny, we're so excited. You come right in, leave your bags there, I'll show you your rooms later. Kenny is in the garden.'

She is small and slight. A cream shift dress flatters her slim figure, her silver hair is beautifully cut in a sleek bob, French polished nails. A necklace of jet beads like shark's teeth with a large gold medallion at the front relieves the paleness of her hair and dress. Her black patent leather sandals must have rubber on the heels because they make hardly a sound on the polished tiles.

She leads the way through a long sunlit corridor to double doors which open into a conservatory running the width of the back of the house. She leads us past the sofas and coffee tables onto a paved patio where a stone dolphin sprays water into a small pond. Beyond this, wide steps, paved in the same golden stone as the patio, drop to the extensive lawn below.

'Kenny, they've arrived!' There is a grunt from the shrubs edging the patio and a tousled head of grey hair appears.

'Welcome! I didn't hear the bell.' He looks older than Mary, a little taller but trim and economic in his movements. He rinses his hands in the water of the fountain, rolls down the sleeves of his red checked shirt and shakes us warmly by the hand.

'Good to see you. It's been a long time, Manny. Maria, he has told us all about you, but he did not say how beautiful you are.' There is a gleam of delight in his piercing blue eyes but beneath I sense an analytical mind and a strong personality. I would not like to be on the receiving end of his judgement as a state magistrate.

'Come and take a seat. You must be tired

from your journey.' says Mary. 'Would you like tea, beer?' She leads us to a set of wrought iron chairs around a table, shaded by roses clambering over a trellis. It reminds me of gardens in Bristol, but everything here is laid out in straight lines with none of the rambling informality of an English garden. I take the cardigan out of my bag and wrap it round my shoulders. It is a sunny afternoon but despite a long-sleeved dress the air feels chilly to skin used to the heat of the Equator.

'This is Mary's favourite place.' comments Kenny. 'Costs me my last dollar to keep these roses fed and watered! Now, how is your little rosebud?' We fill him in on Rose's progress and show him pictures of her sitting with her cousins in Nimule. He and Mary embark on a kindly but intensive interrogation into our families. A young Hispanic woman brings a pot of tea and two beers and places them on the table. As Manny describes the long quest to locate Elizabeth, I observe my surroundings. Everything is neat, from the trimmed edges of the lawn to the rounded shrubs and the smooth paths. The many windows of the conservatory glisten in the afternoon sun. The sofas are arranged symmetrically and a rack, just visible on the back wall stows magazines and newspapers in tidy rows. Kenny seems impervious to the air of tidiness, leaning back in his chair with his legs crossed. Mary occasionally intersperses a question but mostly listens. When the conversation about our families starts to peter out and Kenny asks us about our country, she stands.

'Excuse me, I must check on dinner. Will seven pm give you time to change? Kenny will show you where to go.' She must be in her seventies but there is no sign of stiffness. She glides into the house. Kenny's eyes narrow.

'Mary gets upset about South Sudan, but I want to hear the news. Is it getting easier? How are you making out?' Manny breathes heavily.

'It's not what we hoped.' he admits. 'There are outbreaks of violence, recently on the border with Sudan, near the oilfields. We're still dealing with the accusations of rape and violence to women and children from the attack of Murle tribesmen on Dinka camps. The cuts in the aid budget are affecting food supplies. How can we improve legal structures for the children when the country cannot even feed them?'

'Is there any progress on the judicial structures for young people?' asks Kenny.

'We have policies written but they are not enacted.'

'Will you stay?' Kenny asks. He is soft spoken and kindly but those piercing blue eyes miss nothing. Manny shuffles in his chair.

'There are improvements.' he says. 'All ten states have appointed governors. We're doing better financially; my pay comes through regularly now, so we have been able to save for a house at last.'

'I will be refitting my salon when we get back.' I add. Kenny places the fingers of both hands on the table, letting them down a pair at a time, index fingers first, then middle, then fourth fingers with a heavy gold ring on the left hand, finally little fingers. He does this quickly but deliberately. I imagine him in court, weighing judgement, considering every point of law.

'You've reconnected with your roots. That's

a positive. You're doing well, but have you considered that there are two types of security. The first is home and family, we all long for that. The other aspect is the broader security of our environment. South Sudan has a history of conflict and violence. The government is not stable. Have you considered Rose's future? Where will she be educated? You're a good lawyer, Manny, and your wife is an experienced businesswoman. You still have US citizenship. Return here and visit your families as often as you like. Rose would have the opportunity of an Ivy League University assuming she is as lively minded as you two are. The USA has its problems, but it has always been a country of opportunity.' His words are quiet and measured. They carry authority and experience. He is right, we should do what is best for Rose. I look for the doubt in Manny's eyes, but there is none. My husband leans forward in his chair, fingers pressed together, spread, and flexed against each other.

'The USA has been good to me.' he says. 'Without the government programme for the Lost Boys, I would still be in the refugee camp. This country has given me an education, a career, and a future. I honour your people, but it is not my country. I don't want my children and grandchildren to be without roots. Rose's ancestors' bodies are buried in the soil of South Sudan. I want her to grow up knowing her land. Things are bad, I know, but if everyone seeks the comfort of the west, who will build our nation?' He pauses and wipes the sweat off his forehead with a cotton handkerchief. Kenny gives him a quizzical stare then turns to me.

'What about you, Maria?'

'I want the best for Rose, of course, but family is the most important thing. Rose is loved and cared for.

She will grow up knowing who she is and where she belongs. Life in Juba is difficult, the last two years have been tough, but God will protect us. He has seen us through the conflict with Khartoum and given us a new country. He will not give up on us now. We must bring our people back. I am sure we can do it.'

Kenny leans forward and looks at Manny, then me, with those piercing blue eyes.

'You're certain.' he states. 'I can see it in you. I respect that. People who believed in the future and were willing to endure built this country. What are your plans for tomorrow?'

'Err, I thought we'd make for the Lincoln Memorial and work our way along the Mall.' Manny replies, as disconcerted as I am by Kenny's sudden change of subject.

'Can I make a suggestion?' It is a rhetorical question, and we nod obediently. 'Head for the National Portrait Gallery first and the room with portraits of the founders of the United States. I think you will be inspired. Then you can make your way back to the Mall.

'That would be new for me as well as Maria.' Manny comments.

'You could go on to the Star-Spangled Banner at the Smithsonian Institute. It tells a moving story of nation building.' We look at each other and grin. I can understand why Manny admires Kenny. It feels good to be so fully understood when many are critical of our return to Juba. It feels as though we have passed a test, put our case, carried our point, and been encouraged to pursue it further.

The following morning, we stand outside the National Portrait Gallery. I am already inspired by the breadth of vision of this country. We visited the Lincoln Memorial first and the words spoken at Gettysburg are ringing in my heart.

...we here highly resolve that these dead shall not have died in vain -- that this nation, under God, shall have a new birth of freedom -- and that government of the people, by the people, for the people, shall not perish from the earth.

There has been conflict and hardship here too, between the northern states and the south. The triumph of the north and the freeing of slaves prefigures our own struggles against centuries of slavery. We are still at the stage of bloodshed and turmoil.

The doors of the gallery open and we pass through its cool stone corridors to the early portraits. Washington, Jefferson, Adams, Franklin. Life size pictures of strong faces with distinctive features and personalities; in the eyes of each one a focus on a faraway point. They are staring into the future. Seeking hope in a distant perspective. They did not see what they longed for in their own time. But if they are in heaven now, they can see what a nation they have built. We are doing that too, Manny's meeting with the Lost Boys and our human rights work are our part in building a nation.

On the way out we pass a portrait of Barack Obama. His dark face is lined with the burdens of presidency, his hair touched with grey, but his eyes too have that distant focus, on something that has not been achieved yet, but will come in time, with commitment from those who are willing to be inspired and stay the course. We do not speak, Manny and I, but our hands are tightly clasped. His thicker fingers enclose my narrower hand and there is a strength in both of us. We can feel it. We will do it. We will carry on. We will do our best to build a nation for our child, and for her children too.

'Where are we going next?' I ask. 'Kenny said something about seeing a flag.'

'I have another idea.' says Manny.

Fort McHenry has mown lawns sweeping down to the harbour. It is mid-afternoon and for the first time since I flew to the States, I can feel some warmth in my bones. We sit on a bench at the water's edge. The channel is wide here. The opposite shore is visible as a low line of buildings, dwarfed by the container ship moving slowly past.

We had lunch in a café in the Inner Harbour. Manny showed me the office where he used to work on the east side, and the apartment block on the west side where he lived. There are restaurants and shops around the inner end of the harbour and the water taxis buzz back and forth between them. It is like Bristol but on a grander scale. The windows of the tower blocks glisten. The harbourside is paved in beautiful red brick with stone edging, neat and precise. There is no bare earth or wasteland. Even the trees and flowers have walls around them to keep them tidy. The taps and toilets are spotless wherever we have stayed or eaten. Nothing seems broken or dysfunctional.

We have driven from the Inner Harbour out to Fort McHenry, overlooking Chesapeake Bay.

Manny wants to show me how the stars and stripes flag of the USA originated. The park around the fort is spacious and well kept.

'You could have stayed with all this luxury and order and just visited South Sudan.' I suggest to him.

'It was an empty life.' he replies. 'I only had one room with a galley kitchen and shower room off a small entrance hall. It was more like a hotel room than an apartment, easy to run but not a home. You could see the water from the balcony if you craned your neck a bit. I liked the services. It had a gym in the basement, and I used to run round the harbour most days. But I never felt at ease with the people here. Garang and Jacob are my family but no-one else appreciated where we had come from or how we got here. Even Kenny and Mary didn't understand my restlessness to get back to where I belonged. To find my people. To be in my own land. They speak about the American dream. It's not my dream.' I reach for his hand. In childhood we always had a sense of each other's rhythm, cruelly interrupted by the violence of the 1990's, but our hearts still beat to the same drum.

The waves of Chesapeake Bay slap against the smooth lawns of the park. The trees shiver in the breeze. Faint echoes of African ancestors forced to these shores whisper in the restless air. Their descendants built their lives here, but we have a new dream. Manny jumps up with sudden energy.

'Come,' he says, we haven't got much time.' Hand in hand we walk across the grass and pay our entry fee. The fort is huge, as everything is in this land, a five-sided star extending its arms out to cover every angle of the approach to the Bay. There are gun emplacements around the perimeter, frightening symbols of strength. Inside the fort tells a different story of a fierce battle with the British for independence, where all seemed lost until a home sewn flag was seen flying over the fort on the morning after the fighting.

'It's just a few strips of woollen cloth.' I comment, looking at the huge flag pinned to one the wall.

'But it inspired people and gave them the strength to continue building a country.'

'Our flag of star and stripes represents our land and our people.'

'And the blood shed to gain freedom.' Manny finishes. We stand silently, reading the poem that has become the national anthem of the USA.

'*O! This be it ever when freemen shall stand between their lost homes and the war's desolation.*' I read out. 'That's our dream, Manny, for our homes and families, and recovery from the war. We are just at an earlier stage than this country.'

A few hours later our plane lifts off and the waters of Chesapeake Bay and the lights of Baltimore and Annapolis drop away beneath us. A hostess appears with the drinks trolley, and we choose fruit juices, a last bit of luxury.

'Jane and Rory may fly to Nairobi at the end of August, before Camarg starts his final school year and Carlye starts at primary school.'

'Great, we could find a cheap flight and meet up.'

'We'll have to see how I am.'

'Why, what's wrong?' I lean across and whisper in his ear. 'I went to the pharmacy while you were buying shirts. I did a test when we stopped for lunch. It was positive.'

'You're not talking Covid, are you?' he whispers.

'No, we're going to have another child, Manny. I think I'm six or seven weeks overdue so Rose should have a little brother or sister in the New Year.' He grasps my hand and runs his finger over the veins.

'New Year, new baby, new country.' he takes my other hand and holds both tightly. 'We have to make it work, for the sake of our family.' He has a glass of wine with our meal to celebrate, but I stick to fruit juice, and we toast each other talking excitedly about our plans for a new home, schooling for Rose, reopening the salon and finding a new manager. There are so many ideas gleaned from our trip. Our minds run free, inspired by the stories of people, and places we have visited. We sleep and dream of a better future.

Six hours later we are still over the Atlantic. Another seven interminable hours before we land in Addis Ababa for the flight to Juba. The plane takes us back the way we have come for over an hour until we sink through the clouds and see the olive-green ribbon of the Nile below us, the verdant margins of swamp land and the ochre earth of the suburbs. Aunt Roselyn is there to meet us, Rose rushes towards us, flinging herself at Manny and shouting 'Dada, Dada.' He gathers her up, holding her as she chats incessantly and waves excitedly at other passengers. I follow with our cases, hoping she will like the American eagle cuddly toy we bought her at Fort McHenry.

Jacob greets us outside the terminal, ready to drive us home. Flags fly in the streets; it is only a few days to Independence Day on the ninth of July. Big celebrations are planned to mark ten years of independence, but Jacob tells us there are rumours that the President will close them down due to continuing conflict and Covid. There are posters promoting special wrestling matches and bars advertise television screens for those who want to watch the events. Mixed messages typify our country. There is peace, there is conflict. There is progress, there is corruption. There are plans, there is Covid. The leaders are talking, the leaders are fighting. But we move forwards in tiny steps. Development is coming to Juba. There are opportunities for education, and industry. The oil is flowing again. A line of our own national anthem runs through my head:

We rise, raising flag with guiding star and singing songs of freedom with joy, for justice, freedom and liberty shall for evermore reign. Oh God bless South Sudan.

Further reading

Aida Edemariam *The Wife's Tale* 4th Estate 2019

Gael Faye *Petit Pays* Grassette & Fasquelle 2016

Clyde Ford *The Hero with an African Face* Bantam 1999

Rachel Ibrek *South Sudan's Injustice System* Zed Books Ltd 2019

Peter Martell *First Raise a Flag How South Sudan Won the Longest War but Lost the Peace.* Hurst and Company 2018

Diann Mills *long walk home* Tyndale 2019

Gary Moelk *By Their Fruit Oil, Genocide and Faith A Chronicle of South Sudan*

Alan Moorehead *The White Nile.* Harper and Brothers New York 1960

David van Reybrouck Congo *The Epic History of a People* Fourth Estate 2015

Zach Vertin *A Rope from the Sky The Making and Unmaking of the World's Newest State* Amberley 2018

ABOUT THE AUTHOR

I am a writer and speaker, based in the UK. I chair the board of All Together in Dignity, a global human rights based anti-poverty organization.

I fell in love with East and Central Africa while living and working in a Harambee school in Kenya in the 1970s. In the last five years I have been to South Sudan several times and have listened to many people talk about the trauma they have experienced through conflict and poverty, yet through it all the human spirit shines through.

You can find out more at:
https://letitiamason.wordpress.com

Or follow me on
https://www.facebook.com/MariaofSS/?ref=aymt_homepage_panel